Her Royal Spyness

Her Royal Spyness

Rhys Bowen

DOUBLEDAY LARGE PRINT
HOME LIBRARY EDITION

BERKLEY PRIME CRIME, NEW YORK

THE BERKLEY PUBLISHING GROUP
Published by the Penguin Group Penguin Group (USA) Inc. 375 Hudson Street, New York, New York 10014, USA
Penguin Group (Canada), 90 Eglinton Avenue East, Suite 700, Toronto, Ontario M4P 2Y3, Canada (a division of Pearson Penguin Canada Inc.) Penguin Books Ltd., 80 Strand, London WC2R 0RL, England Penguin Group Ireland, 25 St. Stephen's Green, Dublin 2, Ireland (a division of Penguin Books Ltd.) Penguin Group (Australia), 250 Camberwell Road, Camberwell, Victoria 3124, Australia (a division of Pearson Australia Group Pty. Ltd.) Penguin Books India Pvt. Ltd., 11 Community Centre, Panchsheel Park, New Delhi—110 017, India Penguin Group (NZ), 67 Apollo Drive, Rosedale, North Shore 0745, Auckland, New Zealand (a division of Pearson New Zealand Ltd.) Penguin Books (South Africa) (Pty.) Ltd., 24 Sturdee Avenue, Rosebank, Johannesburg 2196, South Africa

Penguin Books Ltd., Registered Offices: 80 Strand, London WC2R 0RL, England

This book is an original publication of The Berkley Publishing Group.

ISBN-13: 978-0-7394-8815-7

PRINTED IN THE UNITED STATES OF AMERICA

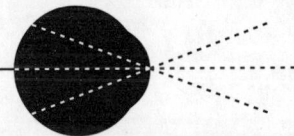

This Large Print Book carries the
Seal of Approval of N.A.V.H.

Notes and Acknowledgments

This is a work of fiction. While some real historical personages make cameo appearances in this book, Georgie and her friends and family exist only in the head of the writer. I have tried to ensure that royal personages do nothing out of character and accurately play themselves.

I would like to thank those who provided valuable input and gentle criticism: fellow mystery writers Jane Finnis and Jacqueline Winspear; my husband, John (who knows what's what about who's who); my daughters Clare and Jane; and my cheering section, my wonderful agents Meg and Kelly.

Thanks also to Marisa Young for lending her name to an English debutante.

Her Royal Spyness

Chapter 1

Castle Rannoch
Perthshire
Scotland
April 1932

There are two disadvantages to being a minor royal.

First, one is expected to behave as befits a member of the ruling family, without being given the means to do so. One is expected to kiss babies, open fetes, put in an appearance at Balmoral (suitably kilted), and carry trains at weddings. Ordinary means of employment are frowned upon. One is not, for example, allowed to work on the cosmetics counter at Harrods, as I was about to find out.

When I venture to point out the unfairness of this, I am reminded of the second item on my list. Apparently the only acceptable destiny for a young female member of the house of Windsor is to marry into another of the royal houses that still seem to litter Europe, even though there are precious few reigning monarchs these days. It seems that even a very minor Windsor like myself is a desirable commodity for those wishing a tenuous alliance with Britain at this unsettled time. I am constantly being reminded that it is my duty to make a good match with some half-lunatic, bucktoothed, chinless, spineless, and utterly awful European royal, thus cementing ties with a potential enemy. My cousin Alex did this, poor thing. I have learned from her tragic example.

I suppose I should introduce myself before I venture any further. I am Victoria Georgiana Charlotte Eugenie, daughter of the Duke of Glen Garry and Rannoch—known to my friends as Georgie. My grandmother was the least attractive of Queen Victoria's daughters, who consequently never managed to snare a Romanov or a Kaiser, for which I am truly grateful and I expect she was too. Instead she was hitched to a dreary Scottish baron who was bribed with a dukedom for taking her off the old queen's hands. In due time she dutifully produced my father, the second duke, before succumbing to the sort of diseases brought on by inbreeding and too much fresh air. I never knew her. I never met my fearsome Scottish grandfather either, although the servants claim that his ghost haunts Castle Rannoch, playing the bagpipes on the ramparts (which in itself is strange as he couldn't play the bagpipes in life). By the time I was born at Castle Rannoch, the family seat even less comfortable than Balmoral, my father had become the second duke and was busy working his way through the family fortune.

My father in turn had done his duty and married the daughter of a frightfully correct English earl. She gave birth to my brother, looked around at her utterly bleak Highland surroundings, and promptly died. Having secured an heir, my father then did the unthinkable and married an actress—my mother. Young men like his uncle Bertie, later King Edward VII, were allowed, even encouraged, to have dalliances with actresses, but never to marry them. However, since Mother was Church of England and came from a respectable, if humble, British family at a time when the storm clouds of the Great War were brewing in Europe, the marriage was accepted. Mother was presented to Queen Mary, who declared her remarkably civilized for someone from Essex.

The marriage didn't last, however. Even those with less zip and zest than my mother could not tolerate Castle Rannoch for long. The moan of the wind through the vast chimneys, coupled with the tartan wallpaper in the loo, had the effect of producing almost instant depression or even insanity. It's amazing, really, that she stuck it out for as long as she did. I think the idea of being a duchess appealed to her in principle. It was only when she realized that being married to a duke meant spending half the year in Scotland that she decided to bolt. I was two at the time. Her first bolt was with an Argentinian polo player. Many more bolts have followed, of course. The French racing driver, so tragically killed in Monte Carlo, the American film producer, the dashing explorer, and most recently, I understand, a German industrialist. I see her from time to time, when she flits through London. Each time there is more makeup and more exotic and expensive hats as she tries desperately to cling on to those youthful looks that made men fight over her. We kiss, cheek to cheek, and talk about the weather, clothing, and my marriage prospects. It's like having tea with a stranger.

Luckily I had a kind nanny, so my upbringing at Castle Rannoch was lonely but not too terrible. Occasionally I was whisked away to stay with my mother, when she was married to someone suitable in a healthy part of the world, but she wasn't really cut out for motherhood and rarely stayed in one place for long, so that Castle Rannoch became my anchor, known and trusted, even if it was gloomy and lonely. My half brother, Hamish (usually known as Binky), was sent away to the sort of boarding school where cold showers and runs at dawn are the norm, designed to mold future leaders of the empire, so I hardly knew him either. Nor my father, really. After my mother's much publicized bolt he sort of lost heart and wafted around the watering holes of Europe, losing more and more money at the tables in Nice and Monte Carlo until the infamous stock market crash of '29. When he learned that he'd lost what remained of his fortune, he went up onto the moors and shot himself with his grouse gun, although how he managed to do it has always been the object of speculation, my father never having been a particularly good shot.

I remember trying to feel a sense of loss when the news was delivered to me in Switzerland. I only had the vaguest image in my brain of what he looked like. I missed the concept of having a father, knowing he was there for protection and advice when really needed. It was alarming to realize that at nineteen, I was essentially on my own.

So Binky became third duke, married a dull young woman of impeccable pedigree, and inherited Castle Rannoch. I, meanwhile, had been shipped off to finishing school in Switzerland, where I was having a spiffing time mixing with the naughty daughters of the rich and famous. We learned passably good French and precious little else except how to give dinner parties, play the piano, and walk with good posture. Extracurricular activities included smoking behind the gardener's shed and climbing over the wall to meet with ski instructors in the local tavern.

Luckily some wealthier members of the family chipped in for my education and allowed me to stay there until I was presented at court and had my season. For those of you who might not know, every young woman of good family has her season—a series of dances, parties, and other sporting events, during which she comes out into society and is presented at court. It's a polite way of advertising "Here she is, chaps. Now for God's sake somebody marry her and take her off our hands."

"Season" is actually a rather grand word for a series of dismal dances, culminating in a ball at Castle Rannoch during the grouse season, to which the young men came to shoot and by evening were all too tired to dance. Few of them knew the Highland dances that were expected at Castle Rannoch anyway, and the bagpipes echoing at dawn from the north turret made several young men realize they had pressing engagements in London that couldn't wait. Needless to say, no suitable proposal was forthcoming and so, at the age of twenty-one, I found myself stuck at Castle Rannoch with no idea what I was going to do for the rest of my life.

Chapter 2

Castle Rannoch
Monday, April 18, 1932

I wonder how many people have had life-changing experiences while on the loo? I should point out that the bathrooms at Castle Rannoch are not the small cubicles one finds in ordinary homes. They are vast, cavernous places with high ceilings, tartan wallpaper, and plumbing that hisses, groans, clanks, and have been known to cause more than one heart attack, as well as such instant fits of insanity that one guest leaped from an open bathroom window into the moat. I should add that the windows are always open. It's a Castle Rannoch tradition.

Castle Rannoch is not the most delightful spot at the best of times. It lies beneath an impressive black crag, at the head of a black loch, protected from the worst of gales by a stand of dark and gloomy pine forest. Even the poet Wordsworth, invited here during his ramblings, could find nothing to say about it, except for a couplet scribbled on a sheet of paper found in the wastepaper basket.

From dreadful heights to lakeside drear
Abandon hope all ye who enter here

And this was not the best of times. It was April and the rest of the world was full of daffodils, blossoms, and Easter bonnets. At Castle Rannoch it was snowing—not that delightful powdery stuff you get in Switzerland but wet, heavy, slushy snow that sticks to the clothing and freezes one in seconds. I hadn't been out for days. My brother, Binky, having been conditioned to do so at school, insisted on taking his morning walks around the estate and arrived home looking like the abominable snowman—sending his son Hector, affectionately known as Podge, screaming for Nanny.

It was the sort of weather for curling up with a good book beside a roaring fire. Unfortunately my sister-in-law, Hilda, usually known as Fig, was trying to economize and only allowed one log on the fire at a time. This was surely a false economy, as I had pointed out on several occasions. Trees were being felled by gales on a daily basis. But Fig had a bee in her bonnet about economizing. Times were hard everywhere and we had to set a good example to the lower classes. This example included porridge for breakfast instead of bacon and eggs and even baked beans as the savory after dinner one night. *Life is drear*, I wrote in my diary. I was spending a lot of time writing in my diary these days. I knew I should be doing something. I was itching to do something, but as my sister-in-law reminded me constantly, a member of the royal family, however minor, has a duty not to let the family down. Her look implied that I was liable to become pregnant or dance naked on the lawn if I went out to Woolworths unchaperoned. My duty apparently was to wait until a suitable match was made for me. Not a happy thought.

How long I would have patiently awaited my doom, I can't really say, if I hadn't been sitting on the loo one April afternoon, trying to avoid the worst of the driving snow that was blowing in upon me by holding up a copy of *Horse and Hound*. Over the moan of the wind, I became aware of voices. Owing to the eccentric nature of the plumbing at Castle Rannoch, installed many centuries after the castle was built, it was possible to overhear conversations floating up from many floors below. This phenomenon probably contributed to the delusions and fits that overcame even the sanest of our guests. I was born to it and had used it to my advantage all my life, overhearing many a thing that had not been meant for my ears. To an outsider, however, lost in contemplation on the loo, and staring in horror alternately at the dark crags outside the window and the tartan wallpaper within, echoing voices booming hollow from the pipes were enough to push them over the edge.

"The queen wants us to do what?" This was enough to make me perk up and pay attention. I was always keen for gossip about our royal kin, and Fig had given a horrified shriek, quite unlike her.

"It's only for a weekend, Fig."

"Binky, I do wish these horrid common Americanisms were not creeping into your conversation. Next thing we know you'll be teaching Podge to say 'mirror' instead of 'looking glass' and 'serviette' instead of 'napkin.'"

"God forbid, Fig. It's just that the word 'weekend' does seem to sum it up quite nicely, doesn't it? I mean, what other word do we have for Friday, Saturday, and Sunday?"

"It implies that we are slaves to a week's labor, which we aren't. But don't try to change the subject. I think it's damned cheek on the part of HM."

"She's only trying to help. Something has to be done for Georgie."

Now I was truly attentive.

"I agree she can't spend the rest of her life moping around here and doing crossword puzzles." Fig's sharp voice echoed alarmingly, making one of the pipes hum. "But then on the other hand, she could prove useful with little Podge. It would mean we wouldn't have to hire a governess for him before he goes to prep school. I suppose they must have taught her something at that ridiculously expensive establishment in Switzerland."

"You can't use my sister as an unpaid governess, Fig."

"Everybody has to pull their weight these

days, Binky, and quite frankly she's not doing anything else, is she?"

"What do you expect her to do, draw
pints behind the local bar?"

"Don't be ridiculous. I want to see your
sister happily settled as much as you do.
But being told I have to invite a prince here
for a house party, in the hopes of foisting
him upon Georgiana—really, that is too
much, even for HM."

Now I positively had my ear pressed
against the pipes. The only prince that
came to mind was my cousin David, the
Prince of Wales. He was certainly a good
catch, to whom I certainly wouldn't say no.
It's true he was a good deal older than I, and
not quite as tall either, but he was witty and
a splendid dancer. And kind too. I'd even be
prepared to wear flat-heeled shoes for the
rest of my life.

"I would say it was a great deal of expense wasted on a hopeless cause." Fig's
sharp voice again.

"I wouldn't call Georgie a hopeless cause.
She's a splendid-looking girl. A little tall for
the average chap, maybe, a little gawky still,
but healthy, good bones, not stupid. A
damned sight brainier than I, if the truth be

known. She'll make a great wife for the right fellow."

"She's turned down everyone we've found for her so far. What makes you think she'll be interested in this Siegfried?"

"Because he's a prince, and heir to the throne."

"What throne? They murdered their last king."

"There is talk of reinstatement of the royal family in the near future. Siegfried is next in line."

"The royal family won't last long enough for him to succeed. They'll all be murdered again."

"Enough of this, Fig. And we don't need to mention any of this to Georgie either. Her Majesty has requested and one does not turn down a request from HM. A simple little house party, that's all. For Prince Siegfried and some of his English acquaintances. Enough young men so that Georgie doesn't get wind of our plans for her right away."

"That's an expensive proposition, Binky. You know how much these young men drink. We can't even offer them a shoot at this time of year. Nor a hunt. What are we

going to do with them all day? I don't suppose this Siegfried will want to climb a
mountain."

"We'll manage it somehow. After all, I am
the head of the family. It is up to me to see
my sister settled."

"She's your half sister. Let her mother find
her somebody. God knows she has enough
castoffs of her own, and most of them millionaires."

"Now you're being catty, Fig. Please reply
to HM telling her we will be delighted to
arrange the house party in the near future."

The speakers drifted out of range. I stood
there at the bathroom window, impervious
to the snow blowing in on me. Prince
Siegfried of Romania, of all people. I had
met him while I was a pupil at Les Oiseaux,
my finishing school in Switzerland. He had
struck me as a cold fish with staring eyes, a
limp handshake, and a look that indicated a
perpetual bad smell under his nose. When
he was introduced to me, he had clicked his
heels and murmured, "*Enchanté.*" The way
he said it made me feel that I should be the
one having the honor bestowed upon me,
not the other way around. I didn't suspect

he'd be any more enchanted to see me again.

"The time has come for action!" I shouted into the storm. I was no longer a minor. I was able to go where I wanted without a chaperon, to make my own decisions and to choose my own life. It wasn't as if I were either the heir or the spare. I was only thirty-fourth in line to the throne. Being a mere woman, I could never inherit the dukedom or Castle Rannoch even if Binky had not produced a son. I was not going to sit around one minute longer waiting for the future to come to me. I was going out into the world to choose my own destiny.

I slammed the loo door and strode down the corridor to my room, where I surprised my maid, hanging up freshly ironed blouses.

"Can you find my trunk in the attic, please, Maggie?" I said. "And pack clothes suitable for city wear. I'm going to London."

I waited until Binky and Fig were taking tea in the great hall, then I breezed in. Actually it wasn't hard to breeze anywhere at Castle Rannoch, since there was usually a howling gale racing along the corridors, making the tapestries flap. Binky was standing with his back to the fire, thus blocking the heat from the one log from reaching the rest of the room. Fig's nose was blue enough to match her blood and I noticed she was cradling the teapot in her hands, rather than let Ferguson, the parlormaid, do the pouring.

"Ah, Georgie, there you are," Binky said heartily. "Had a good day? Beastly out. I don't suppose you went for a ride?"

"I wouldn't be so cruel to my horse," I said. I lifted the silver lid over one of the dishes. "Toast," I said in disappointment. "No crumpets, I see."

"Economy, Georgiana," Fig said. "We can't eat crumpets if the rest of the world can't afford them. It wouldn't be right. Heaven knows we can barely afford them ourselves any longer. It would be margarine if we hadn't a dairy herd."

I noticed she was spreading a generous amount of Fortnum's black currant jam onto her toast, but wisely said nothing. Instead I waited until she had taken a mouthful before I said, "I'm popping down to London for a while, if that's all right with you."

"To London? When?" Fig asked, her sharp little eyes glowering at me.

"Tomorrow, I thought. If we're not snowed in."

"Tomorrow?" Binky asked. "This is a bit sudden, isn't it?"

"Yes, why haven't you mentioned it before?" Fig seconded.

"I only found out myself today," I said, concentrating on spreading butter on toast. "One of my dearest school chums is getting married and she wants me there to help her with the wedding preparations. And since I'm not doing anything useful up here, I thought I should answer her call of distress. Baxter will be able to drive me to the station in the motorcar, won't he?"

I had invented this story on the way downstairs. I was rather proud of it.

"This is most inconvenient, Georgie," Binky said.

"Inconvenient? Why?" I turned innocent eyes upon him.

"Well, you see, it's like this—" He turned to Fig for inspiration, then went on, "We were planning a little house party. Getting some young people up here for you. We realize that it must be boring to be stuck up here with an old married couple like us and no dances or fun."

I went over to him and gave him a kiss on the cheek. "You are an old dear, Binky, thinking of me like that. But I couldn't possibly allow you to spend money on me. I'm not a child. I realize how frightfully tight money is these days and I know you had to pay those awful death duties on the estate."

I could see Binky was in an absolute agony of indecision. He knew that Her Majesty would expect her request to be obeyed, and now I was about to bolt. He couldn't tell me why he wanted me to stay because it was supposed to be a secret. It was quite the most amusing thing that had happened in ages.

"So now you don't have to worry about me," I said. "I'll be mixing with young people in London and helping out a friend and getting on with my life. I may use Rannoch House as my base, may I not?"

I saw a quick glance pass between Fig and Binky.

"Rannoch House?" Fig said. "You want to open up Rannoch House, just for yourself?"

"Not really open it up," I said. "I'd only be using my bedroom."

"We can't spare a servant to go with you," Fig said. "We're down to the bare minimum as it is. Binky could scarcely summon up enough beaters for the last shoot. And Maggie would never leave her invalid mother to go to London with you."

"It's all right," I said. "I shan't want to take a servant with me. I shan't even turn on the central heating."

"But if you're going to help this girl with her wedding, won't you be staying with her?" Fig asked.

"Eventually, yes. But she hasn't arrived from the continent yet."

"A continental, is she, this girl? Not English?" Fig looked horrified.

"We're not English," I said. "At least Binky and I aren't. We're part Scottish with a good admixture of German."

"Let me amend that to British then. You were brought up to be British. That's where the big difference lies. This girl is foreign, is she?"

I was dying to invent a mysterious Russian countess, but it was too cold for the brain to react quickly. "She's been living abroad," I said. "For the sake of her health. She's rather delicate."

"Then I wonder some poor chap wants to marry her," Binky said heartily. "Sounds as if she won't be much good at producing an heir."

"He loves her, Binky," I said, defending my fictitious heroine. "Some people do marry for love, you know."

"Yes, but not in our class," Binky said easily. "We do our duty. We marry someone suitable."

"I like to think that love may come into it a little, Binky," Fig said in a frosty tone.

"If one strikes it lucky, Fig. Like you and I."

He wasn't as stupid as he seemed, I decided. He was without guile, a man of simple needs, simple pleasures, but definitely not stupid.

Fig actually managed a smile. "Will you need to have your tiara brought up from the vault?" she asked, going back to practical matters now.

"I don't think it's a tiara sort of wedding," I said.

"Not St. Margaret's then?"

"No, it's to be a small affair. I told you the bride was delicate."

"Then I wonder she needs help in preparing for it. Anyone can arrange a simple wedding." Fig took another large bite of toast and jam.

"Fig, she has asked for help and I am responding," I said. "I'm just in the way up here and who knows, I may even meet somebody in London."

"Yes, but what will you do for servants?"

"I'll hire a local girl to look after me."

"Make sure you check her references thoroughly," Fig said. "Those London girls can't be trusted. And keep the silver locked away."

"I'm not likely to need the silver," I said. "I'm only going to use it as a place to sleep for a few nights."

"Well, I suppose if you must go, you must. But we'll miss you dreadfully, won't we, Binky?"

Binky went to say something, then thought better of it. "I'll miss you, old thing," he said. It was quite the nicest thing he had ever said to me.

❧

I sat looking out of the train window as we sped southward, watching winter melting into glorious spring. There were new white lambs in fields, the first primroses on the embankments. My excitement grew as we neared London. I was on my own, truly on my own, for the first time in my life. For the first time I'd be making my own decisions, planning my own future—doing something. At this point I had no idea what I should be doing, but I reminded myself that it was the 1930s. Young ladies were allowed to do more than embroider, play piano, and paint watercolors. And London was a big city, teeming with opportunities for a bright young person like myself.

The bubble of enthusiasm had burst by the time I reached Rannoch House. It had started to rain just outside London and by the time we came into King's Cross Station it was coming down in buckets. There were sorry-looking men lining up for a soup kitchen along Euston Road and beggars at every corner. I stepped out of the cab and let myself into a house as cold and dreary as Castle Rannoch had been. Rannoch House is on the north side of Belgrave Square. I remembered it as a place of bustle and laughter, always people coming and going to theaters, dinner parties, or on shopping expeditions. Now it lay shrouded in dust sheets, colder than the grave, and empty. The realization crept over me that this was the first time in my entire life that I had been all alone in a house. I looked back at the front door, half afraid and half excited. Was I stupid to have come alone to London? How was I going to cope on my own?

I'll feel better after a nice bath and a cup of tea, I thought. I went up to my bedroom. The fireplace was empty, the fire unlaid. What I needed was a fire to cheer me up, but I had no idea how one set about laying a fire. In truth I had never seen a fire laid, or lit. One awoke to a merrily crackling fire, never having seen the maid who slipped into the room at six o'clock to light it. Fig expected me to hire a maid of all work, but I had no money to do so. So I was going to have to learn to do things for myself. But I really didn't think I could face learning how to light a fire at this moment. I was tired, travel weary, and cold. I went through to the bathroom and started to run a bath. There was a good six inches of water in it before I realized that both taps were running cold water. The boiler had obviously been turned off and I had no idea what a boiler looked like or how I might get it going. I began to seriously question the folly of my rapid departure. Had I waited and planned better, I could surely have secured an invitation from someone who lived in a warm and comfortable house with servants to run my bath and make my tea.

Now in the depths of gloom, I went downstairs again and braved the door that led below stairs, to the servants' part of the house. I remembered going down there as a small child, sitting on a stool while Mrs. McPherson, our cook, let me scrape out the cake bowl or cut out gingerbread men. The big, half-underground kitchen was spotless, cold, and empty. I found a kettle and I even found a tinderbox and a spill to light the gas. Feeling very proud of myself I boiled some water. I even located a tea caddy. Of course that was when I realized that there was no milk, nor was there likely to be unless I contacted the milkman. Milk arrived on doorsteps. That much I knew. I rooted around in the larder and discovered a jar of Bovril. I made myself a cup of hot Bovril instead with some Jacob's cream crackers and went to bed. *Things are bound to be brighter in the morning*, I wrote in my diary. *I have taken the first steps in a new and exciting adventure. At least I am free of my family for the first time in my life.*

Chapter 3

Rannoch House
Belgrave Square
London
Friday, April 22, 1932

Even the most minor member of the royal family is not supposed to arrive at Buckingham Palace on foot. The proper mode of entry is at the very least a Rolls-Royce motor or, in the case of reduced circumstances, a Bentley or Daimler. Ideally a state coach drawn by a team of perfectly matched horses, although not many of us run to coaches these days. The sight of one female person slinking across the forecourt on foot would definitely have my esteemed relative-by-marriage, Her Royal Majesty and Empress of India, Queen Mary, raise an eyebrow. Well, probably not actually raise the eyebrow, because personages of royal blood are trained not to react, even to the greatest of improprieties. Were a native in some dark corner of the colonies to strip off his loincloth and dance, waggling his you-know-what with gay abandon, not so much as an eyebrow twitch would be permitted. The only appropriate reaction would be polite clapping when the dance was over.

This sort of control is drummed into us at an early age, very much as one trains a gun dog not to react to the sound of a shot fired at close range or a police horse to a rapid movement in the crowd. Miss MacAlister, the governess who preceded my finishing school in Switzerland, used to chant to me, like a litany: A lady is always in control of herself. A lady is always in control of her emotions. A lady is always in control of her expression. A lady is always in control of her body. And indeed it is rumored that some royal personages can dispense with visiting strange water closets for days on end. I wouldn't be crass enough to betray which royal personages can achieve this feat.

Fortunately there are other ways into Buckingham Palace, preferable to facing those formidable gilt-tipped gates and then crossing that vast expanse of forecourt under the watchful eye of those impossibly tall, bear-skinned guards and possibly Her Majesty herself. If you go around to the left, heading in the direction of Victoria Station, you can enter through the Ambassador's Court and the visitors' entrance. Even more desirable, if you follow the high brick wall along that road, you will come across a discreet black door in the wall. I gather it was used by my father's uncle Bertie, who had a short but happy reign as King Edward VII, when he wished to visit the more shady of his lady friends. I expect my cousin David, the current Prince of Wales, has used it from time to time when staying with his parents. I was certainly making use of it today.

Let me say that I am not in the habit of visiting the palace from choice. One does not drop in for afternoon tea and a chat, even if they are relatives. I had been summoned, two days after my arrival in London. My esteemed relative the queen possessed one of the best underground intelligence networks in the country. I didn't think that Fig would have contacted her, but she had found out somehow. A letter had arrived, on palace writing paper, from Her Majesty's private secretary, Sir Giles Ponsonby-Smythe, indicating that Her Majesty would be delighted if I would take tea with her. Which was why I was slinking up the Buckingham Palace Road on a Friday afternoon. One does not refuse HM.

Of course I was more than a little curious to know why I was being summoned. In fact it crossed my mind that HM might sit me down to tea and then produce Prince Siegfried and a convenient Archbishop of Canterbury to perform the wedding ceremony on the spot. In truth I felt as Anne Boleyn must have done when Henry VIII asked her to drop in for a flagon of ale, and not to wear anything with a high neckline.

I didn't remember seeing my exalted relatives since my presentation as a debutante—an occasion I won't forget in a hurry, and I'm sure they haven't either. I am one of those people whose limbs don't always obey them in times of crisis. My gown with its long train, not to mention three ridiculously tall ostrich feathers bobbing in a hair ornament, was a recipe for disaster. I had entered the throne room on cue, heard the booming announcement—"Lady Victoria Georgiana Charlotte Eugenie of Glen Garry and Rannoch!"—and executed the perfect curtsy, as practiced a million times at deb school. However, when I tried to stand up, it seems that my high heel had somehow caught itself in the train. I tried to move, but was tethered by my own heel spike. I tugged, gracefully, conscious of those royal eyes on me. Nothing happened. I felt perspiration trickling down my bare back. (Yes, I know ladies don't sweat, but something was trickling down my back.) I tugged harder. The heel came free and I was catapulted farther into the throne room as if I had been shot from a cannon at the very moment I should have been backing out of the royal presence. Even Her Majesty had looked mildly astonished, but nothing was said, on the occasion or subsequently. I wondered if it would come up over crumpets.

I made a successful entry along a narrow hallway that skirted the palace kitchens, and was making my way along the lower corridor, past various household offices, startling maids and footmen along the way, until in turn I was startled by a horrified voice exclaiming, "You, girl. Where do you think you are going?"

I turned to see an austere old gentleman bearing down on me.

"I don't know you," he said accusingly.

"I am Lady Georgiana, His Majesty's cousin," I said. "I am here to take tea with Her Majesty. I am expected."

There are some advantages to being a minor royal. The old man turned beetroot red.

"My lady, I do apologize. I can't think why I wasn't informed of your arrival. Her Majesty is awaiting you in the yellow sitting room. This way, please."

He led me up a side staircase to the *piano nobile*, which has nothing to do with the musical instrument but is the floor on which most of the royal life of the palace takes place. The yellow sitting room is in the southeast corner, with windows looking down the Mall to Admiralty Arch and also out over the start of Buckingham Palace Road. A great vantage point, in fact. As a room, however, it has never appealed to me. It is furnished largely with objects brought from the Royal Pavilion at Brighton, collected by King George IV at a time when chinoiserie was the height of fashion. Lots of dragons, chrysanthemums, and bright painted porcelain. I found it a little too flowery and garish for my taste.

"Lady Georgiana, ma'am," my stuffy friend said in a low voice.

Her Majesty wasn't at the table in the window, but standing, peering into one of the glass cases that adorned the walls. She looked up briefly as I came in.

"Ah, Georgiana. I didn't see you arrive. Did you take a cab?"

"I walked, ma'am." I should explain that royals are always ma'ams and sirs, even to their closest relatives. I went over to plant the dutiful kiss on the cheek, plus execute a curtsy. The order of these two actions requires the most delicate timing. In spite of a lifetime of practice I always managed to bump my nose on the royal cheek as I stood up from the curtsy.

Her Majesty straightened up. "Thank you, Soames. Tea in fifteen minutes."

The elderly man backed out, closing the double doors. Her Majesty had gone back to peering into the glass case. "Tell me, Georgiana," she said, "am I right in thinking that your late father had a fine collection of Ming? I'm sure I remember discussing it with him."

"He collected lots of things, ma'am, but I'm afraid I wouldn't know one pot from another."

"That's too bad. You must come to the

palace more often and let me educate you. One finds such solace in collecting beautiful objects."

I didn't point out that one needs money to collect beautiful objects and I was currently a pauper.

The queen still didn't look up from the glass case. "Your brother, the current duke, I suppose has little interest in objets d'art and antiques?" she asked casually. "He was raised to be like his grandfather—huntin', shootin', fishin'—the typical country squire."

"That's certainly true, ma'am."

"So it's possible that any number of Ming vases might still be lying around Castle Rannoch—unappreciated?"

There was the slightest of quivers in her voice and I suddenly understood where this conversation was going. She wanted to get her hands on items she lacked in her own collection. She confirmed this by saying, oh so casually, "I wondered if, next time you were home, you could take a look around. There is a smaller vase just like this one that would fit so well in this display. And if your brother isn't really interested . . ."

You want me to pinch it for you, I was dying to say. Her Majesty had an absolute passion for antiques and if she had not been Queen of England and Empress of India, she might have been one of the most skillful hagglers in the history of the antiques trade. Of course she possessed a trump card nobody else held. If she expressed admiration for any object, protocol demanded that it be presented to her. Most noble families hid the good stuff when a royal visit was imminent.

"I won't be going back to Castle Rannoch often anymore, ma'am," I said tactfully. "Now that the house has passed to Hamish and he is married, it isn't really my home."

"A great pity," she said. "But surely you'll pay a visit when you come to stay with us at Balmoral this summer. You will be coming to Balmoral, I take it?"

"Thank you, ma'am. I'll be delighted."

How could one refuse? When one was invited to Balmoral, one went. And the dreaded invitation fell on one or another of us relations every summer. Every summer we tried to come up with suitable excuses as to why we couldn't be there. These ranged from yachting on the Med to making a visit to the colonies. It is rumored that one female relative actually managed to have a baby during the Balmoral season each year, although I think this was being a little excessive. It really wasn't that bad for one brought up at Castle Rannoch. The tartan wallpaper, tartan carpets, the bagpipes at dawn, and the chill wind blasting in through open windows only reminded me of home. Others found it hard to endure, however.

"Then we may go over to Glenrannoch together. Such a pretty drive, I always think." She ushered me away from the glass cases and over to a small tea table. I must remind myself to write to Binky to warn him to lock up the best china and silver this summer I decided. "In fact, I rather suspect that my son David might have it in mind to persuade your brother to invite a certain woman to stay at Castle Rannoch this summer. David knows perfectly well that she would not be welcome at Balmoral, and Castle Rannoch is conveniently close by." She touched my arm as I pulled out a chair for her to sit down. "And I use the word 'woman' advisedly, because she certainly is no lady," she whispered. "An American adventuress, twice married already." She sighed as she took a seat. "Why he can't find someone suitable and settle down I simply can't understand.

He's not getting younger and I would like to see him settled before he has to take the throne. Why can't he marry someone like you, for example? You'd do very well."

"I'd have no objection," I said. "But I'm afraid he sees me as a little girl still. He likes sophisticated older women."

"He likes tarts," Her Majesty said coldly. She glanced up as the doors opened and an array of tea trays was carried in. "Ah, tarts," she repeated, just in case her comment should have reached the ears of the servants.

One by one the dishes were placed on the table. Tiny finger sandwiches with cress poking out of them, cake stands dotted with miniature éclairs and strawberry tarts. It was enough to bring tears to the eyes of one who had been living under Fig's austerity all winter and for the past two days on toast and baked beans. The tears were not of joy, however. I had been to enough royal functions in my life to know the protocol. The guest only eats what Her Majesty eats. And Her Majesty was not likely to take more than a slice or two of brown bread. I sighed, waited for her to take brown bread, then took a slice myself.

"I thought I might employ you as my spy," she said, as tea was poured.

"This summer at Castle Rannoch, you mean?"

"I must find out the truth before that, Georgiana," she said. "I only hear rumors. I want a firsthand account from somebody I can trust. I understand that David has persuaded Lord and Lady Mountjoy to give a house party and May ball and to include this woman and her husband—"

"Her husband?" I knew one should never interrupt the queen. It just slipped out.

She nodded with understanding. "Such behavior may well be considered acceptable in America. She is apparently still living with her husband. He, poor creature, is dragged around to provide respectability and to dispel rumors. Of course one can never dispel rumors. It has been all we can do to keep the press mute on the subject and if David becomes more brazen in his pursuit of her, then I don't think we'll be able to suppress the rumors much longer. I say his pursuit of her, but frankly I believe it to be the other way around. I suspect that this woman is relentlessly pursuing him. You know what he's like, Georgiana. An innocent

at heart, easily flattered, easily seduced."
She put down the slice of brown bread and
leaned a little closer to me. "I need to know
the truth, Georgiana. I need to know whether
this is a mere flirtation for this woman, or
whether she has serious designs on my
son. My worst fear is that, like all Americans, she is fascinated with royalty and
dreams of being Queen of England."

"Surely not, ma'am. A divorced woman?
That's impossible."

"Let us hope it is impossible. The only solution is for the king to go on living until
David becomes too old to be desirable as a
catch. But I fear my husband's health is failing. Never the same after the Great War. The
strain was too much for him."

I nodded with sympathy. "You said you
wanted me to be your spy?"

"I do indeed. The house party at the
Mountjoys' should give you ample opportunity to observe this woman and David together."

"Unfortunately I haven't been invited," I
said.

"But you came out with the Mountjoys'
daughter, didn't you?"

"I did, ma'am."

"There you are, then. I'll let it be known that you are currently in London and would like to renew your acquaintanceship with the Mountjoy girl." (She pronounced it "gell.") "People don't usually turn down my suggestions. And you need to be out in society if you're ever going to find yourself a husband." She looked up at me sharply. "So tell me, what are you planning to do with yourself in London?"

"I've only just arrived, ma'am. I haven't yet decided what I'll be doing."

"That's not good at all. With whom will you be staying?"

"At the moment I'm at Rannoch House," I said.

The royal eyebrow went up. "Alone in the London house? Unchaperoned?"

"I am over twenty-one, ma'am. I have come out."

She shook her head. "In my day a young woman was chaperoned until the day she was married. Otherwise a future husband could not be sure whether or not he was getting—umm—soiled goods, so to speak. No proposals on the horizon?"

"No proposals, ma'am."

"Dear me. I wonder why." She eyed me

critically, as if I were one of her art objects. "You're not unattractive and at least half your pedigree is impeccable. I can think of several young men who would be suitable. King Alexander of Yugoslavia has a son, hasn't he? No, maybe that part of the world is a little too brutal and Slavic. What about the Greek royal family? That delightful little blond boy? But I'm afraid he's too young, even for you. Of course, there's always young Siegfried, one of the Hohenzollern-Sigmaringens of Romania. He's a relative of mine. Good stock."

Ah, yes, Siegfried. She couldn't resist bringing him into the conversation. I had to squash this idea once and for all.

"I've met Prince Siegfried several times, ma'am. He didn't seem much interested in me."

She sighed. "This was all so much simpler in my day. A marriage was arranged and we got on with it. I was originally intended to marry His Majesty's brother, the Duke of Clarence, but he died suddenly. When it was suggested that I marry His Majesty instead, I acquiesced without a fuss. We have certainly been happy enough, and your great-grandmother adored Prince

Albert, as we all know. Perhaps I'll see what I can do."

"This is the 1930s, ma'am," I ventured. "I'm sure I'll meet someone eventually, now that I'm living in London."

"That's what I'm afraid of, Georgiana. Your father was not known for making the most sensible of choices, was he? However, I don't doubt you'll be married one day; one hopes to somebody suitable. You'll need to learn how to run a great house and act as ambassador for your country, and heaven knows you've had no mother to show you the ropes. How is your mother these days? Do you ever see her?"

"When she flits through London sometimes," I said.

"And who is her latest beau, may one ask?" She nodded to the maid who was offering slices of lemon for the china tea.

"A German industrialist, the last time I heard," I said, "but that was a couple of months ago."

I caught the briefest of twinkles in the royal eye. My austere relative might look starchy and forbidding, but deep down she did have a sense of humor.

"I shall take the matter in hand myself,

Georgiana," Her Majesty said. "It's not good for young girls to be idle and unchaperoned. Too many temptations in the big city. I'd take you on as one of my own ladies-in-waiting, but I already have a full complement at the moment. Let me think. It's possible that Princess Beatrice could use another lady-in-waiting, although she doesn't go out as much as she used to. Yes, that might do splendidly. I shall speak to her about it."

"Princess Beatrice, ma'am?" My voice quivered a little.

"You must have met her. The old queen's only surviving daughter. The king's aunt. Your great-aunt, Georgiana. She has a charming house in the country, and a place in London too, I believe, although she rarely comes to town anymore."

Tea came to an end. I was dismissed. And doomed. If I couldn't come up with some brilliant form of employment in the near future, I was about to be lady-in-waiting to Queen Victoria's only surviving daughter, who didn't get out and about much anymore.

Chapter 4

Rannoch House
Friday, April 22, 1932

I came out of Buckingham Palace in deep gloom. Actually the gloom had been deepening ever since my season ended and I realized that I was facing life ahead with no funds and no prospects. Now it seemed that I was to be locked in the country estate of an elderly princess while my royal kin found a suitable husband for me. The only spark of excitement in my dreary future would be the challenge to spy on my cousin David and his latest "woman."

I was in distinct need of cheering up, so I boarded the district line train to visit my favorite person. Gradually city sprawl gave way to Essex countryside. I disembarked at Upminster Bridge and soon I was walking along a row of modest semidetached homes on Glanville Drive, their pocket handkerchief-sized gardens decorated liberally with gnomes and birdbaths. I knocked at the door of Number 22, heard a muffled grunt, "I'm coming, I'm coming," and then a Cockney face peered around the half-open door. The face was perky, beaky, and wrinkled like an old prune. It took a second to register who I was and then lit up in a huge grin.

"Well, blow me down with a feather," he said, flinging the door wide open. "This is a turnup for the books. I didn't expect to see you in a month of Sundays. How are you, my love? Come and give your old granddad a kiss."

I suppose I should have mentioned that while one of my grandparents was Queen Victoria's daughter, my only living grandparent was a retired Cockney policeman who lived in a semidetached in Essex with gnomes in the front garden.

His stubbly face was scratchy on my cheek as he planted a kiss and he smelled of carbolic soap. I hugged him fiercely. "I'm well, thanks, Granddad. How are you?"

"Can't complain. The old chest ain't what it was, but at my age that's what you expect, isn't it? Come on in. I've got the kettle on and a nice bit of seedy cake, made by the old bat next door. She keeps sending round food, in the hopes of showing me what a good cook she is and what a good catch she'd make."

"And would she make a good catch?" I asked. "You have been living on your own for a long while now."

"I'm used to my own company. Don't need no meddling old woman in my life. Come on in and take a pew, ducks. You are a sight for sore eyes."

He beamed at me again. "So what brings you to this neck of the woods? In need of a good meal, by the look of it. You're all skin and bones."

"As a matter of fact, I am in need of a good meal," I said. "I've just come from the palace, where tea consisted of two slices of brown bread."

"Well, I can certainly do better than that. What about a couple of poached eggs on toasted cheese and then some of that cake?"

"Perfect." I sighed happily.

"I bet you didn't tell that lot at the palace where you were coming afterward." He bustled around the meticulously neat little kitchen, breaking two eggs into the poacher.

"They wouldn't have liked that. When you were a little girl, they used to intercept the letters we sent you."

"Surely not."

"Oh, yes. They didn't want no contact with us poor folk. Of course, if your mum had stuck around to do her duty and bring you up proper, we'd have been invited to stay or she could have brought you to see us. But she was off flaunting herself somewhere. We often worried about you, poor little mite, stuck in that big drafty place all alone."

"I did have Nanny. And Miss MacAlister."

He beamed again. He had the sort of smile that lit up his whole face. "And you turned out a treat. I'll have to admit that. Look at you. The proper young lady. I bet you've got the boyfriends lined up and fighting for you, haven't yer?"

"Not exactly," I said. "In fact I'm rather at a loose end, not quite sure what to do with myself. My brother's not giving me an allowance any longer, you see. He claims abject poverty."

"The dirty rotter. Do you want me to come up and give him a piece of my mind?"

"No, thanks, Granddad. There's nothing

you could do. I think they are genuinely hard up, and I'm only a half sister, after all. He told me I was welcome to stay on at Castle Rannoch, but having to amuse little Podge and help Fig with her knitting was really too dreadful. So I bolted, just like my mother. Only not as successfully. I'm camping out in the London house. Binky is letting me live there for the moment but it's freezing cold without the central heating on and I have no servant to look after me. I don't suppose you could show me how to light a fire, could you?"

My grandfather looked at me, then started laughing, a wheezy laugh that turned into a nasty cough. "Oh, you're a proper treat, you are. Teach you how to light a fire? Bless your little heart, I'll come up to Belgravia and light your fire for you, if that's what you want. Or you can always come and camp with me." His eyes twinkled with glee at the thought of this. "Can you imagine their faces if they knew that the thirty-fourth in line to the throne was living in a semidetached in Hornchurch?"

I laughed too. "Wouldn't that be fun? I might just take you up on it, except that it would only make the queen speed up with her arrangements to ship me to some royal aunt as a lady-in-waiting. She thinks I need training in how to run a great house."

"Well, I expect you do."

"I'd die of boredom, Granddad. You can't imagine how dreary it is, after all the excitement of a season, all those coming-out parties and balls, and now I've no idea what to do next."

The kettle started to whistle and he made the tea. "Get yourself a job," he said.

"A job?"

"You're a bright girl. You've been well educated. What's to stop you?"

"I don't think they'd approve."

"They're not supporting you, are they? And they don't own you. It's not like you're taking public money to carry out royal duties. You go out and have fun, my girl. Find out what you'd really like to do with your life."

"I'm sorely tempted," I said. "Girls are doing all kinds of jobs these days, aren't they?"

"Of course they are. Only don't go on the stage like your mum. She was a nice girl, properly brought up, until she got those stars in her eyes and went on the stage."

"She certainly made a success of it,

didn't she? Bags of money and married a duke?"

"Yes, but at what price, ducks? At what price? Sold her soul. That's what she did. Now she's clinging on to those good looks for dear life, dreading the day that no man is interested in her anymore."

"She bought you this house, didn't she?"

"I'm not saying she hasn't been generous. I'm just saying it changed her whole personality. Now it's like talking to a stranger."

"I agree," I said, "but then I never really knew her. I gather she's with a German industrial baron now."

"Ruddy German," he muttered. "Pardon my language, love, but just talking about them gets my goat. And that new chap, that Hitler. He's up to no good, I can tell you. He'll want watching, you mark my words."

"He may be a good thing for them. Help get the country back on its feet again," I suggested.

He scowled. "That country deserves to stay where it is. It don't need no encouragement. You didn't serve in the trenches."

"Neither did you," I reminded him.

"No, but your uncle Jimmy did. Only eighteen he was and he never came home."

I hadn't even known I had an uncle Jimmy. Nobody had ever told me.

"I'm sorry," I said. "It was a horrible war. Let's pray there will never be another one."

"There won't, as long as the old king stays alive. If he kicks the bucket, all bets are off."

He put a large plate of food in front of me and for a while I was silent.

"Blimey," he said. "You can certainly knock that back. You been starving yourself?"

"Living on baked beans," I confessed. "I haven't found a grocer's shop yet in Belgravia. Everyone has things delivered. And frankly I don't have any money."

"Then you'd better come down here and have Sunday dinner with me. I expect I could manage a roast and two veg—got lovely cabbages in the back garden, and of course later in the summer there will be beans. Can't do any better than that, even at your fancy posh restaurants in the West End."

"I'd love to, Granddad," I said and I realized that he needed me as much as I needed him at the moment. He was lonely too.

"I don't like the thought of you living in that big house all on your own," he said, shaking his head. "Some funny types up in the Smoke these days. Not quite right in the head after the war. Don't you go opening the door to any strangers, you hear? I've a good mind to get out my old uniform and patrol up and down outside your front door."

I laughed. "I'd like to see that. I've never seen you in uniform." I knew that my grand-father had been a policeman once, but he'd given it up long ago.

He gave a wheezy laugh. "I'd like to see it too. My jacket would never button up around my middle these days, and my old feet would never hold up in those boots. But I still don't like the thought of you trying to survive in that big place on your own."

"I'll be fine, Granddad." I patted his hand. "So teach me how to light a fire. Teach me how to do the washing up. I need to know everything."

"Lighting a fire starts with going down the coal'ole," he said.

"The coal'ole?"

"Yes, you know. They pour in the coal from a manhole on the street and you shovel it out through a little door at the bottom. I'm sure you'll find that's the way it's done at your place. But it's usually dark and dirty and there are bound to be spiders. I can't see you wanting to do that."

"If it's a choice between getting dirty and freezing, I'll choose getting dirty."

He turned to look back at me. "I must say I like your spunk. Just like your mother. She'd let nothing stand in her way either." He broke off with another fit of noisy coughing.

"That cough sounds terrible," I said. "Have you been to a doctor?"

"On and off all winter," he said.

"And what does he say it is?"

"Bronchitis, love. All this smoke in the air and the winter fogs are bad for me. He says I should give myself a nice holiday at the seaside."

"Good idea."

He sighed. "It takes money to go on holiday, sweetheart. Right now I'm not exactly flush. All those doctor visits last winter. And the price of coal going up. I'm trying to live off the little bit I've got put by."

"You're not getting a police pension?"

"A very small one. I wasn't on the force long enough, see. Got meself involved in a little bit of a fracas, coshed over the head, and then I started getting dizzy spells, so that was that."

"Then ask Mother to help you out. I'm sure she's got plenty."

His face hardened. "I'm not taking German money. I'd rather starve first."

"I'm sure she has money of her own. She's been with an awful lot of rich men in her time."

"She might have managed to put a bit away, but she'll need that for herself when her looks finally go and she's on her own. Besides, she was good enough to buy your grandma and me this house. She don't owe me nothing. And I'm not asking anyone for charity."

I noticed as I carried my plate across to the sink that the kitchen did look bare. An awful thought struck me that he had given me his last two eggs.

"I'll get a job, Granddad," I said. "And I'll learn to cook and then you can come to dine with me at Rannoch House."

That started him laughing again. "I'll believe it when I see it," he said.

I felt terrible as I rode the train back to London. My grandfather needed money badly and I couldn't help him. Now I'd have to get a job in a hurry. It seemed that it wasn't as easy to escape from family as I had thought.

It was a bright, warm evening and I was loath to go back to that dreary, empty house with the furniture covered in dust sheets and rooms that never warmed up enough to be comfortable. I got off at South Kensington and started to walk up the Brompton Road. Knightsbridge was still bustling with elegant couples on their way to an evening's entertainment. You'd never know that there was a depression and that a good portion of the world was lining up for a bowl of soup. Having grown up in such privileged circles, I'd only just become aware of the terrible injustices in the world and they worried me. If I'd been a lady with a comfortable private income, I'd have volunteered at those soup kitchens. However, I was now also one of the unemployed poor. I might be needing that bread and soup myself. Of course, I realized that it was different for me. I only had to agree to go and live with an elderly princess and I'd be dining well and drinking the best wines, without a care in the world. Except that now the thought was creeping into my consciousness that one should care. One should be doing something worthwhile.

I paused as I passed Harrods's windows. All those stylish dresses and shoes! My only attempts at keeping up with the latest fashion had been during my season, when I had received a meager clothing allowance, studied magazines to see what the bright young things about town were wearing this season, and then had the gamekeeper's wife run me up copies. Mrs. MacTavish was good with her needle but they were poor imitations at best. Oh, to have the money to sail into Harrods and choose an outfit, just like that!

I was lost in reverie when a taxi pulled up at the curb, a door slammed, and a voice exclaimed, "Georgie! It is you. I thought I spotted you and I made the taxi driver stop. What a surprise. I didn't know you were in town."

There before me, looking dazzlingly glamorous, was my former schoolfriend Belinda

Warburton-Stoke. She was wearing an emerald green satin opera cape—the kind where the sides are joined together to make the sleeves, thus making most people look like penguins. Her hair was styled in a sleek black cap with a jaunty hair ornament on one side, complete with ridiculous ostrich feather that bobbed as she ran toward me.

We rushed to embrace. "How lovely to see you, Belinda. You're looking fabulous. I would have hardly recognized you."

"One has to keep up appearances or the customers won't come."

"Customers?"

"My dear, haven't you heard? I've started my own business. I'm a fashion designer."

"Are you? How is it going?"

"Frightfully well. They are positively fighting to have the chance to wear my creations."

"How wonderful for you. I'm envious."

"Well, I had to do something. I didn't have a royal destiny, like you."

"My royal destiny doesn't seem too promising at the moment."

She pulled out some coins to pay the taxi driver, then linked arms with me and started to march me up the Brompton Road. "So what are you doing in town?"

"I bolted, taking after my mother, I suppose. I couldn't stand Scotland a minute longer."

"Nobody can, darling. Those awful loos with the tartan wallpaper! I have a permanent migraine when I'm there. Were you on your way somewhere? Because if not, come back and have a drink at my place."

"You're living near here?"

"Right next to the park. Terribly avant-garde. I've bought myself a dear little mews cottage and done it up and I'm living there alone with just my maid. Mother is furious, but I am twenty-one and I've come into my own money so there's not much she can do, is there?"

I allowed myself to be swept up Brompton Road, along Knightsbridge, and into a cobbled back alley where the former mews were now apparently transformed into living quarters. Belinda's cottage looked quaint on the outside but inside was completely modern—all white walls, streamlined, Bakelite and chrome with a cubist painting on the wall, possibly even a Picasso. She sat me on a hard purple chair, then went across to a generously stocked sideboard. "Let me make you one of my cocktails. I'm famous for them, you know."

With that she poured dangerous amounts from any number of bottles into a shaker, finished them off with something bright green, then poured the shaken result into a glass and dropped in a couple of maraschino cherries. "Get that down you and you'll feel wonderful," she said. She took a seat opposite me and crossed her legs, revealing a long expanse of silk stocking and just a hint of gray silk petticoat.

The first sip took my breath away. I tried not to cough as I looked up and smiled. "Very interesting," I said. "I don't have much opportunity to drink cocktails."

"Do you remember those awful experiments creating cocktails in the dorm at Les Oiseaux?" Belinda laughed as she took a long drink from her own glass. "It's a wonder we didn't knock ourselves out."

"We almost did. Remember that French girl, Monique? She was sick all night."

"So she was." Belinda's smile faded. "It already seems so long ago, like a dream, doesn't it?"

"Yes, it does," I agreed. "A beautiful dream."

She looked at me sharply. "So do I gather that life isn't too wonderful for you at the moment?"

"Life is pretty bloody, if you really want to know," I said. The cocktail was obviously already having an effect. "Bloody" wasn't a word I habitually used. "If I don't come up with something to do with myself soon, I'll be shipped out to a stately home in the country until the royal kin come up with some awful foreign prince for me to marry."

"Could be worse. There are some frightfully good-looking foreign princes. And it might be nice to be a queen someday. Think of all those lovely tiaras."

I scowled. "In case you haven't remembered, there are precious few kingdoms left in Europe. And royal families seem to be a disposable commodity. What's more, the suitable young men I have met have been so dull that assassination actually seems preferable than a long life with them."

"Dear me," Belinda said. "We are in a blue mood, aren't we? So your sex life must be pretty dismal at the moment."

"Belinda!"

"Oh, I'm sorry. I've shocked you. The set I mix with now has no qualms about discussing their sex lives. And why not? It's healthy to talk about sex."

"I don't mind talking about it really," I said, although in truth I found myself squirming with embarrassment. "God knows we used to talk about it all the time at school."

"But doing is so much better than talking, don't you agree?" She smiled like a cat with cream. Then she looked horrified. "You're not still a virgin?"

"Afraid so."

"It's no longer required of a potential princess, is it? Don't tell me they still send an archbishop and the lord chancellor to check personally before the marriage can be consummated."

I started to laugh. "I assure you I'm not saving myself from choice. I'd be perfectly happy to rip my clothes off and roll in the hay just as soon as I find the right man."

"So none of the young men we encountered during our season gave you hot pants for them?"

"Belinda, your language!"

"I've been mingling with Americans. Such fun. So naughty."

"If you want to know, the young men I have encountered have all been insufferably dull. And from my limited experience of groping and gasping in the backseats of taxies, I think sex must be overrated anyway."

"Oh, trust me, you'll like it." Belinda smiled again. "It is quite delish, with the right man, of course."

"Anyway, there is no point in talking about it, because I'm not likely to get in much practice, unless it's with gamekeepers like Lady Chatterley. I'm being banished to the country to be lady-in-waiting to an aged relative."

"They can't banish you. Don't go."

"I can't stay in London indefinitely. I've nothing to live on."

"Then get a job."

"Of course I'd love to get a job, but I suspect it won't be as easy as that. You've seen men queueing up for work. Half the world is looking for nonexistent jobs at the moment."

"Oh, the jobs are there for the right people. You just have to find your niche in life.

Find a need and fill it. Look at me. I'm having a whale of a time—nightclubs, all the social life I could wish for, my picture in *Vogue*."

"Yes, but you obviously have a talent for dress design. I've no idea what I could possibly do. Our schooling equipped us only for marriage. I can speak passable French, play the piano, and I know where to seat an archbishop at table. This hardly makes me employable, does it?"

"Of course it does, darling. All those nouveau riche middle-class snobs will positively snap you up, just to boast about you."

I stared at her in horror. "But I couldn't let them know who I really was. It would get back to the palace and I'd be whisked away to marry a prince in Outer Mongolia before I had time to catch my breath."

"You don't have to tell them who you are. One look at you and anyone can see you are top drawer. So get out there and have some fun."

"And earn some money, more to the point."

"Darling, are you stony broke? What about all the rich relatives?"

"Money comes with strings in my family.

If I go as a lady-in-waiting, I'll obviously get an allowance. If I agree to marry Prince Siegfried, I'm sure they'll come up with a wonderful trousseau."

"Prince Siegfried? The one we met at Les Oiseaux? The one we called Fishface?"

"The very same."

"Darling, how frightful. Of course you couldn't possibly marry him. Apart from the fact that Romania's monarchy is in a bit of disarray at the moment. Exile can be remarkably dreary."

"I'm not sure that I want to marry any prince," I said. "I'd rather build a career of my own, like you're doing. I just wish I had some talent."

She eyed me critically, just as the queen had done. "You're tall. You could be a model. I have connections."

I shook my head. "Oh, no. Not a model. Not walking up and down in front of people. Remember the debutante fiasco."

She giggled. "Oh, yes. Maybe not a model then. But you'll find something. Secretary to a film star?"

"I can't take shorthand or type."

She leaned across and patted my knee. "We'll find something for you. What about

Harrods? It's on the doorstep and it would be a good place to start."

"Working behind the counter at a department store?" I sounded shocked.

"Darling, I'm not suggesting you work as a belly dancer in the casbah. It's a perfectly respectable department store. I shop there all the time."

"I suppose it might be fun. But they wouldn't take me on with no experience, would they?"

"They would if someone who was a well-known society figure and woman-about-town wrote you a fabulous letter of recommendation."

"Who are you suggesting?"

"Me, you idiot." Belinda laughed. "When I've finished my letter, nobody would dare turn you down."

She took out pen and writing paper and started to write. "What name will you use?" she asked.

"Florence Kincaid," I said after a moment's thought.

"Who on earth is Florence Kincaid?"

"She was a doll my mother brought me back from Paris when I was little. Mother wanted me to call her Fifi La Rue, but I decided that Florence Kincaid sounded nicer."

"You'd probably be offered more interesting jobs if you called yourself Fifi La Rue," Belinda said with a wicked smile. She sucked on the end of her pen. "Now, let me see. Miss Florence Kincaid has been in my employ for two years as my assistant in the organization of charity fashion shows. She is of impeccable character and breeding, shows great initiative, poise, charm, and business sense, and has been a joy to work with. I release her with profound reluctance, realizing that I can no longer offer the scope that her kind of talent and ambition needs to blossom. How does that sound?"

"Fabulous," I said. "You are wasted as a fashion designer. You should become a writer."

"Now, I'll write it out neatly and you can take it round to Harrods in the morning," she said. "And now that I know you're living on my doorstep, we must get together more often. I'll introduce you to some naughty men-about-town. They'll show you what you've been missing."

That sounded like an interesting proposition. I had yet to meet any really naughty young men. The only ones who had verged on the naughty were the ski instructors who frequented the inn across the street from Les Oiseaux and our interaction with them was limited to throwing notes out of the windows or, on a couple of occasions, drinking a glass of mulled wine with their arms around our shoulders. The young Englishmen were revoltingly proper, maybe because our chaperons lurked in the background. If they took one outside for a stroll and tried a quick and hopeful grope, one stern rebuke would make them gush out apologies. "So sorry. Damned bad form. Can't think what came over me. Won't happen again, I promise."

Now I was twenty-one. I had no chaperon and I was dying to see what naughty young men had to offer. From what I had heard, I was somewhat confused about sex. It sounded rather horrid, and yet Belinda obviously enjoyed it—and my mother had done it with oodles of men on at least five different continents. It was, as Belinda had said, about time I found out what I had been missing.

Chapter 5

Rannoch House
Saturday, April 23, 1932

I woke the next morning determined to take Belinda up on her other suggestion—the one for gainful employment. Armed with Belinda's glowing recommendation, I sat facing the head of personnel at Harrods. He was eyeing me suspiciously and waved the letter in my direction. "If you had indeed proved so satisfactory, why did you leave this position?"

"The Honorable Belinda Warburton-Stoke is going through a difficult period, as one does when setting up a new business, and had to give up charity events for the time being."

"I see." He examined me critically, as several other people had done in the past twenty-four hours. "You're well enough spoken and you've been well educated, that is obvious. You say your name is Florence Kincaid? Well, Miss Kincaid, don't you have family connections? I'm wondering why you would want a job like this. Not just for fun, I hope, when so many poor souls are on the brink of starvation."

"Oh, indeed not, sir. You see, my father died some years ago. My brother has inherited the property and his new wife doesn't want to have me there any longer. I'm as much in need of a job as anyone else."

"I see." He frowned at me. "Kincaid. That wouldn't be the Worcester Kincaids, would it?"

"No, it wouldn't."

We stared at each other for a while, then my impatience got the better of me. "If you have no position vacant, please inform me immediately, so that I can take my skills to Selfridges."

"To Selfridges?" He looked horrified. "My dear young lady, you need no skills at Selfridges. I'll take you on trial. Miss Fairweather could use some help on the cosmetics counter. Follow me."

And so I was handed a smock in an unflattering salmony pink that made me, with my Celtic reddish blond hair and freckles, look like a large cooked prawn, and installed in cosmetics, under the disapproving glare of Miss Fairweather—who eyed me with a more superior stare than I had ever seen coming from one of my austere relatives.

"No experience at all? She's had no retail experience? I don't know how I'm ever supposed to find the time to train her." She sighed. She spoke with the kind of ultra-posh upper-class accent developed by those of humble birth who want to conceal this fact.

"I'm a quick learner," I said.

She sniffed this time. Frankly I thought she was a poor choice to put in charge of cosmetics, as no amount of cream, powder, or rouge would make that face look either soft, appealing, or glamorous. It would be like powdering granite.

"Very well, I suppose you'll have to do," she said. She gave me a rapid tour of our products and what they were supposed to do. Until now I had thought that cosmetics consisted of cold cream, a brushing of the lips with Natural Rose, and powdering one's nose with baby powder or those handy *papiers poudres*. Now I was amazed to see the selection of powders and creams—and the prices too. Some women obviously still had money in this depression.

"If a customer asks you for advice, come to me," Miss Fairweather said. "You have no experience, remember."

I murmured humble acquiescence. She moved to the other side of the counter like a ship in full sail. Customers started arriving. I called Miss Fairweather when necessary and I was just feeling that I was getting the hang of it and it wouldn't be too odious a job after all when a voice said imperiously, "I need a jar of my very special face cream that you always keep hidden away, just for me."

I looked up and found myself face-to-face with my mother. I'm not sure who was the more horrified.

"Good God, Georgie, what on earth are you doing here?" she demanded.

"Trying to earn an honest living like everybody else."

"Don't be ridiculous, darling. You weren't raised to be a shopgirl. Now take off that horrible smock at once. It makes you look like a prawn. And let's go and have some coffee at Fortnum's."

She still had that china-doll look that had made her the darling of the London stage, but the eyelashes were definitely too long to be real and there were circles of rouge on both cheeks. Her hair was black this time and she was wearing a pillar box red jacket of obvious Parisian design and a matching jaunty red beret. Around her neck was a silver fox, complete with beady-eyed head. I had to admit that the effect was still stunning.

"Would you please go away," I hissed at her.

"Don't tell me to go away," my mother hissed back. "Is that any way to talk to your mother, who hasn't seen you in months?"

"Mummy, you'll get me dismissed. Please just go away."

"I certainly won't go away," my mother said in her clear voice that had charmed audiences in the London theaters before my father snapped her up. "I have come to buy face cream and face cream I shall have."

A floorwalker appeared miraculously at her side. "Is there some problem, madam?"

"Yes, this young person doesn't seem to be able or willing to help me," my mother said, wafting a distressed hand in his direction. "All I need is some face cream. That shouldn't be too difficult, should it?"

"Of course not, madam. I'll have our senior assistant assist you as soon as she is finished with her customer. And you, girl. Fetch a chair and a cup of tea for madam."

"Very well, sir," I said. "I was perfectly willing to help madam,"—put emphasis on the word—"but she wasn't able to tell me the brand of face cream she needed."

"Don't answer back, girl," he snapped at me.

Seething with annoyance, I went to get my mother a chair and a cup of tea. She accepted both with a smirk. "I need cheering up, Georgie," she said. "I am quite desolate. You heard about poor Hubie, of course?"

"Hubie?"

"Sir Hubert Anstruther. My third husband, or was it my fourth? I know we were definitely married because he was the straightlaced type who wouldn't countenance living in sin."

"Oh, Sir Hubert. I remember him." I did too, with a warm kind of glow. He was one of the few husbands who had actually wanted me around and I still had fond memories of the time I spent at his house when I was about five. He was a big bear of a man who laughed a lot and had taught me how to climb trees, ride to hounds, and swim across his ornamental lake. I was broken-hearted when my mother left him and moved on to pastures new. I had rarely seen him since, but I received the occasional postcard from exotic parts of the world and he sent me a most generous check for my twenty-first.

"He's had an awful accident, darling. You know he's an explorer and mountaineer. Well, apparently he's just had a terrible fall in the Alps. Swept away by an avalanche, I believe. They don't expect him to live."

"How horrible." Instant feelings of guilt that I hadn't been to see him recently, or even written anything more than thank-you letters.

"I know. I've been devastated ever since I heard. I adored that man. Worshipped him. In fact I believe he was the only man I truly loved." She paused. "Well, apart from dear old Monty, of course, and that gorgeous Argentine boy."

She shrugged, making the silver fox around her neck twitch in a horribly lifelike way. "Hubert was very fond of you too. In fact he wanted to adopt you, but your father wouldn't hear of it. But I believe you're still mentioned in his will. If he does die, and they say his injuries are absolutely frightful, you won't have to work behind shop counters anymore. What do the royals think about this, anyway?"

"They don't know," I said, "and you are not to tell them."

"Darling, I wouldn't dream of telling them anything, but I really can't come to London never knowing when I'm going to be served by my own daughter. It just isn't on. In fact . . ."

She looked up with a charming smile as Miss Fairweather approached. "I am so sorry to keep you waiting like this, your ladyship. It is still your ladyship, isn't it?"

"No, I'm afraid not. Just plain Mrs. Clegg these days—I believe I am still legally married to Homer Clegg. What an awful name to be stuck with but Homer is one of these straightlaced Texan oil millionaires and he doesn't believe in divorce, unfortunately. Now, my needs are very simple today. Just a jar of that very special face cream you always keep hidden away for me."

"The one we import specially from Paris, madam, in the crystal jar with the cherubs on it?"

"That's the one. You are an angel to remember." My mother gave her brilliant smile and even the stern-faced Miss Fairweather flushed coyly. I could see how my mother had made so many conquests in her life. As Miss Fairweather went to hunt out the face cream, my mother straightened her hat in the mirror on the counter. "Poor Hubert's ward must be quite crushed by the news too," she said, without looking up at me. "He worshipped his guardian too, poor little chap. So if you happen to bump into him, do be kind to him, won't you? Tristram Hautbois." (She pronounced it "Hote-boys," naturally. It is the done thing to anglesize any French name when possible.) "You two were great chums when you were five years old. I remember you stripped off your clothes together and went romping in the fountains. Hubie did laugh."

At least I had had some illicit adventures with the opposite sex in my life, even if I was too young to remember them.

"Mother, about Granddad," I said in a low voice, not wanting to miss this opportunity. "He's not very well. I think you should go and see him—"

"I'd love to, darling, but I'm catching the

boat train back to Cologne this afternoon. Max will be pining. Tell him next time we're over, all right?"

The cream was brought, packaged, and charged to my mother's account. She was escorted out with much bowing and gushing. I watched her go, feeling that annoyance I always felt after any encounter with my mother—so many things I wanted to say and never a chance to say them. Then the floorwalker and Miss Fairweather returned to the counter, muttering together. She gave me a frosty stare and a sniff as she went around to her side.

"And you, girl, take off that smock," the floorwalker said.

"Take off my smock?"

"You are dismissed. I heard the tone of voice you used to one of our best customers. And Miss Fairweather claims she even heard you telling the customer to go away. You may have ruined Harrods's reputation forever. Go now. Turn in your smock and be gone."

I couldn't defend myself without revealing myself as a liar and a fraud. I went. My experiment with gainful employment had lasted all of five hours.

It was about two o'clock when I came out into a glorious spring afternoon. The sun was shining, the birds in Kensington Gardens were chirping, and I had four shillings I had earned in my pocket.

I wandered aimlessly through the afternoon crowds, not wanting to go home, not knowing what to do next. It was Saturday and the streets were packed with those who had a half day off work. I'd never get a job in another store now, I decided miserably. I'd probably never get another job anywhere and I'd die of starvation. My feet started hurting me and I felt almost dizzy with hunger. I realized they hadn't even given me a lunch break. I stopped and looked around me. I didn't know much about restaurants. People I knew didn't pay to go out to eat. They ate at home, unless they were invited to dine with a friend or neighbor. When we had been in London for my season we had eaten supper at the various balls. I had been taken to tea at the Ritz by a friend's aunt, but I could hardly go to the Ritz with four shillings in my pocket. I knew Fortnum and Mason, and the Café Royal, and that was about the extent of my restaurant knowledge.

I realized I had walked until the Kensington Road had become Kensington High Street. I recognized Barkers and knew that it would have a tearoom, but I had determined never to set foot in a department store again. In the end I went into a dismal Lyons, ordered a pot of tea and a scone, and sat feeling sorry for myself. At least I'd eat well as lady-in-waiting to a princess. At least I would be addressed politely and wouldn't have to put up with people like Miss Fairweather and that floorwalker. And I wouldn't risk bumping into my mother.

I looked up as a shadow hovered over me. It was a dark-haired young man, slightly unkempt, but not at all unattractive, and he was grinning at me.

"My goodness, it is you," he said in a voice that bore traces of an Irish brogue. "I couldn't believe my eyes as I walked past and saw you in the window. That's never her ladyship, I said to myself, so I had to come in to see." He pulled out the chair opposite me and sat without being invited to do so, still studying me with amused interest. "So what are you doing, seeing how the other half lives?"

He had unruly dark curls and blue eyes

that flashed dangerously. In fact he so un-
nerved me that I resorted to type. "I'm sorry,
I don't believe we've been introduced," I
said. "And I don't speak to strange men."

At that he threw back his head and
laughed. "Oh, that's a good one. Strange
men. I like that. Do you not recall dancing
with me at a hunt ball at Badminton a couple of years ago? Obviously not. I'm mor-
tally wounded. I usually make a far greater
impression on a girl I've held in my arms."
He held out his hand. "Darcy O'Mara. Or
should I say the Honorable Darcy O'Mara,
since you obviously care about such things.
My father is Lord Kilhenny, a peerage that
goes back far longer than your own admirable family's."

I took his hand. "How do you do?" I said
tentatively, because in truth I was sure I'd
have remembered meeting him and especially being in close contact in his arms.
"Are you sure you're not mistaking me for
someone else?"

"Lady Georgiana, is it not? Daughter of
the late duke, sister to the boring Binky?"

"Yes, but . . ." I stammered. "How can I
possibly not remember dancing with you?"

"Obviously you had more desirable partners that night."

"I assure you I didn't," I said hotly. "All the young men I remember were as dull as ditchwater. They only wanted to talk about hunting."

"There's nothing wrong with hunting," Darcy O'Mara said, "in its place. But there are many preferable occupations when in the presence of a young woman."

He looked at me so frankly that I blushed and was furious with myself.

"If you'll excuse me, I'd like to drink my tea before it gets cold." I looked down at the grayish, unappetizing liquid.

"Don't let me stop you," he said, waving expansively. "Go ahead, if you think you'll survive the experience without being poisoned. They lose a customer a day here, you know. Just whip them quietly out the back entrance and go on as if nothing has happened."

"They do not!" I had to laugh.

He smiled too. "That's better. I've never seen such a grim face as you were making earlier. What's wrong? Have you been dumped by a deceiver?"

"No, nothing like that. It's just that life is

insufferably gloomy at the moment." And I heard myself telling him about the room in the cold house, the embarrassment at Harrods, and the prospect of banishment to the country. "So you see," I concluded, "I've not much to look cheerful about at the moment."

He eyed me steadily, then he said, "Tell me, do you have a posh frock with you?"

"Posh as in dressing for dinner posh, or as in going to church posh?"

"As in attending a wedding posh."

I laughed again, a little uneasily this time. "Are you suggesting we run off and get married to cheer me up?"

"Good Lord, no. I'm a wild Irish boy. It will take a lot to tame me and drag me to the altar. So do you have a suitable outfit within reach?"

"Yes, as a matter of fact I do."

"Good. Go and put it on and meet me at Hyde Park Corner in an hour."

"Do you mind telling me what this is all about?"

He touched his finger to his nose. "You'll see," he said. "A damned sight better than tea and scones at Lyons anyway. Are you going to do it?"

I looked at him for a moment, then sighed. "What have I got to lose?"

Those roguish eyes flashed again. "I don't know," he said. "What have you?"

You are quite, quite mad, I said to myself several times as I washed, dressed, and attempted to tame my hair into the sleekness required by fashion. Going out on a whim with a strange man about whom you know nothing. He could be the worst sort of imposter. He could be running a profitable white slave ring, pretending to know young girls and luring them to their doom. I stopped what I was doing, rushed down to the library, and pulled out a copy of Burke's Irish Peerage. There it was all right: Thaddeus Alexander O'Mara, Lord Kilhenny, sixteenth baron, etc. Having issue: William Darcy Byrne . . .

So a real Darcy O'Mara did exist. And it was midafternoon. And the streets were crowded. And I wouldn't let him take me to a low-down dive or sleazy hotel. And he was awfully good-looking. As he said, what had I got to lose?

Chapter 6

Rannoch House
Saturday, April 23, 1932

I almost didn't recognize Darcy O'Mara as he came toward me on Park Lane. He was wearing full morning suit, his wild curls had been tamed, and he looked remarkably presentable. The quick once-over glance he gave me told me that he thought I also passed muster.

"My lady." He gave me a very proper bow.

"Mr. O'Mara." I inclined my head to reciprocate the greeting. (One never calls anybody honorable, even if they are.)

"Please forgive me," he said, "but was I correct in addressing you as 'my lady' and not 'your royal highness'? I'm never quite sure of the rules when it comes to dukes."

I laughed. "Only the male children of royal dukes can use the HRH," I said. "I, being a mere female, and my father not being a royal duke, even though of royal blood, am simply 'my lady.' But just plain Georgie will do."

"Not at all plain Georgie. It was good of you to come. I assure you you won't regret it." He took my elbow and steered me through the crowd. "Now let's get out of here. We look like a couple of peacocks in the hen coop."

"Do you mind telling me where we're going?"

"Grosvenor House."

"Really? If you're taking me to dine, isn't it a little early, and if you're taking me to tea, aren't we overdressed?"

"I'm taking you to a wedding, as I promised."

"A wedding?"

"Well, the reception part of it."

"But I haven't been invited."

"That's all right," he said calmly as we started down Park Lane, "neither have I."

I wrenched my arm free of him. "What? Are you out of your mind? We can't go to a wedding reception to which we haven't been invited."

"Oh, it's all right," he said. "I do it all the time. Works like a charm."

I eyed him suspiciously. He was grinning again. "How else would I get a decent meal once a week?"

"Let me get this straight. You intend to gate-crash a wedding at Grosvenor House?"

"Oh, yes. As I told you, there's never a problem. If you look right and you speak with the right accent and you know how to behave, everyone takes it for granted you are a legitimate guest. The groom's side thinks the bride's must have invited you and vice versa. You, being absolutely top drawer—they'll be proud and happy to have you there. Raises the tone of the whole occasion. Afterward they can say to each other, 'I hope you noticed we had a member of the royal family present.'"

"Just a distant relative, Darcy."

"Nonetheless, a catch. They'll be thrilled, you'll see."

I pulled away from him. "I really can't do this. It's not right."

"Are you backing out because it's not right or because you're afraid of getting caught?" he asked.

I glared at him. "I was brought up to behave properly, which may not have been the case in the wilds of Ireland."

"You're scared. You're afraid there's going to be a scene."

"I am not. I just don't think it's the right thing to do."

"Stealing their food by false pretense, you mean? As if anyone who can afford a wedding reception at Grosvenor House would notice if anyone took a couple of illegal slices of cold salmon." He took my hand. "Come on, Georgie. Don't back out on me now. And don't say you're not interested. Anyone who was attempting to eat one of Lyons's scones is obviously in need of a good meal."

"It's just that . . ." I began, conscious of his hand holding mine. "If I'm caught there might be a frightful stink."

"If they notice you and realize that they didn't invite you, they'll only feel mortified that they left you off the list and glad that you came."

"Well . . ."

"Look at me. Do you want smoked salmon and champagne or to go home to baked beans?"

"Well, if you put it that way, lead on, Mac-duff."

He laughed and took my arm. "That's the ticket," he said and swept me along Park Lane.

"If you're really Lord Kilhenny's son," I asked, my courage returning, "why do you need to gate-crash other people's weddings?"

"Same story as your own," he said. "The family's penniless. Father invested heavily in America, lost it all in '29; then there was a fire in his racing stables. Lost all that too. Had to sell the property and when I turned twenty-one he told me there was nothing for me so I'd have to make my own way. I'm making it the best I can. Ah, here we are."

I glanced up at that formidable red and white brick building on Park Lane as Darcy swept me up the steps under the colonnade and into the front entrance of Grosvenor House Hotel.

The doorman saluted as he opened the door. "You're here for the wedding reception, sir? To your right, in the blue ballroom."

I was whisked across the foyer and suddenly found myself in a queue for the reception line. I was expecting doom to fall at any moment, when the bride and groom would look at each other. I could hear them saying loudly, "But I didn't invite her, did you?" Luckily brides and grooms must be in a state of shock on such occasions. The bride's mother murmured, "So kind of you to come." The bride and groom were momentarily involved with the person ahead of us and Darcy took the opportunity to steer me toward a passing tray of champagne.

After a few minutes of feeling that my heart was going to leap into my mouth, expecting at any second to feel that hand on my shoulder, that voice barking, "She's a gate-crasher, please have her escorted from the premises," I started to relax and look around me. It certainly was very pleasant. The event was not being held in the grand ballroom, to which I had been for a ball during my season; it was in a smaller room, big enough for only two hundred or so, and now richly decorated with early spring flowers— the scent was heavenly. At the far end was a long, white-clothed table on which I could glimpse the many tiers of a cake. In one corner an orchestra (composed, as they so often are, of elderly men) was playing Strauss waltzes. I took a hot vol-au-vent from a passing tray and began to enjoy myself.

Darcy had been quite right. If you behave as if you should be there, then nobody questions it. People who half recognized me drifted up and there were several conversations along the lines of, "So, have you known old Roly long?"

"Can't say I know him well at all."

"Oh, so you're one of Primrose's lot then. Stunning girl."

"You see how easy it is?" Darcy whispered. "The only difficulty arises when there is a sit-down banquet with assigned places at the table."

"What on earth do you do then?" I asked, the panic returning as I looked around to detect evidence of an adjoining dining room.

"I make my apologies for having to catch a train and I melt away before it starts. But this one is only nibbles and cake. I checked first. I usually do."

"You're amazing."

He laughed. "We Irish have learned to live by our wits after centuries of being occupied by you English."

"If you don't mind, I happen to be Scottish. Well, one-quarter Scottish anyway."

"Ah, but it was your great-grandmother who went around subjugating half the world. Empress of all I survey, and all that. You must have that quality somewhere in your makeup."

"I've never had a chance to subjugate anybody yet, so I can't really say," I confessed, "but I'm frequently amused and she never was, apparently. At least not after Albert died. In fact, given my grim list of ancestors, I'd say I'm pretty normal."

"I'd say you turned out pretty damned well, for someone who is more than half English," he said and, to my annoyance, I blushed again.

"I think I'll go and try some of that crab," I said and turned away, only to bump into a familiar face.

"Darling!" Belinda cried excitedly, "I had no idea you were coming to this bash. Why didn't you tell me? We could have taken a cab together. What fun, isn't it? Who'd have thought that Primrose would settle down with someone like Roly?"

"Primrose?" I glanced across the room to glimpse the bride's back, hidden beneath a long veil around which everybody was cautiously stepping.

"The bride, darling. Primrose Asquey d'Asquey. She was at school with us, don't you remember? Well, for one term anyway. She was expelled for giving the new girls a lecture on how to use the Dutch cap."

We looked at each other and started to laugh.

"I do remember," I said.

"And now she's marrying Roland Aston-Poley. Military family. Which means she's gone from being Primrose Asquey d'Asquey to being Primrose Roly Poley. Not a happy choice, if you ask me."

I laughed with her.

"So you're part of Roly's brigade then," she said. "I didn't realize you had army connections."

"Not really." I started to blush again, then grabbed her arm and dragged her out of the main crush of guests. "Actually I'm here with an extraordinary chap. Darcy O'Mara. Do you know him?"

"Can't say that I do. Point him out to me."

"Over there by that flower arrangement."

"I say. Not bad. You can introduce me anytime you want to. Tell me all about him."

"That's just it," I whispered. "I'm not really sure if he's who he claims to be or a confidence trickster."

"Has he asked you to lend him money?"

"No."

"Then he's probably all right. Who does he say he is?"

"Lord Kilhenny's son. Irish baron."

"There's a million of them. I wouldn't doubt it for a moment. So he's the one who knows Roly?"

I leaned even closer. "He doesn't know either of them. We're gate-crashers. Apparently he does this sort of thing often, just to get a free meal. It's shocking, isn't it? I can't believe I'm doing this."

To my horror, she started to laugh. When she had controlled her mirth, she leaned toward me. "I'll let you into a little secret. I'm doing exactly the same thing. I wasn't invited either."

"Belinda! How could you?"

"Easily. Exactly the same way you could. My face is sort of familiar. I'm seen at Ascot and the opera, so nobody ever questions whether I was invited or not. It works wonderfully."

"But you said you were doing so well in your career."

She made a face. "Not all that well, actually. It's tough to start up a business, especially if you want to design clothes for the fashionable set. They never want to pay, you see. They gush over the dress I've designed for them and tell me they positively adore it and I'm the cleverest person they've ever met. Then they wear it to the opera and when I remind them they haven't paid, they point out that they have been advertising my dress just by wearing it and I should be grateful. I'm sometimes owed several hundred pounds, and the fabrics are not cheap."

"How awful for you."

"It's difficult," she agreed, "because if I make a fuss and upset one of them, she'll tell the rest of her set and they'll drop me like a hot potato."

I did see that this was likely to happen. "So what are you going to do? You can't keep financing their new clothes forever."

"I'm hoping for the big break, I suppose. If one of the royal family—or one of the Prince of Wales's lady friends—decides she likes my dresses, then everyone in the world will want them. That's where you could be most helpful, you know. If you are going to be mingling with your royal cousin and his set, I'll lend you one of my designs to wear and you can gush about me."

"I wouldn't guarantee that my cousin's women would pay up any quicker than your current clients," I said. "But I don't mind trying for you. Especially if it allows me to wear a slinky new dress."

"Splendid!" Belinda beamed at me.

"I'm sorry you're going through such a tough time," I said.

"Oh, there are a few honest ones among them—mostly old money, you know. Properly brought up, like you. It's those dreadful nouveau riche women who try to wriggle out of paying. I could name one society belle who looked me straight in the eye and insisted she had already paid, when she knew as well as I did that she hadn't. They're just not like us, darling."

I squeezed her arm. "At least you are out and about in society. You're bound to meet a rich and handsome man and then your money worries will be over."

"So will you, darling. So will you." She glanced across the room. "I take it that handsome Irish peer's son does not come with a fortune?"

"Penniless," I said.

"Dear me. Not a wise choice then, in spite of his looks. Although after last night's little conversation about sex lives, he might be just the one to . . ."

"Belinda!" I hissed as Darcy was making in our direction. "I've only just met him and I have no intention—"

"We never have, darling. That's just the problem. We never have." Belinda turned to meet Darcy with an angelic smile.

The afternoon went on. Smoked salmon came around, and shrimp and sausage rolls and savory éclairs. My spirits began to rise with the champagne intake until I was actually enjoying myself. Darcy had vanished into the crowd and I was standing alone when I noticed a potted palm tree swaying by itself as if in a strong wind. Since no wind is allowed to blow through ballrooms at Grosvenor House I was intrigued. I made my way to the corner and peered around the palm tree. A vision in alarming royal purple satin stood there, holding on to the palm tree as it swayed. What's more, I recognized her. It was another old school chum, Marisa

Pauncefoot-Young, daughter of the Earl of Malmsbury.

"Marisa," I hissed.

She attempted to focus on me. "Oh, hello, Georgie. What are you doing here?"

"More to the point, what exactly are you doing—dancing with a palm tree?"

"No, I came over all dizzy so I thought I'd retire to a quiet corner, but the damned tree won't stay still."

"Marisa," I said severely, "you're drunk."

"I fear so." She sighed. "It was all Primrose's fault. She insisted on having a very boozy breakfast to pluck up courage before the ceremony and then I got rather depressed all of a sudden and champagne does have a wonderful way of lifting the spirits, doesn't it?"

I took her arm. "Come on, come with me. We'll find somewhere to sit and get you some black coffee."

I led her out of the ballroom and found two gilt chairs in a hallway. Then I hailed a passing waiter. "Lady Marisa isn't feeling well," I whispered. "Do you think you could rustle up some black coffee for her?"

Black coffee appeared instantly. Marisa sipped and shuddered alternately. "Why can't I ever be a happy drunk?" she demanded. "One too many and my legs won't hold me up any longer. This is very sweet of you, Georgie. I didn't even know you were coming."

"Neither did I until the last moment," I said truthfully. "So tell me, why were you so depressed?"

"Look at me." She made a dramatic gesture at herself. "I look as if I've been swallowed by a particularly unpleasant variety of boa constrictor."

She wasn't wrong. The dress was long, tight, and purple. Since Marisa has no figure to speak of and is almost six feet tall, the effect was something like a shiny purple drainpipe.

"And I thought Primrose was my friend," she said. "I was flattered when she invited me to be bridesmaid, but now I see that she only did it because we are cousins and she had to, so she made damn sure that I wouldn't outshine her going up the aisle. Actually I could hardly totter up the aisle, due to the tight skirt. And it was so dark in St. Margaret's that I bet I looked like a floating head with a couple of disembodied arms on either side clutching this hideous bouquet. I'm not going to forgive her in a hurry."

She sighed and drained the last of the black coffee. "And then I got here and I thought at least being bridesmaid usually has its perks. You know, a quick kiss and cuddle with an usher behind the potted palms. But look at them—not a single grab and grope among the lot of them. Most of them are Roly's older brothers, and they've all brought their wives along. And the others are not that way inclined—daisy boys, you know."

"You mean pansy boys," I said.

"Do I? Well, you know what I'm getting at, don't you? So not the teeniest bit of titilla-tion all afternoon. No wonder I turned to drink. It was good of you to rescue me."

"Not at all. What are school friends for?"

"We did have fun at Les Oiseaux, didn't we? I still miss it sometimes, and all the old friends. I haven't seen you in ages. What have you been doing with yourself?"

"Oh, this and that," I said. "I'm newly ar-rived in town and I'm hunting for a suitable job."

"Lucky you. I do envy you. I'm stuck at home with Mummy. She hasn't been too well, you know, and she won't hear of my going off to London alone. How I'm ever going to meet a potential husband, I can't think. The season was a hopeless failure, wasn't it? All those dreadful clod-hopping country types who held us as if we were sacks of potatoes. At least Mummy is talking about taking a place in Nice for the rest of the spring. I certainly wouldn't say no to a French count. They have those wonderful droopy come-to-bed eyes."

She looked up as a burst of applause came from the ballroom.

"Oh, dear. They've started the speeches. I should be there, I suppose, when Whiffy proposes a toast to the bridesmaids."

"Do you think you can stand without swaying now?"

"I'll try."

I helped her to her feet and she tottered uncertainly back into the ballroom. I slipped into the back of the crowd, which now clustered around the podium with the cake.

The cake was cut and distributed. Speeches began. I was also beginning to feel the effects of three glasses of champagne on a relatively empty stomach. There is nothing worse than speeches about

someone you don't know, made by someone you don't know. How my royal kin manage to sit there, day after day, and look interested through one deadly dull speech
after another inspires my highest admiration. I looked for Darcy but couldn't see him,
so I prowled the back of the crowd, hoping
to find a chair I might sit on unobtrusively.
The only chairs were occupied by elderly
ladies and an extremely ancient colonel with
a wooden leg. Then I thought I spotted the
back of Darcy's head and I moved back into
the crowd again.

"My lords, ladies, and gentlemen, pray
raise your glasses for the loyal toast," the
toastmaster boomed out.

I accepted another glass of champagne
from a passing tray. As I was raising it, my
elbow was jogged violently and the champagne splashed up into my face and down
my front. Before I could do any more than
gasp I heard a voice saying, "I'm most
frightfully sorry. Here, let me get you a napkin." Like many young men of our class, he
could not, or would not, say the letter *r* and
pronounced it "fwightfully."

He reached across to a nearby table and
handed me a piece of linen.

"That's a tray cloth," I said.

"I'm so sorry," he said again. "It's all I could find."

I dabbed at my face with the tray cloth and was now able to focus on him. He was tall and slim, like an overgrown schoolboy who is wearing his big brother's morning suit. An attempt had been made to slick down his dark brown hair but it still flopped in boyish fashion across his forehead and his earnest brown eyes were now pleading with me in a way that reminded me of a spaniel I once had.

"I've ruined your lovely dress. I really am the most clumsy ox," he went on as he watched me dry myself off. "I'm absolutely hopeless at events like this. The moment I put on a morning suit or a dinner jacket, I am positively guaranteed to spill something, trip over my shoelaces, or generally make an utter fool of myself. I'm thinking of becoming a hermit and living in a cave somewhere on a mountaintop. In Scotland, maybe."

I had to laugh at that. "I don't think you'll find the food is as good," I pointed out. "And I think you'd find a Scottish cave incredibly cold and drafty. Trust me, I know whereof I speak."

"You do have a point." He observed me and then said, "I say, I think I know who you are."

This was not good. It was bound to happen, I suppose. Just in case things got awkward, I tried to spot Darcy in the crowd. However, I was completely unprepared for what the young man said next: "I believe that you and I are related."

I went through a quick mental list of cousins, second cousins, and second cousins once removed.

"Really?" I said.

"Well, sort of related. At least, not actually related, but your mother was once married to my guardian, and we played together when we were little. I'm Tristram Hautbois, Sir Hubert Anstruther's ward."

All I could think was what terrible twist of fate had christened somebody Tristram who could not say his *r*s properly. He pronounced it "Twistwam."

"We ran through the fountains naked, apparently," I said.

His face lit up. "You remember it too? We thought we'd get into frightful trouble, because a lot of important people had been invited to tea on the lawns, but my guardian thought it was frightfully funny." His face became solemn again. "You've heard what's happened, I suppose. Poor old Sir Hubert's had a terrible accident. He's in a coma in a Swiss hospital. They don't expect him to live."

"I only heard about it this morning," I said. "I'm very sorry. I remember him as such a nice man."

"Oh, he was. One of the best. So good to me, you know, even though I was only a distant relative. My mother was his mother's cousin. You knew his mother was French, I suppose. Well, my parents were killed in the Great War and he took frightful risks coming over to France to rescue me. He has raised me as if I were his own son. I owe him a huge debt of gratitude that I'll never be able to repay now."

"So you're actually French, not English?"

"I am, but I'm afraid my mastery of the language is no better than the average schoolboy's. I can just about manage '*la plume de ma tante*' and all that. Shameful, really, but I was only two years old when I was brought to Eynsleigh. It's a lovely house, isn't it? One of the prettiest in England. Do you remember it well?"

"Hardly at all. I have a vague memory of the lawns and those fountains, and wasn't there a fat little pony?"

"Squibbs. You tried to make him jump over a log and he bucked you off."

"So he did."

We looked at each other and smiled. I had thought him the usual run-of-the-mill mindless twit until now, but the smile lit up his whole face and made him look quite appealing.

"So what will happen to the house if Sir Hubert dies?" I asked.

"Sold, I expect. He has no children of his own to inherit. I am the closest he has to a son, but he never officially adopted me, unfortunately."

"What are you doing with yourself now?"

"I've just come down from Oxford and Sir Hubert arranged for me to be articled to a solicitor in Bromley in Kent, of all places. I'm not sure that I'm cut out for the law, but my guardian wanted me to have a stable profession, so I suppose I've got to stick with it. Frankly I'd much rather be off on adventures and expeditions like him."

"A little more dangerous," I pointed out.

"But not boring. How about you?"

"I've just arrived in London and I'm not sure what I'm going to be doing with myself. It's not quite as easy for me to just go out and get a job."

"No, I suppose it wouldn't be," he said. "Look, now that you're in London, maybe we can do some exploring together. I happen to know the city quite well and I'd be delighted to show you around."

"I'd like that," I said. "I'm staying at the family home. Rannoch House on Belgrave Square."

"And I'm in digs in Bromley," he said. "A slight difference."

Another young man in a morning coat approached. "Buck up, old thing," he said to Tristram. "We need all the groomsmen outside toot sweet. We've got to sabotage the car before they drive away."

"Oh, right. Coming." Tristram gave me an apologetic smile. "Duty calls," he said. "I do hope we meet again soon."

At that moment Darcy appeared. "Are you ready to go, Georgie? The bride and groom are about to leave and I thought . . ." He broke off when he saw I was standing beside Tristram. "Oh, I'm sorry. I didn't mean to interrupt. How are you, Hautbois?"

"Pretty fair. And yourself, O'Mara?"

"Can't complain. Will you excuse us? I have to take Georgie home."

"I turn into a pumpkin at six o'clock," I attempted to joke.

"I look forward to seeing you again, Lady Georgiana," Tristram said formally.

As Darcy turned away and attempted to fight his way through the crowd to the door, Tristram grabbed my arm. "Watch out for O'Mara," he whispered. "He's a bit of a cad. Not quite trustworthy."

Chapter 7

Rannoch House
Saturday, April 23, 1932

We came out to a mild April evening. The setting sun was streaming across the park.

"There," Darcy said, taking my arm to help me down the steps. "That wasn't so bad, was it? You survived perfectly well and you're considerably better fed and wined than you were a couple of hours ago. In fact there are now nice healthy roses to your cheeks."

"I suppose so," I said, "but I don't think I plan on doing it again. Too hair-raising. There were people who knew me."

"Like that twerp Hautbois?" Darcy said scathingly.

"You know Tristram, then?"

"I can't say I actually socialize with him these days. We were at school together. At least, I was a couple of years above him. He snitched to the masters and got me a beating once."

"For doing what?"

"Trying to take something from him, I believe," he said. "Sniveling little brute that he was."

"He seems quite pleasant now," I said.

"Has he asked to see you again?"

"He's offered to show me around London."

"Has he now."

With a thrill I realized that he might be jealous. I grinned.

"So how on earth do you know him?" Darcy went on. "He can't have been one of your partners at those dreary deb balls, surely?"

"We were practically related once. My mother was married to his guardian. We used to—to play together." Somehow I couldn't use the word "naked" with Darcy.

"I'd imagine you are probably practically related to a good many people on several continents," he said and raised an eyebrow.

"I think my mother only actually married the first few bolts," I said. "In those days she was conventional enough to still believe she should marry them. Now she just—"

"Lives in sin?" Again that challenging smile that did something to my insides.

"As you say."

"That would never work for me," he said. "As a Catholic, I'd be damned to hell if I kept marrying and divorcing. The church considers marriage sacred and divorce a mortal sin."

"And if you kept living in sin with somebody?"

He grinned. "I think the church would prefer that, given the options."

I glanced up at him as we waited to cross Park Lane. Penniless, Irish, and a Catholic too. Quite unsuitable in every way. If I were still being chaperoned, I'd have been bundled into the nearest cab and whisked away instantly.

"I'll see you home," he said, taking my arm again when I teetered as we crossed the street.

"I'm perfectly capable of finding my own way home in broad daylight," I said, although I had to admit that my legs weren't exactly steady after all that champagne and with the heady prospect of his walking beside me.

"I'm sure you are, but wouldn't you rather

have my company to enjoy this lovely evening? Were I currently in funds, I'd have arranged a horse-drawn carriage and we'd clip-clop slowly along the leafy avenues. As it is, we can still walk across the park."

"All right, then," I said, rather ungraciously. Twenty-one years of strict upbringing were shouting that I should have no more to do with a man whom I had been warned was a cad and unreliable, as well as being penniless and a Catholic. But when had I ever had such a tempting chance to stroll through the park with someone so devastatingly handsome?

There is nothing as lovely as a London park in springtime. Daffodils among the trees, new green emerging on those spreading chestnuts, elegantly turned-out horses crossing from the riding stable toward Rotten Row, and courting couples strolling hand in hand or sitting rather too close to each other on the benches. I stole a glance at Darcy. He was striding out, looking relaxed and enjoying the scene. I knew I should be making conversation at this moment. At all those training sessions at Les Oiseaux, when we had to dine with each of the mistresses in turn, it was drummed into us that it was a mortal sin to allow a silence to descend upon a dinner party.

"Do you actually live in London?" I asked Darcy.

"At the moment. I'm sleeping at a friend's place in Chelsea while he's on his yacht in the Med."

"That sounds awfully glamorous. Have you been to the Med yourself?"

"Oh, yes. Many times. Never in April though. Not smooth enough. I'm a rotten sailor."

I tried to form the question I was dying to ask him. "So do you have some kind of profession? I mean, if you have to gate-crash functions to get a good meal and your father has cut you off without a penny, how do you survive?"

He looked down at me and grinned. "I live by my wits, my girl. That's what I do. And it's not a bad life. People invite me to make upon even number at dinner parties. I'm awfully well house-trained. I never spill soup on my dinner jacket. They invite me to dance with their daughters at hunt balls. Of course they don't all know what I've told you about being penniless. I'm Lord Kilhenny's son. They think I'm a good catch."

"You will be Lord Kilhenny one day, won't you?"

He laughed. "My old man is likely to live forever, just to spite me. He and I have never been the greatest of pals."

"And what about your mother? Is she still living?"

"Died in the flu epidemic," he said. "So did my little brothers. I was away at school so I survived. The conditions were so brutal there, the food so bad, that even the influenza bugs didn't think it worth visiting." He smiled, then the smile faded. "I think my father blames me for living."

"But you'll have to do something with yourself someday. You can't go on sneaking in to eat at other people's functions."

"I expect I'll marry a rich heiress, probably an American, and live happily ever after in Kentucky."

"Would you like that?"

"Good horses in Kentucky," he said. "I like horses, don't you?"

"Adore them. I even adore hunting."

He nodded. "It's in the blood. Nothing we can do about it. That's the one thing I regret, the destruction of our racing stable. We had some of the finest thoroughbreds in Europe at one time." He stopped as if the idea had just struck him. "We must go to Ascot together. I know how to pick winners. If you come with me, you'll win yourself a tidy amount."

"If I can win myself a tidy amount, why don't you win tidy amounts for yourself and thus not be quite so penniless?"

He grinned. "And who says I don't win myself very tidy amounts from time to time? It's a great way to keep my head above water. I can't do it too often, though, or I'd find myself in trouble with the bookmakers."

I looked up and saw to my regret that we were approaching Hyde Park Corner and Belgrave Square lay just on the other side.

It was one of those rare spring evenings that holds the promise of summer. The sun was about to set and the whole of Hyde Park was glowing. I turned to savor the scene.

"Don't let's go indoors yet. It's lovely to be outside. I'm afraid I was brought up to be a country girl. I hate looking out of my window at chimneys and rooftops."

"I feel the same way," Darcy said. "You should see the views from Kilhenny Castle—all those lovely green hills and the sea

sparkling in the distance. Can't beat it anywhere in the world."

"Have you been around the world?" I
asked.

"Most of it. I went to Australia once."

"Did you?"

"Yes, my father suggested I try to make
my fortune there."

"And?"

"Not the right sort of place for me.
They're all plebs, all mates together. They
actually enjoy roughing it and going to a loo
in the backyard. Oh, and they actually expect one to work by the sweat of one's
brow. I'm afraid I was made for civilization."
He found a bench and sank onto it, patting
the seat beside him. "Good view from here."

I sat beside him, conscious of the close-
ness and warmth of his leg against mine.

"So tell me," he said. "What do you plan
to do with yourself now that Harrods is no
more?"

"I'll have to look for another job," I said,
"but I rather fear that Her Majesty is making
her own plans. At the moment it is a choice
between marrying a ghastly foreign prince
or becoming lady-in-waiting to a great-aunt,
Queen Victoria's last surviving daughter, in

the depths of the countryside where the height of entertainment will be holding her knitting wool or playing rummy."

"So, tell me"—he looked at me with interest—"how many people actually stand between you and the throne?"

"I'm thirty-fourth in line, I believe," I said. "Unless somebody's had a baby in the meantime and pushed me further back."

"Thirty-fourth, eh?"

"I hope you're not thinking of marrying me in the hopes of gaining the crown of England one day!"

He laughed. "That would be a trump card for the Irish, wouldn't it? King of England, or rather Prince Consort of England."

I laughed too. "I used to do that when I was small—lie in bed and work out ways to kill off all those ahead of me in the line of succession. Now I'm grown up, you couldn't pay me enough to be queen. Well, actually that's a lie. If my cousin David proposed, I'd probably accept."

"The Prince of Wales? You think he's a good catch?"

I looked surprised. "Yes, don't you?"

"He's a mama's boy," Darcy said scornfully. "Haven't you noticed? He's looking for a mummy. He doesn't want a wife."

"I think you're wrong. He's just waiting to find a suitable one."

"Well, this latest flame won't be suitable," Darcy said.

"Have you met her?"

"Oh, yes."

"And?"

"Not suitable. Charming enough, but definitely an older woman and far too worldly-wise. They'd never let her be queen."

"Do you think she wants to be?"

"Well, as of now she's still married to someone else, so it's probably a moot point," he said. "But I shouldn't keep your own hopes up. Your cousin David is never going to pick you as his consort. And frankly, you'd soon tire of him."

"Why? I think he's most amusing, and he's a topping dancer."

"He's a lightweight," Darcy said. "No substance to him. A moth flitting around, trying to find out what to do with himself. He'll make a rotten king."

"I think he'll step up when the time comes," I said huffily. "We have all been brought up with duty thrust down our throats. I'm sure David will do his one day."

"I hope you're right."

"Anyway," I whispered confidentially, "I've been asked to spy on her." I realized as I said it that too much champagne had loosened my tongue and I should not be confiding things like this to strangers, but by the time I had processed this information, it was too late.

"To spy on her? By whom?" Darcy was clearly interested.

"The queen. I'm supposed to attend a house party to which the prince and his lady friend have both been invited, then report back to HM."

"You'll probably have nothing good to say about her." Darcy grinned. "Men universally find her delightful and women universally find something catty to say about her."

"I'm sure I shall be very fair in my assessment," I said. "I am not prone to cattiness."

"That's one of the things I think I might like about you," Darcy said. "And there are others." He looked around. The sun had gone down and it had become instantly chilly. "Best get you home before you freeze in your posh frock."

I had to agree that I was now feeling the cold, especially since the champagne down my front hadn't quite dried yet. And no maid to sponge away the stains. What was I going to do about that?

He took my hand and dragged me across the traffic at Hyde Park Corner.

"Well, here I am," I said unnecessarily as I stood outside my front door and fumbled in my purse for the key. As usual in moments of stress, my fingers weren't obeying very well. "Thank you for a lovely afternoon."

"Don't thank me, thank the Asquey d'Asqueys. They paid for it. Aren't you going to invite me in?"

"I don't think I'd better. I'm living alone, you see."

"And you're not even allowed to have a young man in for a cup of tea? I didn't realize the royal rules were still so strict."

"It's not royal rules." I laughed nervously. "It's just that—I'm afraid none of the rooms fit for entertaining are open. And I have no servants yet. I'm just sort of camping out in one bedroom and the kitchen, where my culinary talents don't stretch beyond baked beans and tea. I did take cooking classes at school, but all useless items like petit fours that I never could master."

"I prefer petit fives myself," he said, making me smile.

"I never learned to make those either."

I glanced into the gloomy interior of the front hall and then back at Darcy. The thought of being alone with him was tempting. Twenty-one years of training won out. "Thank you for a lovely afternoon," I said again, and held out my hand. "Good-bye then."

"Good-bye then?" He gave me the most appealing little lost boy look. I almost melted. But not quite. "Look, Darcy, I would love to invite you in, but it is getting late, and . . . you do understand, don't you?"

"Turned out alone into the snow. How cruel." He pulled a tragic face.

"You said five minutes ago that it was a lovely afternoon."

"Ah well," he said. "I can see you're not going to be moved whatever I say. Twenty-one years of royal upbringing. Never mind, there will be other occasions." He took my hand, brought it to his lips, and this time he kissed it, sending a shiver all the way up my arm.

"If you like, I'll take you to a party at the Café de Paris next week," he said casually, releasing my hand again.

"Are you crashing this one too?"

"Of course. It's given by Americans. They just love British nobility. When they hear you are related to the royal family, they'll be kissing your feet and plying you with cocktails and inviting you to stay on their ranches. Will you come?"

"I expect so."

"I can't remember which day, offhand. I'll let you know."

"All right," I said. I lingered, feeling awkward. "Thank you again."

"The pleasure was all mine." He made that somehow sound sinful. I fled into the house before he caught me blushing again. As I closed the door behind me and stood in that cold, dark front hall with its black and white checked floor and dark embossed walls, a disturbing thought came into my mind. It occurred to me that Darcy might now be using me to gate-crash even more events. Perhaps I was now a guaranteed entry ticket to places he had been barred from before.

Indignation rose up for a second. I didn't

like the thought of being flattered and used, or being flirted with as if he really meant it. But then I had to agree that it was more fun than the humdrum life I had been leading recently. Certainly better than doing cross-word puzzles at Castle Rannoch or sitting in the subterranean kitchen eating baked beans. As I had said earlier, what had I got to lose?

Chapter 8

Rannoch House
Saturday, April 23, 1932

I was about to go upstairs to take off my posh frock, as Darcy called it, when I noticed some letters were stuck in the box. Hardly anybody knew I was in town yet so letters were a novelty. There were two of them. I recognized my sister-in-law's writing on one of the envelopes, and the Glen Garry and Rannoch crest (two eagles, trying to disembowel each other over a craggy mountaintop), so I opened the other one first. It was the predicted invitation. Lady Mountjoy would be so delighted if Lady Georgiana could join them at their country estate for a house party and a masked fancy dress ball.

There were a couple of postscripts. The first a formal one: *Please bring fancy dress costumes with you as there is nowhere in* the neighborhood that rents out such things.

And the second, less formal: *Imogen will be so delighted to see you again.*

Imogen Mountjoy was among the dullest, stodgiest girls in the world. She and I had scarcely exchanged more than two words during our season, and those were both about hunting, so I truthfully couldn't imagine her being delighted at the thought of seeing me, but it was a kind gesture and I resolved to RSVP as soon as I had read the missive from Fig.

Dear Georgiana,
Binky has just informed me that he has to pop up to town on Monday on a matter of urgent and unforeseen business. With the world in its current sorry state and everybody being asked to economize, I thought it seemed silly and wasteful to go to the expense of sending staff in an advance party to open up the house when you are already there. Since you are living "grace and favor" as it were, I hope it won't be too much to ask to have Binky's bedroom and study aired out for him, and

maybe just the little morning room for him to read the newspapers. (You have ordered the Times, *I hope.)*

I'm sure he'll be dining at his club so you don't have to worry too much about the food side of things. I expect the house will be quite chilly. Maybe you could have a fire going in Binky's bedroom on the day he arrives. Oh, and a hot water bottle in his bed too.

Your loving sister-in-law, Hilda

She always was known for her stuffy formality. Nobody ever called her by her real name. And I could see why. A more ridiculous name for a duchess I have never heard. If I had been called Hilda, I would have drowned myself in the nursery bathtub rather than grow up saddled with such a burden.

I stared at the letter for a moment. "What cheek," I said out loud and it was echoed back from the high ceiling of the hallway. *Not only are they no longer supporting me, but now they're treating me like a servant. Perhaps she forgets that I'm here all alone, without a maid, even. Does she want me to dust and make beds and light fires myself?*

Then I realized that it probably had never occurred to Hilda that I was living here without servants. She obviously expected that I had hired a maid by now.

After I had calmed down, I supposed it wasn't such an unreasonable request. I was able-bodied enough to take off a few dust sheets and even run a carpet sweeper over a floor or two, wasn't I? I had grown up never having to make my own bed, never having got myself a glass of water until I went to school, but I was capable of doing both. I was making splendid progress really. I hadn't actually attempted to light a fire yet, of course, even though Granddad had given me the most basic instruction the previous day. It was the thought of that coal'ole, as he called it—the dreaded coal cellar replete with spiders—that put me off. But it would have to be tackled sometime. With all those ancestors who fought at Bannock Burn and Waterloo and every battle in between, I should have inherited enough spunk to face a coal cellar. Tomorrow was Sunday, when I was expected for lunch with my grandfather. I'd have him take me through the complete fire-lighting experience. Never let it be said that a Rannoch was defeated by anything!

On Sunday morning I was up, bright and early, ready to tackle my task. I put on an apron I found hanging in a cupboard below stairs and I tied a scarf around my hair. It was actually quite fun to whip off dust sheets and shake them out of the window. I was dancing around with the feather duster when there was a knock at the front door. I didn't stop to think about the way I was dressed as I opened it and found Belinda on the doorstep.

"Is her ladyship at home to callers?" she asked, then she started as she recognized me. "Georgie! What on earth? Are you auditioning for the role of Cinderella?"

"What? Oh, this." I glanced down at the feather duster. "On the orders of my dear sister-in-law. She wants me to get the house ready for the arrival of my dear brother, the duke, tomorrow. Come on in." I led her down the hallway and up the stairs to the morning room. The windows were open and a fresh breeze stirred the lace curtains.

"Do sit down," I said. "The seat has been newly dusted."

She looked at me as if I had turned into a new and dangerous creature. "Surely she didn't mean that you were to take it upon yourself personally to clean the house?"

"I'm afraid that's exactly what she did mean. Do take a seat."

"What was she thinking?" Belinda sat.

"I think the word for my sister-in-law is frugal, at best. She didn't want to pay for the extra train tickets to send down the servants ahead of Binky. She reminded me of my grace and favor status, thereby suggesting that I owed Her Grace a favor."

"What nerve," Belinda exclaimed.

"My own sentiments exactly, but she obviously assumes I've hired a maid by now. She gave me a long lecture on the untrustworthiness of Londoners and how I should check all references."

"Why didn't you bring a maid with you?"

"Fig wouldn't release one of ours and frankly I couldn't afford to pay her anyway. But, you know, it's not too bad. In fact it's been quite fun. I'm getting rather good at it. It must be that humble ancestry on my mother's side coming out but one gets quite a satisfaction from polishing things."

Then suddenly it was as if I was hit with a

flash of divine inspiration. "Wait," I said. "I've just had a marvelous idea—I wanted a paying job, didn't I? I could do this for other people and be paid for it."

"Georgie! I'm all for standing on your own feet, but there are limits. A member of the house of Windsor acting as a char lady? My dear, think of the stink there would be when it was found out."

"They don't need to know it's actually me, do they?" I gave a couple of whisks with the feather duster as I warmed up to the idea. "I can call myself Coronet Domestics and nobody need ever know that I, and I alone, am Coronet Domestics. It's better than starving, anyway."

"What about the lady-in-waiting thing? How does one turn down the request of a queen?"

"Very cautiously," I said. "But luckily nothing in the palace happens overnight. By the time HM has it arranged, I shall tell her that I am fully occupied and financially stable."

"Well, good luck then, I suppose," Belinda said. "You wouldn't find me cleaning lavatories."

"Oh, dear," I said, coming down to earth with a bump. "I hadn't counted on lavatories. I was thinking more a quick whisk with my handy duster. That much I can handle."

She laughed. "I fear you may have a rude awakening. Some people are absolute pigs, you know." She leaned back against the velvet upholstery and crossed her legs in a move that must have been practiced and designed to drive young men wild. It had no such effect on me except to elicit a wave of envy over her silk stockings.

"So how did you enjoy your outing with the attractive Mr. O'Mara?" she asked.

"He is quite dashing, isn't he?"

"What a pity he's penniless. Not exactly the escort you need at this stage of your life."

"Maybe we go together well," I said.

"You've tried, have you?" Belinda asked.

"Tried what?"

"Going together."

"We've only just met, Belinda. Although he did kiss my hand on the doorstep and suggest that I invite him inside."

"Did he? How terribly un-British."

"I have to confess I did enjoy the hand-kissing part and I almost relented and let him into the house."

She nodded. "He's Irish, of course. They

are a wild race, but more fun, one has to admit, than the English. Heaven knows Englishmen have no idea at all about the gentle art of seduction. The best most of them can manage is to slap you on the behind and ask if you fancy a spot of the old rumpy-pumpy."

I nodded. "That does sum up my experience so far."

"There you are then. So he may well be the one."

"To settle down with? We'd starve."

"Not to settle down with." She shook her head at my stupidity. "To rid you of the burden around your neck. Your virginity, I mean."

"Belinda! Really!"

She laughed at my red face. "Someone has to before you turn into a sour old maid. My father always says that once women turn twenty-four, they are beyond redemption, so you've only got a year or so." She looked at me, expecting an answer, but I was still lost for words. Discussing my virginity did not come easily to me. "You are seeing him again?" she asked.

"He's taking me to a party at the Café de Paris next week."

"Oh, my dear. Very swank."

"Gate-crashing again, I'm afraid. He says it's given by Americans and they'll fall over backward to have a member of the royal family present, even if it's a minor one."

"He's absolutely right. When is it?" She produced a small diary from her bag.

"Belinda, you're as bad as he is."

"Maybe we're kindred spirits. You should keep us apart. I think I might rather fancy him myself, although I'd never step on the toes of an old school chum. And being penniless does limit the desirability. I do have horribly expensive tastes." She jumped up and grabbed the feather duster from me. "I almost forgot what I came for. I bumped into another old school chum at the wedding yesterday. Sophia, that round little Hungarian countess. Didn't you see her?"

"No, I didn't. There were so many people and I was attempting to lie low."

"Well, anyway, she invited me to a little party on a houseboat in Chelsea this afternoon and I asked if I could bring you. I tried to find you, but you'd vanished."

"Darcy and I melted away before the party dispersed."

"So will you come to the party on the houseboat?"

"It does sound rather fun. Oh, wait a minute. No, I'm afraid I can't come after all. I've just remembered that I promised to have Sunday lunch with my grandfather. In fact"—I glanced at my watch—"I have to run and get changed instantly."

"Your nonroyal grandfather, I take it?"

"The other one is long dead, so that would have to be a séance and no lunch."

"And your living one? Don't I remember that your family discouraged any communication with him? Why was that?"

"He's a Cockney, Belinda, but he's an old dear, quite the nicest person I know. I just wish I could do more for him. He's not exactly in funds at the moment and he needs a good holiday by the sea." I brightened up again. "So maybe my housecleaning experiment will be so successful that I can send him on his holiday and all will be well."

Belinda eyed me suspiciously. "I am not normally one to look on the dark side of things, but I think you are courting disaster, my sweet. If news of your new career choice ever made it back to the palace, I fear you'd be married off to the frightful

Siegfried and locked away in a castle in Romania before you could say Ivor Novello."

"This is a free country, Belinda. I am twenty-one years old and nobody's ward and I'm not next in line to the throne and frankly I don't give a hoot what they think!"

"Well said, old thing." She applauded. "Come on then, let me help you compose your advertisement before you depart."

"All right." I went over to the writing desk and took out pen and paper. "Do you think the *Times* is preferable to the *Tattler* in attracting the right clientele?"

"Do both. Some women never read a newspaper but always look at the *Tattler* to see if they are in it."

"I'll bite the bullet and pay for both then. I hope a commission comes along quickly or I'll be standing in a bread line myself in a week or so."

"It's a pity you can't come to the party with me this afternoon. Sophia is a robust girl in that typically middle-European way, so I'm sure food will feature prominently. And she mixes with all kinds of delightful bohemians—writers and painters, that kind of thing."

"I wish I could, but I'm sure food will

figure prominently at my grandfather's too. He's promised me a roast and two veg. So what shall we say in this advertisement?"

"You have to make it quite clear that you are not interested in scrubbing their loos, just light dusting and opening their houses up for them. How about: 'Coming to London but want to leave your staff at the country seat?'"

I scribbled away. "Oh, that's good. Then we could say Coronet Domestics Agency will air out your house and make it ready for your arrival."

"And you have to give an endorsement from someone of status."

"How can I do that? I can hardly ask Fig to recommend me and she's the only one for whom I've ever cleaned a house so far."

"You endorse yourself, you chump. As used by Lady Victoria Georgiana, sister of the Duke of Glen Garry and Rannoch."

I started laughing. "Belinda, you are positively brilliant."

"I know," she said modestly.

⁂

Lunch was a huge success—lovely leg of lamb, crispy roast potatoes and cabbage from Granddad's back garden, followed by baked apple and custard. I felt the occasional pang of guilt as I wondered whether he could really afford to eat in this way, but he was taking such obvious pleasure from watching me eat, that I let myself enjoy every bite.

"After lunch," I said, "you really must teach me how to light a fire. I'm not joking. My brother will be arriving tomorrow and I've been instructed to have a fire lit in his bedroom."

"Well, blow me down. Of all the cheek," he said. "What do they think you are—a skivvy? I'm going to give that brother of yours a piece of my mind."

"Oh, it's not Binky," I said. "He's actually quite a dear. Very vague, of course, never notices anything. And not very bright. But essentially a kind person. And it is my fault partly, I suppose. My sister-in-law took it for granted that I'd be hiring staff as soon as I got to London. I should have made it quite clear that I couldn't afford to do so. Stupid pride."

My grandfather shook his head. "I told you, my love. If you want to light a fire, you'll have to go down the coal cellar."

"If I must, I must," I said. "I'm sure plenty of servants have been down into the coal cellar and survived. What then?"

He talked me through it, from the newspaper to the right way to lay the sticks and then the coal on top, and all about opening dampers. It sounded daunting.

"I wish I could come up and do it for you," he said. "But I don't think your brother would take kindly to my being in the house."

"I wish you could come up and live with me for a while," I said. "Not to look after me, but to keep me company."

He looked at me with wise dark eyes. "Ah, but that would never work, would it? We live in different worlds, ducks. You'd want me to sleep above stairs in your house and I wouldn't feel right doing that, but then I wouldn't feel right sleeping below stairs, like a servant either. No, it's better this way. I welcome your visits, but then you go back to your world and I stay in mine."

I looked back longingly as I walked up Glanville Drive past the gnomes.

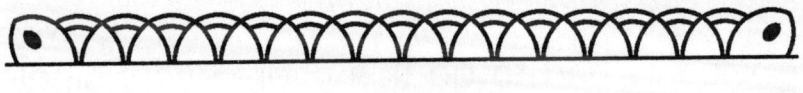

Chapter 9

Rannoch House
Sunday, April 24, 1932

When I arrived back at Rannoch House I changed into my servant garb, tied up my hair, and ventured downstairs until I located the dreaded coal hole. As Granddad had predicted, it was awful—a dark opening in the outside well, only a couple of feet high. I couldn't find a shovel and I wasn't going to reach my arm into that dark unknown. Who knows what was lurking in there? I went back into the kitchen and discovered a large ladle and a towel hanging on a rack. Then I used the ladle to scrape out bits of coal, one at a time, then picked them up with the towel to put into the coal scuttle. By this method it took a good half hour to fill the scuttle but at least I didn't touch any spiders and my hands remained clean. Finally I staggered upstairs with it, with new admiration and respect for my maid, Maggie, who obviously had to do this chore every single morning.

I experimented with lighting a fire in my own room and by the end of the evening I had a very smoky room, but a crackling blaze going. I was quite proud of myself. Binky's bedroom was ready for him, with clean sheets and windows opened. I laid a fire in his grate and went to bed satisfied.

On Monday morning I went into the *Times* office and placed an advertisement for the front page. I provided a post office box to reply to, as I didn't think Binky would take kindly to requests for a char lady coming to Rannoch House. Then I went to the *Tattler* and repeated the process.

I had just returned home when there was a knock at the front door. I went to answer it and found a strange man on the doorstep. He was a sinister-looking figure, dressed from head to toe in black—long black over-coat and broad-brimmed black hat tilted forward so that it was hard to see his eyes. What I could see of his face I didn't like. He might have been good-looking once, but he had one of those faces that has started to sag. And it had the pasty pallor of one who is not often in the fresh air. Nobody at Castle Rannoch ever had such a complexion. At least the biting wind produced the rosiest of cheeks.

"I am 'ere to see zee duke," he said in what sounded like a French accent. "You will inform him immediately that Gaston de Mauxville has arrived."

"I'm sorry but the duke hasn't arrived himself yet," I said. "I don't expect him until this afternoon."

"Most inconvenient," he said, slapping one black leather glove against the palm of his other hand.

"He's expecting you, is he?"

"Of course. I shall come in and wait." He attempted to push past me.

"I'm afraid you won't," I said, taking an instant dislike to the man's arrogant manner. "I don't know you. I suggest you come back later."

"Why, you impudent girl. I'll have you dismissed." He raised a glove and I thought for a moment he was going to strike me. "Do you know to whom you are speaking?"

"More to the point, do you know to whom you are speaking?" I said, giving him my most frosty stare. "I am the duke's sister, Lady Georgiana."

At this his bluster subsided, but he continued to splutter.

"But you open the door like a 'ousemaid. Most irregular, most embarrassing."

"I'm sorry," I said, "but the staff are still in Scotland, I am in the house alone, and I'm sure you would agree that my brother would not want me to entertain a strange man, unchaperoned."

"Very well," he said. "You will inform your brother that I expect to see him the moment he arrives. I am staying at Claridge's."

"I'll inform him, but I don't know of his plans," I said. "Do you have a card?"

"Somewhere," he said, patting various pockets, "but in this instance a card will not be necessary, I believe."

He turned as if to leave, then looked back suddenly. "This is the only property you own apart from Castle Rannoch?"

"Yes," I said. "I don't own it. My brother does."

"Naturally. And Castle Rannoch—what is it like?"

"Cold and drafty," I said.

"Most inconvenient, but it can't be

helped. And the estate—it produces a good income?"

"I have no idea what kind of income the estate produces," I said, "and if I knew, I should not be discussing it with a stranger. Forgive me, but I have things I must attend to."

With that I closed the door. Horrible man. Just who did he think he was?

Binky arrived around four, also rather flustered as he had traveled without a manservant.

"I couldn't find a porter and had to carry my own bag across the station," he said grouchily. "I'm so glad to find you still here. I thought you'd be off helping with some wedding or other."

"That's not for a couple of weeks," I said, glad he had reminded me of the story I had concocted to facilitate my escape. "And I gather the bride's house is packed full of relatives, so I'll be staying on here, if that's all right."

He nodded absentmindedly. "I'm quite frazzled, Georgie. A good soak in the tub and then tea and crumpets should revive me, I think."

"You still take cold baths, do you?" I asked.

"Cold baths? I had to have them every day at school, of course, but not lately by choice."

"Well, that's the only choice at the moment," I said, secretly rather enjoying it. "The boiler has not been lit."

"Why on earth not?"

"Because I have been here alone, dear brother, and your wife did not give me permission to turn on the boiler, even if I had any idea how to perform such a feat. I have been heating a pan of water to wash in the mornings, and I'm afraid you'll just have to do the same."

"That's a dashed unpleasant blow to a chap after he's come all the way from Scotland on a beastly cold train." He broke off, as my words had finally penetrated. "Here all alone, you say? No servants or anything?"

"Just me," I said. "Fig wouldn't lend me any of your staff and I have no money to hire staff of my own, as you very well should know, since you were the one who cut off my allowance on my twenty-first birthday."

He went red. "Look here, Georgie. You

make me sound like an ogre. I really didn't want to but, dash it all, I just haven't the income to support you for the rest of your life. You're supposed to marry, you know, and let some other poor blighter take care of you."

"Thank you for those kind words," I said.

"So what you're saying is, in effect, that there is nobody here to run my bath, nobody to make me tea and crumpets, nothing?"

"I can make you tea and toast, which is almost as good as crumpets, as your wife pointed out."

"You know how to make things? Georgie—you're a bloody genius."

I had to laugh. "I hardly think that tea and toast constitute genius," I said, "but I have learned a thing or two in the past week. You'll find a fire going in your bedroom, laid and lit by me."

I turned to lead the way up the stairs, opening his bedroom door with a flourish.

"How on earth did you manage that?"

"My grandfather showed me how to do it."

"Your grandfather? He was here?"

"Don't worry. He wasn't here. I went to visit him."

"Out in Essex?" He sounded as if I had made the journey by camel, across the Gobi Desert.

"Binky, contrary to popular belief, people have made it to Essex and back and lived to tell the tale," I said. I ushered him into his bedroom and waited for him to compliment me on my fire and the sparkling clean state of the place. Being a man, he wasn't impressed by either, but started to unpack his overnight bag.

"By the way, you had a visitor this morning," I said. "A most unpleasant fat Frenchman called Gaston something. Extremely arrogant. Where on earth did you meet him?"

Binky's face had turned pale. "I've never actually met him yet. We have only corresponded," he said, "but he is the reason I have come to London now, in the hopes of sorting things out."

"Sorting what things out?"

Binky stood there, clutching his pajamas. "I suppose you have a right to know. I haven't even told Fig yet. I dare not tell Fig.

I don't know how I'll ever tell Fig, but she'll have to know eventually."

"Know what?" I demanded.

He sank to the bed. "That man, Gaston de Mauxville. Apparently he is some kind of professional gambler, and apparently he used to play cards with Father in Monte Carlo. I suppose you've guessed that Father wasn't a very good gambler. Apparently he lost what was left of the family fortune at those tables. And now apparently he lost even more than the family fortune."

"Would you stop saying 'apparently,'" I snapped. "If this is all hearsay, I'm not interested."

"Oh, it's more than hearsay." Binky gave a big sigh. "Apparently—no, *actually*, this bounder de Mauxville claims that Father bet Castle Rannoch in a card game, and lost."

"Father lost our family home? To that horrible rude, flabby foreigner?" I heard myself screeching in most unladylike tones.

"Apparently."

"I don't believe it. The man is a confidence trickster."

"The man claims he has a watertight document in his possession. He is going to present it to me today."

"It would never hold up in a British court, Binky."

"I'm due to see the family solicitors to-morrow, but de Mauxville claims that the document has been witnessed and nota-rized in France and will stand up in any court in the world."

"How awful, Binky." We stared at each other in horror. "No wonder he was asking about Castle Rannoch this morning. I'm so glad I told him it was cold and drafty. If only I'd known I'd have said it was haunted too. You don't think he really wants to live there?"

"I think what he really wants is for me to buy him off."

"Can you afford to buy him off?"

"Absolutely not. You know we're flat broke, Georgie. What with Father losing in Monte Carlo and then saddling me with the death duties when he shot himself—" He looked up hopefully. "That's it. I shall chal-lenge him to a duel. If he's a man of honor, he'll accept. We'll fight for Castle Rannoch, man to man."

I went over and put a hand on his shoul-der. "Binky, my sweet, I hate to remind you, but apart from Father you are without doubt the worst shot in the civilized world. You have never managed to hit a grouse, a deer, a duck, or anything that moves."

"De Mauxville won't move. He'll be standing there. And he's a big target. I can't actually miss."

"He will undoubtedly fire first and he's probably the best shot in all of France. I don't want a dead brother as well as no family home."

Binky sank his head into his hands. "What are we going to do, Georgie?"

I patted his shoulder. "We'll fight it. We'll find some way. At very worst we'll take him up to Scotland to show him his new home and he'll get pneumonia within the week. And if he doesn't, I'll take him up the crag to show him the view over the whole estate and push him off!"

"Georgie!" Binky looked shocked and then laughed.

"All's fair in love and war," I said, "and this is war."

Binky didn't return home until late that evening. I had waited up for him, impatient to know how he had fared with the horrible

Gaston de Mauxville. When I heard the front door slam, I ran downstairs in time to see Binky trudging wearily up toward me.

"Well?" I said.

He sighed. "I met with the fellow. An absolute cad, I'm sure, but I fear the document is genuine. It certainly looked like Father's handwriting to me, and it's been witnessed and sealed too. The rotter wouldn't let the original out of his possession, but he's given me a copy to show our solicitor in the morning. Frankly I'm not too hopeful."

"Why don't you call his bluff, Binky? Tell him he can have Castle Rannoch. Tell him you're glad to get rid of it. He wouldn't last a week there."

"But that wouldn't work at all," he said. "He's not interested in living in the place. He's going to sell it—turn it into a school or a golfing hotel."

"A school maybe," I said. "It would take considerable improvements before anyone would actually pay to stay there."

"It's no laughing matter, Georgie," Binky snapped. "It's our home, damn it. It's been in the family for eight hundred years. I'm not just handing it over to some Continental gambler."

"Then what are we going to do?"

He shrugged. "You're the bright one. I hoped you might come up with a brilliant idea to save us."

"I've already thought of pushing him off the mountain. Pushing him out of the train on the way north, maybe?" I smiled at him. "I'm sorry, Binky. I wish I could think of something. Let's hope the solicitors will know a legal way out of this in the morning."

He nodded. "I'm going straight to bed," he said. "I'm exhausted. Oh, and just a simple breakfast in the morning, I think. A few kidneys, and maybe some bacon, and the usual toast, marmalade, coffee."

"Binky!" I stopped him. "I've told you we have no servants. I can manage a boiled egg, toast, and tea. That's it."

His face fell. "Dash it all, Georgie. You can't expect a chap to face the world fortified only by a boiled egg."

"As soon as I get a job I'll engage a servant who will cook you all the kidneys and bacon you want," I said, "but in the meantime you should be grateful for a sister who is willing to cook for you."

Binky stared at me. "What did you just say? Get a job? A job?"

"I'm planning to stay on in London and make my own way in life. How else do you think I'm going to support myself?"

"I say, Georgie. People like us don't get jobs. It's just not done."

"If Castle Rannoch goes to de Mauxville, you may have to face finding a job yourself or starving."

He looked utterly horrified. "Don't say that. What on earth could I do? I'd be hopeless. I'm all right pottering about the estate and all that. I've got a reasonably good seat on a horse, but apart from that I'm an utter failure."

"You'd find something if you had to support your family," I said. "You could always become a butler to rich Americans. They'd be tickled pink to have a duke waiting on them."

"Don't even say that in jest," he groaned. "The whole thing is just too dreadful to contemplate."

I took his arm. "Go to bed," I said. "Things may look better in the morning."

"I hope so," he said. "You're my rock, Georgie. An absolute brick. I'm counting on you."

I came to London to escape from my

family, I thought as I made my way to my own bedroom. But it seemed that escape was not as easy as I had thought. For an instant marrying Prince Siegfried didn't seem such a bad option after all.

Chapter 10

Rannoch House
Tuesday, April 26, 1932

In the morning I insisted on going with Binky to our solicitors'. After all, it was my family home too. I wasn't about to give it away without a darned good fight. Messrs. Prendergast, Prendergast, Prendergast, and Soapes were in chambers just off Lincoln's Inn. Binky and I arrived early so that we could speak with them before the dreaded Gaston arrived. We were informed that Young Mr. Prendergast would be delighted to see us and ushered into a wood-paneled room in which a man of at least eighty sat. I found myself wondering, if this was Young Mr. Prendergast, what Old Mr. Prendergast might look like. I was already so tense that I started to giggle. Binky turned and glared at me, but I couldn't stop.

"I'm sorry," Binky said to Young Mr. Prendergast, "the shock has been too much for her."

"I quite understand," the old man said kindly. "It has been a shock to all of us. We at Prendergast, Prendergast, Prendergast, and Soapes have represented your family for the past two centuries. I would hate to see Castle Rannoch fall into the wrong hands. May I see the offending document?"

"This is just a copy. The bounder wouldn't let the original out of his hands." Binky handed it to him.

The old man clucked as he studied it. "Dear me. Dear me," he said. "Of course, the first step will be to have a handwriting expert study the original to make sure it is not a forgery. We have your father's hand-written will and signature on file here. Then I shall need to consult an expert on international law, but I rather fear that this will have to be contested in the French courts—an expensive and frustrating proposition."

"Have we no other avenues open to us?" I asked. "No other options?"

"We could try to prove that your father was not of sound mind when he signed the document. That, I fear, would be our best hope. We would need to bring in character witnesses to prove that he had been acting strangely and irrationally, maybe a doctor to testify that insanity ran in the family—"

"Wait a minute," I interrupted. "I'm not having my father ridiculed in a court of law. And I'm not having any hints of insanity in the family either."

Mr. Prendergast sighed. "It may come down to that or losing your home," he said.

Binky and I emerged in deep gloom after an hour or so with the solicitor. De Mauxville had agreed to meet with a handwriting expert. He seemed so confident that I couldn't help thinking that the document was indeed genuine and that Castle Rannoch was on its way to becoming a golfing hotel for rich Americans.

It was only when Binky was reading the *Times* in the cab on the way back to our house that I remembered my advertisement. I glanced at the front page and there it was. Now all I had to do was to await my first reply. In spite of the awful gravity of our situation, I couldn't help feeling the teeniest bit excited.

I didn't have to wait long. The first response arrived the next day. It was from a Mrs. Bantry-Bynge, who had a house on the crescent beside Regent's Park. She had to come up to London unexpectedly for a dress fitting on Thursday, and finding my advertisement was a godsend, as her household staff were becoming frail and elderly and no longer traveled well. She would be traveling alone and dining with friends. All she needed was a place to lay her head that night.

Essentially she just wanted clean linens on the bed, everything given a good dusting, and a fire laid in the bedroom grate. It sounded easy enough. I went into a public telephone booth and dialed the number she had given me, confirming that I would have everything in perfect order before she arrived in the evening. She sounded delighted and told me that the key could be obtained from the housekeeper of the house next door. She asked me to return the following morning after her stay, bundle the sheets into a laundry bag, and deposit them with the same housekeeper when I returned the key. Then she asked me what my fee would be. I hadn't really thought that one through.

"The agency charges two guineas," I said.

"Two guineas?" She sounded shocked.

"It is a specialized service, madam, and we have to make sure our staff is the finest."

"Of course you do."

"And it's probably cheaper than bringing your staff up from Hampshire."

"Of course it is. Very well, I'll leave the money in an envelope you'll find when you come to strip the bed in the morning."

I hung up the phone with a big smile of satisfaction on my face.

Now there was just the question of what I was going to wear. I went below stairs and rummaged in the servants' cupboard until I found a suitable black housemaid's dress and white apron. I even added a jaunty little white cap for style. I couldn't be seen leaving Belgrave Square wearing it, of course.

I was creeping downstairs in my maid's uniform, trying not to wake Binky, when suddenly he called to me from the library.

"Georgie, old thing, would you come in here? I thought I'd do a little research into the history of Castle Rannoch," he said. "I thought that maybe there might be something in our family history or documents granting us peerage that states that the Glenrannoch property can never be bequeathed away from the family."

"Good idea," I said, standing in shadow on the stairs so that Binky wouldn't notice what I was wearing.

"And it's frightfully chilly in here, so I wondered, since you're a wizard at lighting fires, whether you'd get me a small blaze going in here."

"Sorry, old thing, but I have an appointment," I said. "I'm just dashing out the door. You'll have to find a scarf and gloves, I'm afraid, until I get back."

"Confound it, Georgie, how can I be expected to turn pages with gloves on? Can't you be a teeny bit late?" He poked his head around the door, sounding petulant. "Aren't women supposed to be late for everything? I know Fig always is. Spends hours doing things to her eyebrows, I believe, but you always look—" He broke off when he saw me. "Why are you wearing that extraordinary garb? It looks like something the servants would wear."

"It's for a silly hen party, Binky," I said breathlessly. "We're all to come dressed as maids. One of these prewedding things, you know."

"Oh, right. Oh, yes, I see." He nodded.

"Oh, all right then. Off you go. Have a good time and all that."

I grabbed my overcoat to cover the maid's uniform and fled. Outside the house I heaved a sigh of relief. That was a close one. I hadn't thought of the problems that could be caused by having to avoid people I knew.

I did say a silent prayer, as I approached the house on Regent's Park Crescent where I was to pick up the key, that nobody would recognize me. Luckily Regent's Park is not quite as top drawer as Belgravia or Mayfair. Not likely to be frequented by my family and acquaintances. However, I did look around as I went up the steps and knocked on the adjoining front door. The maid looked me up and down with a look of utter disapproval, and didn't invite me in while she summoned the housekeeper. The housekeeper opened her mouth in horror when she saw me standing there.

"What on earth were you doing, ringing the front doorbell as if you were company?" she demanded. "In this household servants use the tradesmen's entrance."

"I'm sorry," I muttered. "I didn't see where it was."

"Down the steps at the side, same as every house," she said, still looking at me with disdain. "No good comes of getting ideas above your station, my girl, even if you do work for one of those fancy domestic agencies."

She regarded me in the most patronizing manner.

"I hope you'll do a good job for Mrs. Bantry," she said. She spoke in that quaite, quaite exaggeratedly posh accent so often affected by the lower classes when they want to sound educated. "She has a lot of lovely things in that house. Quaite the world traveler, she and her husband, the colonel. You are from a locally hired firm, I believe."

"That's right," I said.

"I hope she's had your references checked."

"We come highly recommended by the Lady Georgiana, sister of the Duke of Glen Garry and Rannoch," I said, humbly surveying the milk bottles on the step.

"Oh, well, in that case . . ." She let the rest of the sentence dangle in midair. "That's almost as good as royalty, isn't it? I saw her once at a party, you know. A lovely young thing. Quite as pretty as her mother, who was a former actress, you know."

"Oh, yes," I said, deciding on the spot that her eyesight was probably defective.

"It's my belief that the Prince of Wales should look no further," she said, confidentially now. "It's about time he took a bride, and a good English one is what we'd all like. Not one of these foreigners, especially not a German."

Since my ancestry was a quarter Scottish and had a good admixture of German, I stayed silent.

"Thank you for the key," I said. "I'll return it tomorrow after I've straightened up the place."

"Good girl." She smiled at me in almost a kindly fashion now. "I like it when girls are well spoken. It's all very well to make an effort to better yourself. Just don't get those ideas above your station."

"No, madam," I said, and beat a hasty retreat.

I climbed the steps to the Bantry-Bynge house triumphant, with the key in my hand. First test accomplished. I turned the key and the door swung open. Second test, ditto. I stepped inside and savored the quiet of a sleeping house. A quick tour revealed that this job would be a piece of cake. The reception rooms lay swathed in dust sheets. I went up the stairs and located Mrs. B-B's bedroom easily enough. It was all pink and white and frothy with garlands of roses on the wallpaper. Expensive perfume lingered. Very much a lady's room. I wondered how often the colonel was invited in. I set to work, opening the windows and letting in the good, fresh air, whisking off dust sheets and shaking them out of the window. There were lots of little ornaments and crystal jars around so I was extra careful with my dusting, knowing my tendency to clumsiness. Then I found that they had a vacuum cleaner. I had never used one before but it looked like fun—and a lot less work than pushing a carpet sweeper up and down. I turned it on. It promptly raced across the carpet with me holding on for dear life and started sucking up the lace curtains. Finally I managed to turn it off before the whole curtain rod came down. Fortunately I also managed to rescue the curtain, which survived with only a slight chewing in one corner. After that I decided that the carpet sweeper might just be safer.

Then I found the linen closet and made up the bed. The sheets were trimmed with lace and smelled of roses. Finally I went down to the coal cellar, which was properly equipped with tongs and shovel this time, and laid the bedroom fire. A few weeks ago this would have been a task beyond my wildest imagination.

I was just putting the finishing touches to the room when the front doorbell rang. I had intended to be out and gone before Mrs. B-B herself showed up, but then she wouldn't be ringing her own doorbell, would she?

I went down and opened it. A rather dashing man stood there, his hair parted in the middle and slicked down, a neat line of mustache on his upper lip. He was wearing a blue blazer and flannels, carrying a bouquet of freesia, and had a silver-tipped cane tucked under one arm.

"Hello," he said, giving me a smile that showed too many white and even teeth. "Are you a new maid? I didn't think she usually brought servants with her."

"No, sir. I'm employed by a domestic service. Mrs. Bantry-Bynge hired me to open up the house and get a bedroom ready for her."

"Did she, by jove. Excellent idea." He attempted to come inside.

"I'm sorry, sir, but she hasn't arrived yet," I said, blocking his path.

"That's all right. I expect I'll find something to amuse myself," he said. This time he pushed past me and took off his gloves in the hallway. "I'm Boy, by the way, and you are . . . ?"

"Maggie, sir," I said, my own maid's name being the first thing that came into my head.

"Maggie, eh?" He came rather too close to me and put a finger under my chin. "Lively little Maggie, eh? Good show. So you've been getting a bedroom ready, have you?"

"Yes, sir." I didn't like the way he was looking at me. Leering would be closer, actually.

"Why don't you show me what a good job you've been doing? I hope you have done a good job, because if not, I may just have to give you a good spanking."

His finger that had been under my chin was now tracing its way down my throat. For a second I was too shocked to react but before it reached anything crucial I leaped away. It took all my self-control not to behave as I would normally and tell him what I thought of him. In my head I was screaming that maids do not stamp on toes, kick in shins, or employ any other known method of self-defense without being dismissed on the spot. "I'll just put these flowers in water for you, sir," I said. "They look as if they are about to wilt."

Then I fled in the direction of the kitchen. I had heard whispered stories about men having their way with servants, but it had never crossed my mind that this might be a hazard of my new profession. I was still in the kitchen when I heard voices and came back to find a woman in the front hall. She was on the chubby side with peroxide blond hair set in neat little waves, a lot of face makeup, and an expensive-looking fur draped around her neck. She was also surrounded by an aura of perfume. Mrs. Bantry-Bynge had arrived. Saved by the bell, I thought.

Mrs. Bantry-Bynge looked decidedly flustered. "Oh, you're still here. I hadn't realized. I thought—you see, I came up by an earlier train," she gushed. "And I see my—cousin—has arrived to drive me around in his motor. Isn't that nice? How kind of you, Boy."

I gave what I hoped would pass as a suitable bobbed curtsy. "I'm all finished, madam," I muttered. "Just about to go."

"Splendid. That's wonderful. I do hope Boy has not been—getting in your way." The look she gave implied that he had got in the way of a great many females.

"Oh, no, madam," I said. "I have just been putting these flowers he brought you in water."

She took the vase from me and buried her face in them. "Freesias. How divine. You know I adore freesias. You are so sweet to me."

She peeped at him seductively over the top of the flowers. Then she remembered I was still there.

"Thank you. You may go now. I've told your employer that the money will be on the bedside table when you return to strip the bed and tidy up the room tomorrow."

"Yes, madam. I'll just get my coat and I'll be off then."

I was rather worried that she might notice the coat was cashmere, but then perhaps she'd think it was a hand-me-down from a very kind former employer. As it was, she and Boy only had eyes for each other as I tiptoed past them. When I returned in the morning, the rumpled state of the bed gave me to think that a visit to the dressmaker had not featured in the trip to London at all.

Chapter 11

Rannoch House
Thursday, April 28, 1932

My next assignment, which came in the afternoon post that day, was not going to be as simple as Mrs. Bantry-Bynge's. It was from none other than Lady Featherstonehaugh (pronounced "Fanshaw," to the uninitiated), the parent of one Roderick Featherstonehaugh, usually known as Whiffy, with whom I had danced at debutante balls and who had been best man at last week's wedding. They were coming up to town for a few days, arriving on Sunday, bringing staff with them, but would like the place aired out and dusted first, fires laid ready to be lit and hot water bottles placed in Sir William and Lady Featherstonehaugh's bedrooms. Their son, Roderick, might be joining them if he could get time off from his regiment, but this was unlikely. I was remarkably glad that it was unlikely. I had no wish to bump into Whiffy when I was in full cleaning mode. Bumping into Binky had been bad enough, but he was easy to fool. I couldn't think how I'd explain myself away to someone stiff and correct like Whiffy Featherstonehaugh. Regent's Park was one thing. I could pass there without being recognized, but I knew practically everyone who lived in Eaton Place.

Binky moped around the house, sunk in gloom, and I couldn't think of anything to cheer him up. Because, frankly, the news was not reassuring. The document was deemed to be genuine and Binky started questioning whether it would be too-too awful to claim that Father had been off his rocker for years. "He did always have that rubber duck in his bathtub, didn't he?" he demanded. "That's not normal, is it? And remember when he took up Eastern meditation and stood on his head?"

"Lots of people stand on their heads," I said. "And it is well known that all aristocrats are eccentric."

"I'm not eccentric," Binky said hotly.

"Binky, you go around the estate talking to the trees. I've heard you."

"Well, that's just common sense. Things grow better when you talk to them."

"I rest my case," I said. "And you'd have to prove that Father was practically foaming at the mouth before the court would say he was too incompetent to sign that document."

"He did foam at the mouth once," Binky said hopefully.

"When he swallowed that piece of soap on a bet."

Binky sighed.

He was normally such a cheery soul and I hated to see him like this, but I couldn't think of anything I could do. It even crossed my mind that I might borrow a vampish dress from Belinda and try to seduce de Mauxville, thus obtaining the document from him in the heat of passion. But frankly I didn't think I'd be very good at it.

Friday morning I set out for Eaton Place, my black servant's uniform disguised under my cashmere coat, my cap tucked into my pocket to be put on at the last minute. I scurried down into the tradesmen's entrance and put on my cap before I turned the key I had been given and let myself in.

I stood in a cavernous entry hall, decorated with the heads of hunted African beasts and the odd ceremonial spear. Once inside, my enthusiasm waned. The house was even bigger than our London place and it was full of objects brought back from generations of army postings around the world. I'm sure some of them were valuable and even attractive in their own way, but they were on every surface—curved daggers, ebony masks, statues, jade elephants, carved ivory goddesses—all highly breakable, by the look of them. There were walls full of paintings, mostly of great battles. There were regimental flags, glass-topped tables full of medals, and swords of all kinds of shapes hanging everywhere. The Featherstonehaughs had clearly been a military family of distinction for generations—which explained why Whiffy was in the Guards. There was enough to keep me dusting all day. I went from room to room, wondering if they needed all the large formal rooms on the ground floor opened up, or whether the pretty little drawing room on the first floor would do just as well for a short visit.

There was a vast fireplace at the far end of a ballroom-sized main reception room and I said a silent prayer of thanks that they hadn't wanted that one laid. On every wall there were crossed swords, shields, even suits of armor. It seemed that the Feather-stonehaughs had been killing people suc-cessfully for quite a few generations.

I went upstairs and was relieved to find the bedrooms were not equally full of arti-facts, in fact were rather austere. I was about to start on the bedrooms when I heard a tap dripping in a bathroom. I looked inside and was not thrilled with what I saw. The bathtub had a disgusting black line around it. There were several towels dropped in a heap on the floor and the loo was also not the cleanest. That dripping tap in the basin had left a trail of lime. If this is how they leave their house, I thought, then they don't deserve a good cleaning. Then it occurred to me that someone might actually have been living in the house, and that someone might be Whiffy. I crept from room to room until I was satisfied I was in the house alone.

Then my pride and conscience got the better of me. I didn't want them to think I did shoddy work. I set to attacking that disgust-ing bathroom. I picked up the towels and disposed of them into a laundry hamper. I scrubbed at the basin; I even got down on my knees and attacked the ring around the bathtub. But as for sticking my hand down someone else's lavatory . . . there were limits, after all. In the end I found a brush hanging up behind a door. I tied a cloth around this and, standing suitably far away and averting my eyes, I gave the toilet bowl a quick going-over. Afterward I hurriedly dropped the offending cloth into the nearest rubbish bin and hung up the bath brush as if nothing had happened. It was only as I replaced it on its hook that it occurred to me that it was probably hung there to scrub the hard-to-reach parts of someone's back. Oh, dear. They need never know what it had been used for, I decided.

And of course I realized at that very moment that we upper classes are open to all kinds of fiendish tricks with which our servants can vent their anger and frustration. I'd heard once about a butler who peed into the soup. I wondered what the servants did at Castle Rannoch. The motto is obviously always to treat servants as one would wish to be treated. The golden rule does make a lot of sense.

Feeling more satisfied now, I started in

the back bedrooms and removed the dust covers very carefully. I swept. I even went down to the coal cellar and I laid fires. That went smoothly enough, although I was out of breath after carrying a full coal scuttle upstairs several times. Then I came to the main bedroom, looking out onto Eaton Place.

This room was dominated by a giant four-poster bed, the sort that Queen Elizabeth had obviously slept in on her way north. It was a ghastly affair with faded velvet curtains. The rest of the room was no more conducive to a good night's sleep. On one wall was a hideous mask with tusks, on another a print of a battle scene. As I went to shake out the satin quilt that covered the bed, I misjudged its weight. It flew up, knocking that mask off the wall. Almost as if in slow motion, I watched the mask fall and, in its turn, knock a small statue off the mantelpiece. I flung myself across the room to grab it, but I was too late. It hit the fender with a neat clunk and broke in half. I stared at it in horror.

"Stay calm," I told myself. "It's just one small statue in a house full of ornaments."

I picked up the two pieces. It looked like

some kind of Chinese goddess with several arms, one of which had now snapped off at the shoulder. Luckily it was a clean break. I stuffed both pieces into my apron pocket. I'd take it away, have it repaired, and then slip it back into the house later. Hopefully nobody would notice. I could bring up another, similar piece from downstairs to replace it until I could return it.

I had just heaved a sigh of relief when I froze. Was I now oversensitive, or had I heard footsteps down below? I stood, holding my breath, until I heard the unmistakable creak of a stair or floorboard. Someone was definitely in the house with me. Nothing to get alarmed about, I told myself. It was broad daylight in a fashionable London square. I'd only have to open the window and shout for help and any number of maids, chauffeurs, and delivery boys would hear me. Remembering how Mrs. Bantry-Bynge and her friend Boy had arrived earlier than originally planned, I presumed it was a member of the Featherstonehaughs' entourage. I just prayed it wasn't Whiffy.

There was a big wardrobe in the bedroom and I was tempted to hide. Then the voice of reason won out. Since servants were supposed to be not seen and not heard, I decided I shouldn't announce my presence. A servant would just go on with her work, no matter what was happening around her in the household.

The footsteps came closer. It was hard to keep making that bed without turning around. In the end I just had to peek.

I jumped a mile as Darcy O'Mara stepped in through the bedroom door. "Holy mother of God, what an impressive bed," he said. "This certainly rivals the Princess and the Pea, doesn't it?"

"Darcy, what are you doing here?" I demanded. "You almost gave me a heart attack."

"I thought I saw you crossing Belgrave Square earlier, looking rather furtive, so I decided to follow you. I watched you go in the tradesmen's entrance of the Featherstonehaughs' house when I knew they were still in the country. And I was intrigued. Being of a curious nature I wanted to know what the hell you were doing in someone else's empty house. I waited. You didn't reemerge, so I came to take a look for myself. You didn't lock the door after you, naughty girl."

"All right," I said. "You've discovered my guilty secret."

"Your secret pleasure is to go around making other people's beds? Sigmund Freud would find that interesting."

"No, silly. I've started a new career. I'm running a domestic service to get people's houses ready for them when they want to come to London and save them the expense of sending staff in advance."

"Brilliant notion," he said. "Where is the rest of your team?"

"It's just me so far," I said.

He burst out laughing. "You're doing the housecleaning yourself?"

"I don't see what's so funny about that."

"And when have you ever cleaned a house? I bet you've been polishing the floors with the stuff they use to clean the silver."

"I didn't say I was doing the spring cleaning," I retorted. "My service offers to air out and dust off a few rooms. Make ready the house, that's all. I can run the carpet sweeper, put clean sheets on the beds, and do a good dust."

"I'm impressed—but I bet your family wouldn't be."

"We'll just make sure they don't know. If I start doing well enough, I can hire a staff to do the actual work."

"Very enterprising of you. I wish you luck." His gaze strayed back to the bed, now in half-made disarray. "My, but that is a fine-looking bed," he said. He gave the mattress an experimental push to test the springiness. "Who knows what notable historical characters might have had a romp on this bed? Henry the Eighth, do you think? Nell Gywnne and King Charlie?" Then he looked up at me.

He was standing very close, so close that I found it unnerving, especially given the subject matter of the conversation and the way he was looking at me.

I moved away. "I don't think the Featherstonehaughs would approve if they arrived early and found a strange man in their house, bothering the servants."

He smiled, his eyes flashing a challenge. "Oh, so you're getting bothered by me, are you?"

"Not at all," I said haughtily. "I am being paid to do some work and you are keeping me from carrying out my duties, that's all."

He was still smiling. "I see," he said. "Very

well, I'll go. I can tell when my presence is not wanted. Although I can name a long list of girls who would have found the chance to be alone in such surroundings with an attractive man like myself too good to turn down."

I realized with a pang of regret that I may have given the impression that I wasn't at all interested, which wasn't exactly true.

"You said something about taking me to a party this week?" I said as he turned away. "At the Café de Paris? With Americans?"

"It turned out not to be suitable for you after all." He was looking away from me, and it came to me that he had taken someone else in my place.

"What were they, drug fiends?"

"Journalists. And you can bet they'd just love a scoop on a real royal personage gate-crashing their party."

"Oh, I see." Now I didn't know whether he was genuinely concerned for my welfare or had just decided that I was too straight-laced and boring to be bothering with anymore. He must have noticed my face fall.

"Don't worry about it. The world is full of parties. You haven't seen the last of me, I promise you that," he said. He put a finger under my chin, drew me toward him, and brushed my lips with the lightest of kisses. Then he was gone.

And I stood there, watching the dust motes dance in the morning sunlight, half wishing for what might have been.

I had finished the bedrooms and finally plucked up courage to attack that drawing room. There was no way I was going to take out those Persian rugs and beat them, the way any good servant would have done. I ran a sweeper over them and then started to sweep the dust off that vast parquet floor. I was down on my hands and knees, sweeping the area around the drawing room fireplace, when I heard men's voices. Before I could do anything sensible such as hide behind the nearest suit of armor, the voices came closer. I kept my head down and brushed away furiously, praying that they wouldn't come in here, or at least not pay any attention to me.

"So your parents are arriving today?" One of the voices floated toward me, echoing from all that marble in the foyer, even though he was speaking softly.

"Today or tomorrow. Not sure. Better stay away, just in case, or I'll have the mater going on at me again. You know what she's like."

"So when will I see you?"

The voices had reached the open doorway on the far side of the living room. Out of the corner of my eye I recognized the stiff, upright bearing of the son of the house, the Hon. Roderick (Whiffy) Featherstonehaugh, and behind him, in shadow, another tall and lanky young man. I turned my back to them and kept sweeping, hoping to build up a cloud of dust around me. The sounds of my brush hitting against the brass fender must have startled them.

There was a pause and then Whiffy said, *"Pas devant la bonne."*

This was the standard phrase for times when something was about to be discussed not suitable for servants' ears. It means, "Not in front of the maid," for those of you who are not conversant with French.

"What?" The other man asked, then obviously spotted me. "Oh *oui*, I see. *Je vois*." Then he continued in atrocious French. *"Alors. Lundi soir, comme d'habitude?"* (Meaning, "Monday night as usual?")

"Bien sûr, mon vieux. Mais croyez vous que vous pouvez vous absenter?" ("But do you think you'll be able to get away?") Whiffy's French was marginally better, but still with a ghastly English accent. Really, what do they teach these boys at Eton?

"J'espère que oui." ("I hope so.") Then the speaker reverted to English as they headed out of the room again. "I'll let you know how it goes. I think you may be wunning a fwightful wisk."

I froze with my brush in midair. The other speaker had been Tristram Hautbois. I heard their voices disappearing down the hallway, but I had no idea which room they had gone into. It took all my self-control to finish my sweeping, gather up my cleaning paraphernalia, and deposit it in the broom cupboard before escaping through the servants' entrance.

My heart was thumping wildly as I crossed Eaton Place. This scheme of mine was madness. Already, on my second day of work, it had led to two embarrassing encounters. Next time I couldn't count on being so lucky and getting away unscathed. I felt my cheeks glowing pink at my choice of words.

Getting away unscathed—that was pre- cisely what had happened to me in the bed- room. If Darcy had decided to force his at- tentions upon me, as the older generation so quaintly worded it, I'm not sure I would have been strong-minded enough to have resisted him.

A fierce wind sprang up as I crossed Eaton Place and I held my coat around me as I hurried home, looking forward to a cup of tea—no, make that a brandy—to calm my rattled nerves. It had been quite a morn- ing. I let myself into Rannoch House and stood in the marble-tiled hallway.

"Binky," I called. "Are you home? I am in desperate need of a glass of brandy. Do you have the key to the liquor cabinet?"

There was no answer. I felt the emptiness of the house pressing down on me. It wasn't usually the brightest of places but today it felt positively chilly. I shivered and went up- stairs to take off my maid's uniform. As I passed the bathroom on the second floor I heard a loud drip, drip, drip. Then I saw a trickle of water, coming out from under the bathroom door.

Really, Binky was just too hopeless, I de- cided. He must have decided to have another attempt at a bath and had forgotten to turn the tap off properly. I threw open the bathroom door and stopped short, my mouth open in alarm. The bathtub was full to overflowing, and occupied. For a moment I thought it was Binky lying there.

"Frightfully sorry," I muttered, then I took a second look.

A fully clothed man was lying submerged in the bath, not moving, his face under the water and his eyes wide open, staring upward. What's more, I recognized him. It was Gaston de Mauxville.

Chapter 12

**Rannoch House
Friday, April 29, 1932**

I had never actually seen a dead body before and I stared at him in fascination. He
can't really be dead, I told myself. It's some
kind of macabre French joke, or he's trying
to frighten me. Or maybe he's sleeping. But
his eyes were open and staring vacantly at
the ceiling. I tugged experimentally on a
black-patented toe that was sticking out of
the water. He sloshed around a bit, sending
more water onto the floor, but his expression didn't change. That's when I admitted
what I had known all along. Gaston de
Mauxville was lying dead in my bathtub.

A cold dread seized me. Binky had been
in the house earlier. Had the same madman
also murdered him? "Binky!" I shouted, running out of the bathroom. "Binky, are you all
right?"

I searched his bedroom, the study, the morning room. No sign of him. Then panic really overtook me and I pictured his body hidden under one of the dust sheets, so I ran from room to room, tearing them off, looking in wardrobes, under beds. I even went down to the servants' quarters and poked around there. There was no trace of him, not even in the coal'ole. I went back into his bedroom, and I noticed his clothes were gone. A terrible suspicion began to take shape. I remembered Binky's brave assertion that he would challenge de Mauxville to a duel. Could he possibly have killed de Mauxville? Then I shook my head firmly. Binky was brought up to be the honorable sort. He'd mentioned challenging de Mauxville to a duel. I could picture any kind of fair play and may the better man win, although I thought it hardly likely that Binky would turn out to be the better man in any kind of combat. But drowning somebody in a bathtub? Binky would never resort to such demeaning behavior, even to his worst enemy, and even if he were strong enough to hold a large chap like de Mauxville under the water long enough to drown.

I went back to the bathroom, half hoping

that the body might have disappeared. But he still lay there, eyes staring upward, black overcoat bobbing in the water. I had no idea what to do next, but an extraordinary idea came to me: the document. Maybe he carried it on his person. Fighting back waves of revulsion, I reached into his pockets and extracted a soggy envelope. I was in luck. It contained the document. I proceeded to tear it into little pieces and flushed it down the lavatory. I was immediately appalled by what I had done, of course, but it was too late to retrieve it. At least the police would find no incriminating evidence on him when they arrived.

I paced up and down the second-floor landing, trying to put my thoughts in order. I knew I ought to summon the police, but I hesitated to do so. Our nemesis was lying dead in our bath, and any policeman would leap to the conclusion that one of us must have killed him. I didn't think I could persuade the police to believe that a stranger had chosen our bathtub, out of the whole of London, in which to commit suicide.

But I had just destroyed the incriminating evidence, hadn't I? So who knew, apart from us, that he was our nemesis? Oh, blast and damnation. Our solicitors, of course. They even held a copy of the document and I didn't think they'd be easily persuaded to hand it over, or destroy it, even given their two hundred years of loyalty to our family. And I also didn't think I could persuade them not to mention our association with de Mauxville when the news of his death was made public.

I peeped into the bathroom again. Absurd thoughts were now flashing through my head. Would it be possible for Binky and me to remove the body and drop it into the Thames when nobody was looking? One drowning would appear pretty much like another. But it all seemed rather daunting: de Mauxville was heavy in life, for one thing, and for another, we had no loyal servants or means of transportation in London. I could hardly see us hiring a taxi and propping the body between us while saying, "The Embankment, my good man, and make it a deserted stretch of river." And even if it could be accomplished, it would somehow be letting down generations of fierce Scotsmen whose motto had been Death Before Dishonor. I'm not so sure about the Hanoverian ancestors. I think they could be quite devious when they wanted to.

I was still in midthought when the doorbell rang. I nearly jumped out of my skin. Should I answer it? What if it was only Binky, who was quite likely to have forgotten his key? Whoever it was, they might only come back if the door wasn't answered now. I would just have to get rid of them. I shuddered at that particular choice of words. Not the best in current circumstances. I started down the two flights of stairs, was just about to open the front door, and suddenly realized I was still wearing my maid's uniform. I grabbed my coat from the hall rack and slipped it on, wrapping it tightly around me. Then I opened the door.

"Oh, hello, may I speak to Lady—oh, my gosh, Georgie, it's you."

Tristram Hautbois stood there, his dark hair flopping boyishly over his forehead, beaming at me.

"Tristram. Oh. What a surprise," I stammered.

"Sorry to show up unexpectedly like this," he said, still with that expectant smile on his face, "but the old boy at the solicitors I work for sent me to deliver some papers to an address just around the corner and I thought it seemed too tempting not to see where you lived and say hello. It feels like ages since I saw you last."

Since I had seen him less than an hour ago, I didn't know what to say to this. Obviously he didn't associate the kneeling sweeper in black uniform with me. I pulled the coat more tightly around me.

"Were you just going out?" he asked.

"No, just got home. Haven't had time to take off my coat yet," I said.

"Are you under the weather?"

"No, why?"

"It's not that cold out today," he said. "In fact it's quite mild. I'm not even wearing an overcoat and here you are, all bundled up."

"The house is always so chilly with these high ceilings." I could hear myself babbling and tried to regain my composure.

"What a piece of luck that my timing was so good then, wasn't it?" he said. "I hope you don't mind my showing up on your doorstep like this. So this is Rannoch House. I must say it's pretty impressive. I'd love you to show me around. I understand that your father was something of a collector and you've some fine paintings."

"I'd be happy to show you around, Tristram, but now isn't the best of times," I said, cutting off the end of his sentence.

His face fell. He had the most schoolboyish of faces, his joy or despair clearly showing for all to see.

"I thought you might be pleased to see me," he said in a small voice.

"I am pleased to see you," I said, "and any other time I'd be delighted to invite you in, but I'm in the house alone, and you know what my royal relatives would say if I entertained a man, unchaperoned, even in the middle of the day, so I'm afraid . . ."

"I do understand," he said, nodding earnestly. "But don't the servants count as chaperons?"

"No servants either," I said. "I'm living here alone at the moment until I can hire a maid."

"Gosh, that's awfully daring of you," he said. "So modern."

"I'm not trying to be modern and daring," I said. "Simply lack of funds. I have to find a way to support myself."

"Then we're in the same boat." He beamed again. Truly he had a most endearing smile. "Abandoned and fighting the cruel world."

"Not exactly," I said. "Not like those poor wretches on the bread lines."

"Well, no," he admitted.

"And at least you have gainful employment. When you've finished your articles you'll have a profession. I, on the other hand, am qualified only for marriage and I'm only qualified for that by my pedigree. My family is determined to marry me off to some awful foreign prince who is bound to be assassinated within the year."

"You could always marry me," he said, pronouncing it, of course, "mawwy."

I laughed. "What, and trade a freezing and empty house for a bedsitter in Bromley? It's a sweet offer, Tristram, but I hardly think you're in a position to support a wife, nor will be for some time."

"I may be," he said. "If I come into my guardian's fortune . . ."

"What a horrid thing to say," I snapped, my nerves close to breaking point by this time. "You almost sound as if you're hoping Sir Hubert dies."

"Not hoping. Good Lord, no," he stammered. "Nothing's further from the truth. I worship the old boy. He couldn't have been kinder to me. But I'm only going by what the quacks have said and they have impressed upon me that the outcome is not likely to be good. Bad head injuries, you know. In a coma."

"So sad," I said. "If it's head injuries, then I'd rather he died. Such an energetic man could never be a lifelong invalid."

"My sentiments exactly," Tristram agreed. "So I'm trying to hope for the best, but prepared to accept the worst."

Suddenly I couldn't stand there chatting a second longer without exploding. "Look, Tristram, I am most pleased to see you, but I have to go now. I'm . . . meeting someone for tea and I have to change."

"Another time, maybe? At the weekend? I had promised to show you London, had I not?"

"Yes, you had. And I'm looking forward to it, but I'm not sure what I'll be doing on Saturday and Sunday." (I can't use the word "weekend," even in moments of stress.) "My brother is in town, you know. I may have family matters to attend to."

"Your brother? I don't believe I've met him."

"You probably wouldn't have. He's my half brother, actually, and he would have been away at school when I came to stay with my mother at Sir Hubert's."

"Where did he go to school?"

"Gairlachan. That formidable place in the Highlands."

"With the cross-country runs and cold showers at dawn? Just like the Spartan boys. The weak die and the strong become empire builders."

"That's the one."

"Sir Hubert threatened to send me there if I didn't pull my socks up, but he settled for Downside instead, since Mama was a Catholic and he wanted to honor her wishes. I must say I was relieved. Those monks like their creature comforts."

"That's where you were at school with Darcy?"

"O'Mara, you mean?" His face clouded. "Yes, he was a couple of years above me but we were in the same house." He leaned closer to me, even though we were the only two people on a deserted pavement. "Look, Georgie, I meant what I said the other day. He's a bad egg, you know. Untrustworthy, just like a typical Irishman. Shake hands and then stab you in the back as soon as you turn away." He paused and looked at me. "You're not—er, involved with him, are you?"

"He's just a casual acquaintance," I said, half wanting to lie and watch Tristram's face when I said that we were lovers. "We met at a hunt ball, apparently, and then at that wedding. That is the sum total of our acquaintanceship." I didn't mention the unsettling little scene in the Featherstonehaughs' bedroom.

Relief flooded his boyish features. "That's good, only I wouldn't like to see a nice girl like you ending up with her heart broken, or worse."

"Thank you, but I have no intention of anybody breaking my heart," I said, my hand already itching to close that front door. "I must go now, Tristram. Please excuse me."

"So may I see you again soon? Maybe I could take you to lunch somewhere? Nothing too fancy, I'm afraid, but I know some good cheap Italian places. You know, spaghetti Bolognese and a glass of red plonk for one and sixpence."

"Thank you," I said. "I'm sorry about today, but I really must go. Now." With that I turned and fled into the house. Once I'd closed the door, I stood for some time, leaning against the solid coldness of the oak while my heart regained its normal pace.

Chapter 13

Rannoch House
Friday, April 29, 1932

At least that little interlude had helped me get my thoughts into order. First I must find Binky, I decided. Before I summoned the police, I had to know for certain that he had no part in the killing of de Mauxville, and the most likely place to find him would be his club. He had been taking his meals there since coming to London and it was where he felt comfortable. I tried to think positively: maybe his disappearance had nothing whatever to do with the body. Perhaps he had finally decided that it would be easier to take a room at his club and avoid walking home after dinner and several brandies.

He might have mentioned it to me, I thought angrily. Typical Binky.

I dialed the telephone exchange and

asked to be connected to Brooks, which had been my grandfather's club, my father's, and was now Binky's.

"May I help you?" said a quavering old voice.

"Could you please tell me if Lord Rannoch is currently in residence?" I asked.

"I'm afraid not, madam."

"You mean he's not in residence or you can't tell me whether he is or isn't?"

"Precisely, madam."

"I am Lady Georgiana Rannoch, the duke's sister, and I wish to speak to him on a matter of great urgency. Now, could you tell me whether he is in residence?"

"I'm afraid not, my lady." The voice was unperturbed and it was quite clear that the old man was prepared to die rather than disclose the whereabouts of a club member to one of the opposite sex. There was nothing for it but to go there myself.

I went upstairs and changed out of the maid's uniform, trying not to look at the bathroom door as I went past. The fact that Binky's clothes had gone presumably meant that he wasn't intending to come back. And I could only conclude the worst—that he had seen the body and panicked. Now I just hoped he wasn't some-where spilling the beans.

I took pen and paper and wrote him a note, in case he returned before I did. *Binky. There is a corpse in the upstairs bathtub. Don't do anything until I return. Above all, don't telephone the police. We need to talk about what we should do. Love, Georgie.*

I set off at a brisk pace up Picadilly to St. James's Street, home of the oldest London clubs, went up the austere steps of Brooks, and rapped on the front door. It was opened by an extremely ancient hall porter with wa-tery blue eyes, fine white baby hair, and a perpetual tremor.

"I'm sorry, madam. This is a gentlemen's club," he said, giving me a look of such hor-ror that one might think I was standing on the doorstep dressed as Lady Godiva.

"I know it's a gentlemen's club," I said calmly. "I am Lady Georgiana Rannoch and I telephoned a few minutes ago. I need to know immediately whether my brother, the duke, is on the club premises. If he is, I wish to speak to him on a matter of great ur-gency."

I was doing quite a good imitation of my esteemed great-grandmother—the Empress of India, not the one who had sold fish in the East End, although I gather she had a commanding presence and was also good at getting her own way.

The hall porter quivered but did not budge. "It is against club policy to reveal which members are in residence, m'lady. If you care to write His Grace a message I will see that it is delivered to him, should he appear in the club at any time."

I stared at the porter, wondering what would happen if I pushed past him and took a quick look at the guest book. He was definitely smaller and frailer than I. Then I decided that such unforgivably boorish behavior would get back to HM within the hour and by the end of the week I'd be a lady-in-waiting in deepest Gloucestershire. I wrote my note to Binky and sensed the smug look on the hall porter's face as he took it from me.

Now I had no idea what to do next. Really it was too bad of Binky to have vanished into thin air at a moment like this. I stood at the edge of Green Park, feeling warm spring sunshine on me, watching nannies pushing their little charges for an outing in the fresh air, and found it hard to believe that all around me life was going on as normal. It came to me that I had never been truly alone in my life before. A feeling of utter desolation swept over me. I was alone, unprotected, abandoned in the big city. To my horror I felt tears welling up in my eyes. What on earth had made me bolt to London without any sensible preparations? If only I'd stayed in Scotland, I'd never have found myself in this mess. I had the strongest urge to pack my bags and catch the next train home—which, of course, I realized was exactly what Binky must have done. It's that built-in homing instinct common to generations of Rannochs who crawled back to Castle Rannoch, wounded and exhausted after the latest skirmish against the English/Vikings/Danes/Romans/Picts or whomever they were fighting at the time. I was now absolutely sure that Binky had gone home, but there wasn't much I could do about it. Even if he had fled on discovering the body, he would be on a Scotland-bound train for hours yet, and then he'd have to make his way to Glenrannoch, which meant he probably wouldn't arrive home until sometime tonight.

I pulled out my handkerchief and surreptitiously dabbed my eyes, utterly ashamed of this weak behavior. A lady never showed her feelings in public, according to my governess. And a Rannoch certainly didn't crumble at the first small hurdle in her life. I reminded myself of my ancestor Robert Bruce Rannoch, whose right arm had been hacked off in the battle of Bannockburn and had promptly transferred his sword to his left hand and gone on fighting. We Rannochs did not give in. If Binky had let down the family by running away, I wasn't about to do the same. I would take action, and immediately.

I started to walk back to Rannoch House, trying to decide what to do next. I couldn't leave the body in the bath indefinitely. I had no idea when bodies started decomposing but I had no wish to find out. And I certainly wasn't going to sleep in a house with a body floating yards away. I heard a clock strike four and my stomach reminded me that it was teatime and I hadn't even had lunch. I realized that all my life I had been guided, protected, cocooned by nannies, governesses, servants, chaperons. Other people of my age had learned to think for themselves. I had never had to make a major decision for myself. In fact the first important decision I had made was to run away from Castle Rannoch. That one hadn't turned out too wonderfully so far.

I needed help, and swiftly, but I had no idea to whom I could turn in this hour of need. Certainly not to my kin at the palace. Then the vision of food made me think of my grandfather—the live one, not the ghost who played bagpipes. He was such an obvious choice that a great sense of relief swept over me. He'd know what to do. I was just about to find the nearest underground station when I stopped short: he had, after all, been a policeman. He would be horrified that I hadn't called the police immediately and would make me do so. And then, of course, I'd have to explain why I had fled to Essex rather than reporting a murder right away.

So not my grandfather then. What I needed at this moment was someone to talk to. I realized that making the right decision at this moment was vital. A problem shared is a problem halved, as my nanny used to say. I almost wished I had let Tristram come in when he had appeared on my doorstep and shown him the body in the bath. He was, after all, practically a relative.

Not that he'd have had the slightest idea what to do about my current predicament (he'd probably have fainted on the spot), but at least I'd have shared my problem with someone.

Apart from Tristram, whom did I know in London? There was Darcy, who might well know how to make a corpse disappear. But I wasn't sure that I completely trusted Darcy, and anyway, I had no idea where he lived. Then I remembered Belinda. She had been wonderful in a crisis at school, like that time we had caught the potting shed on fire.

Belinda was just the sort of person I needed at this moment. I set off for her little mews cottage at top speed, uttering a silent prayer that she would be home. I was quite out of breath and feeling horribly hot in my tweed suit by the time I got there, the day having turned out warmer than I had expected. (Of course I could never admit that I was hot. Another thing that my governess used to say was that the words "hot," "lot," and "got" were not part of a lady's vocabulary.) I rapped on the door, which was opened by her maid.

"Miss Belinda is resting and not to be disturbed," she said.

"It's an emergency," I said. "I simply have to talk to your mistress right away. Please go and wake her."

"I can't do that, miss," the maid said, looking as imperturbable as that wretched hall porter at Brooks's. "She gave strict instructions that she was not to be disturbed come hell or high water."

I had had enough of being rebuffed by loyal retainers for one afternoon.

"This is both hell and high water," I said. "A matter of life and death, in fact. If you don't go and wake her, I shall do so myself. Kindly tell her that Lady Georgiana is here on a matter of great urgency."

The girl looked frightened, although whether it was of me or of waking her mistress, I wasn't sure. "Very good, miss, I mean your ladyship," she stammered. "Although she's going to be awful cross, because she didn't get 'ome until three this morning and she's due out again tonight."

She turned reluctantly from the front door and dragged her feet toward the staircase. But at that moment a dramatic figure appeared at the top of the stairs. She was wearing a scarlet Japanese kimono and a mask, pushed up just above her eyes, and she stood in dramatic film star pose, one wrist raised to her temple.

"What is all this racket, Florrie?" she asked. "Didn't I tell you I wasn't to be disturbed?"

"It's me, Belinda," I said. "I have to speak to you."

She raised the mask a little higher. Bleary eyes focused on me.

"Georgie," she said.

"I'm sorry to wake you but it's a real crisis and I couldn't think of anyone else I could turn to." To my horror my voice trembled at the end of this sentence.

Belinda started to grope her way down the stairs in a good imitation of Lady Macbeth in her sleepwalking scene. "Make us some tea, please, Florrie," she said. "I suppose you'd better sit down, Georgie." She collapsed onto the sofa. "God, I feel like hell," she muttered. "Those cocktails must have been lethal and I did have an awful lot of them."

"I'm sorry to be disturbing you like this," I repeated. "I really am. I wouldn't have come if I could have thought of anywhere else to go."

"Sit down and tell Aunt Belinda everything." She patted the sofa beside her.

I sat. "She can't overhear us, can she?" I muttered. "This is strictly for your ears only."

"The kitchen's at the back. So go on. Spill the beans."

"I'm in awful trouble, Belinda," I blurted out.

Her perfectly plucked eyebrows shot up in surprise. "It was only just over a week ago that you expressed interest in losing your virginity. You can't possibly be pregnant already!"

"No, it's nothing like that," I said. "There is a body in my bathtub."

"A dead body, you mean?"

"That's exactly what I mean."

Belinda was now wide awake. She perched on the edge of the sofa, and leaned in closer. "My dear, how absolutely fascinating. Anyone you know?"

"Actually, yes. He was an awful Frenchman called de Mauxville, who was trying to claim ownership of Castle Rannoch."

"A long-lost relative, then?"

"Good Lord, no. Nothing to do with us. He won the house from Father in a card game, or so he was trying to claim."

"And now he's lying dead in your bath. Have you called the police yet?"

"No, I didn't want to do that until I could find Binky and now he's vanished, so I don't know if he had anything to do with it or not."

"It won't look good—you both have an awfully good motive for killing him, after all."

"I know that."

"So what are you planning to do—dispose of the body somehow? Does Rannoch House have a back garden? Flower beds?"

"Belinda! I couldn't bury him in the back garden—it simply isn't done."

"It would be the simplest solution, Georgie."

"No, it wouldn't. For one thing he's rather large and I don't think even two of us could drag him out to the garden successfully. For another, someone is bound to be looking out of a window and see us, and then I'd be in worse trouble than I am now. At least at this moment I can face the police with true innocence. And don't forget that the Rannoch family motto is Death Before Dishonor."

"I bet you'd have done it if he'd been a small man and you'd had a wilderness behind the house," Belinda said, grinning.

I had to smile too. "Maybe I would."

"Who else would know that this de Mauxville had come to claim Castle Rannoch?"

"Our solicitors, unfortunately. Apart from them, I couldn't say."

She sat frowning for a moment. Then she said, "I think your best approach is to play your trump card."

"Trump card?"

"Your royal connection, my dear. You summon the police, acting with righteous indignation. You have just found a body in your bathtub. You have no idea who he is or how he got there. Kindly have it removed instantly. Think of your great-grandmother. The lower classes are always in awe of anything royal."

"And if they ask me if I know him? I can't tell a lie."

"Be suitably vague. You think he came to the house once to see your brother. Of course you were never personally introduced to him, so officially you don't know him."

"That's true enough. I never was introduced." I sighed.

She patted my knee. "You do have a good alibi, don't you?"

"Me? Not one I can divulge to them. I was cleaning somebody's house. I can't let anyone know about that."

"No, of course you can't. Oh, dear, then we'd better give you one. Let's see. You and I went shopping at Harrods together in the morning and then we lunched together at my place, and arrived, together, at Rannoch House. You went up to change and discovered the body, after which we summoned the police immediately."

I looked at her with admiration. "Belinda—you'd do that for me?"

"Of course. Think of what we went through together at Les Oiseaux. I'll never forget all those times you covered for me when I was in a pickle. That time I got locked out and had to climb up the ivy—"

I smiled. "Oh, yes. I remember."

"There you are, then. We'll have some tea. I'll get dressed and we'll go to face the music."

Chapter 14

Rannoch House
Still Friday afternoon

"There he is." I pushed open the bathroom
door and pointed dramatically at the body,
which hadn't moved since I'd seen him last.

Belinda went over and eyed him critically.
"What a nasty-looking man. Was he equally
unpleasant in life?"

"Worse," I said.

"Then you have obviously done society a
favor. The world is less one horrid person."

"I had nothing to do with his death, Belinda, and I'm sure Binky didn't either. We've
just provided the bath."

She peered closely at him, utterly un-
squeamish about the revolting spectacle.
"So how did he get into your bath, do you
think?"

"I have no idea. I went out to do my domestic duties, leaving Binky in the house. I

came home to find the front door unlocked, water all over the floor, and this man lying here."

"And what does Binky say about it?"

"I'm afraid he's done a quick getaway back to Scotland."

"How frightfully unchivalrous of him— leaving you to face the music. You don't think this is his doing, then?"

I weighed it in my mind. "I really don't think so," I said at last. "I simply can't picture Binky drowning someone in a bathtub. He's too clumsy, for one thing. He'd have slipped on the soap or something. And if he had made up his mind to do away with de Mauxville, he would hardly have left him lying in our own bathtub, would he?"

"It's certainly not the brightest thing to have done," she said, "but your brother was never noted for his high intellect, was he?"

"Even Binky couldn't be that stupid, surely." I heard the note of uncertainty creep into my voice. "Anyway, I suspect he's on a train heading north at the moment. I'm waiting for him to arrive home in Scotland, so that I can telephone him and find out the truth. But in the meantime, what should I do? We can't just leave de Mauxville lying there."

Belinda shrugged. "If you don't want to try burying him in the back garden, which I personally think is an excellent idea, you'll simply have to call the police."

"I suppose so," I agreed. "After all, why should I be afraid? I am innocent. I have nothing to hide—"

"Apart from the small fact that you dress up as a maid and go to scrub other people's lavatories," Belinda reminded me.

"Well, apart from that."

"Don't worry. I'm here at your side," Belinda said. "It would take a formidable policeman to get the better of the two of us."

I managed a weak smile. "All right. I'll do it."

I went downstairs to the telephone, then we waited, perched side by side on the stairs, staring at the front door, listening to a clock ticking somewhere in the emptiness of the house.

"Who do you think could have done it?" Belinda asked at last. "What was he doing here in the first place?"

"I suppose he must have come to see Binky."

"But if Binky didn't kill him, who did?"

I shrugged. "Someone else. A stranger, I suppose."

She shook her head. "You want the police to believe that a complete stranger broke into your house while you were out and drowned somebody in your bathtub? That would take a great deal of nerve and planning, Georgiana, as well as a great deal of luck."

"I know. It hardly seems feasible, does it? I mean, who could possibly know that de Mauxville was coming here? Hardly anybody even knew we were in London. And surely de Mauxville can't have many acquaintances here."

She stared thoughtfully at the chandelier. "This de Mauxville," she said, "is he one of us, or strictly NOCD?" (Which, in case you don't know, is shorthand for "not our class, dear.")

"I really couldn't say. He was rather rude, but then I know plenty of rude peers and I expect you do too."

"Do you know where he was staying?"

"Claridge's."

"That does imply money but no club."

"He's French, Belinda. Would a French-man belong to a London club?"

"If he had London connections and made frequent trips across the Channel, he would. So staying at Claridge's implies that he doesn't know people here and doesn't come here often."

"Not very helpful," I said.

"You need to find out all about him. If you found him unpleasant, he may have annoyed any number of people who were just waiting to drown him in somebody's bath. So find out what he does when he comes to England—when he's not trying to get his hands on your castle, I mean."

"I agree, but how?"

"I know an awful lot of people," she said. "Including people who spend half the year on the Continent. People who frequent the casinos in Nice and Monte Carlo. I could ask questions for you."

"Belinda—would you really? You are an absolute brick."

"I shall find it rather fun, actually. Belinda Warburton-Stoke, girl detective."

In spite of the tension, I had to laugh. "Girl detective," I echoed.

"I'm sure I shall be better at it than the

dreary, plodding policeman they are bound to send to investigate."

As if on cue there was a thunderous knocking at the front door. I shot Belinda a look and went down to open it. Several blue uniforms were standing on the front steps and in their midst was one fawn raincoat and trilby. Beneath the trilby was a tired-looking face—a sort of fawn-colored, washed-out face with an expression that indicated life was always unutterably awful, and a fawn mustache that matched the raincoat. The trilby was raised halfheartedly.

"Good evening, miss. Inspector Harry Sugg. I understand that somebody at this address reported a dead body on the premises."

"That is correct. Won't you come in, Inspector?"

He was regarding me suspiciously. "I take it there really is a dead body and this isn't one of those pranks that you bright young people seem to find so amusing—like stealing policemen's helmets?"

"I can assure you there is a body and it's not at all amusing," I said.

I turned and led the way back into the house. Belinda had stood up and was waiting halfway up the stairs. The trilby was raised to her. "Good evening, madam. Are you the owner of this establishment?"

"No, she's not," I said shortly. "This is Rannoch House, owned by the duke."

"What duke would that be, miss?" he asked, taking out a notepad and pencil.

"The Duke of Glen Garry and Rannoch," I said. "My brother. I am Lady Georgiana Rannoch, great-granddaughter to the late Queen Victoria, cousin to His Majesty. This is my friend Belinda Warburton-Stoke."

He didn't seem particularly impressed— not bowing and scraping as Belinda had suggested.

"How do you do, miss?" He nodded to her. "All right then. Supposing you show me this body."

"This way," I said. I realized I had taken an instant and completely irrational dislike to him. I led him up the first flight of stairs, across the landing, and then up the second flight. I noticed he was puffing a little by the time we got to the top. Not used to climbing Scottish crags, obviously.

"He's in the bath," I said.

He still looked as if he wasn't taking me seriously and was dying to prove me an idiot. "In the bath, eh? Are you sure that one of your friends didn't have a drop too much and is now sleeping it off?"

"I doubt it. He's underwater, for one thing. See for yourself." I pushed open the bathroom door. He stepped inside, then visibly recoiled.

"I do see what you mean," he said. "Yes, he's definitely dead, all right. Rogers! In here! You better get on the blower to headquarters and tell them we'll want the fingerprint kit, the camera with the flash, the lot."

He stepped out of the bathroom and turned to me. "This is nasty. Very nasty indeed. Unless he decided to end his own life, it looks very much as if someone ended it for him."

"Why would he choose to end his own life in Lady Georgiana's bathtub?" Belinda said.

"And if he were going to do so, he wouldn't have worn his overcoat," I added.

"Unless he found the water a trifle chilly, or he wanted it to weigh him down," Belinda said, with the faintest of twinkles in her eyes. I could tell she was finding this rather fun, but then she wasn't the prime suspect. I found myself wondering if those of royal blood still had the privilege of being hanged with a silken cord, then decided that having my neck irritated by coarse hemp would be the least of my worries.

Inspector Sugg looked around, as if seeking inspiration. "Is there somewhere we can sit down and talk while I wait for my team to get here?"

"The morning room is opened up," I said. "It's this way."

"The morning room," he echoed. I wondered if he was playing with the word, or thought I had meant "mourning." He followed me back down the stairs. We sat. I was wondering what the protocol was at this juncture and whether I should offer to serve tea. Since I had no servant and did not want to put myself into that role in front of the inspector, I declined.

"Right, let's get to business," he said. "Who was it found the body?"

"I did," I said.

"And I was right behind her at the time," Belinda added for good measure.

"What time was that, miss?"

I was obviously still going to be "miss" to him even though I had told him that I was the duke's sister. Perhaps he'd never learned to use "my lady" or even "your ladyship." Perhaps he was a socialist of the most egalitarian brand. Perhaps he was just plain thick. I decided not to let it rankle.

"We had been shopping together all morning, then we had a spot of lunch together, and came back here about fifteen minutes ago," I said, repeating our carefully rehearsed plan. "I went upstairs to change, saw water on the floor, opened the bathroom door, and found the body."

"Did you touch anything?"

"I started to rescue him, until I realized he was dead," I said. "I had never seen a dead body before so it was rather a shock."

"And who is he?"

"I'm not really sure," I said. I couldn't make myself tell an outright lie. "I believe I've seen him before, but I certainly was never introduced to him. An acquaintance of my brother, perhaps."

"Your brother, the duke?"

"That's right."

"And he is where?"

"In Scotland, I believe, at the family seat."

"So what was his friend doing here then?"

That one I could answer. "He wasn't my brother's friend, I can assure you. And I have absolutely no idea what he was doing here. He certainly wasn't here when I left the house this morning and when I returned he was lying dead in our bath."

"So who else was in the house?" The inspector chewed at his pencil—a nasty habit that Nanny had cured me of at four.

I hesitated, just for a second. "Nobody," I said.

Then I simply couldn't leave it at that. "My brother had been in London on business, but he had been staying mainly at his club."

"When did he leave London?"

"I couldn't tell you. He is a rather vague person and doesn't communicate his plans to me."

"And what about servants? Where were they today?"

"We have no servants down here," I said. "The family residence is in Scotland. I came down alone. My Scottish maid didn't want to leave her invalid mother and I haven't had time to hire a local maid yet. I'm really only using this as a pied-à-terre, until I settle my future plans."

"So you are, essentially, living in the house alone?"

"That's right."

"So let me get this straight: you left the

house this morning, spent the day with your friend here, came back this afternoon to find a body in your bathtub—someone you don't even recognize. And you have no idea who let him in or what he was doing here?"

"That is correct."

"And a little hard to believe, wouldn't you say?"

"I agree, it seems completely impossible, Inspector," I said, "but it's the truth. I can only conclude that there is some kind of sick-minded madman running around London."

"You simply can't stay in this house alone any longer, Georgie," Belinda interrupted. "Pack some things and you can sleep on my sofa."

The inspector now turned his attention to her, which was, perhaps, what she wanted.

"Miss Warburton-Stoke, did you say?"

"That's right." She flashed him a dazzling smile.

"And your address is . . . ?"

"I live in a dinky little mews cottage. Three Seville Mews. Just a stone's throw away in Knightsbridge, actually."

"And you were with your chum when she discovered the body?"

"I was with Lady Georgiana, yes," she said. "At least, she went upstairs to change while I waited downstairs. I came when I heard her scream."

"Have you seen the body, miss?"

"I certainly have. Horrid-looking man, I'd say. He didn't even look as if he'd shaved today."

"And you'd never seen him before?"

"Absolutely not. Never seen him in my life. And believe me, Inspector, I'd remember a nasty face like that."

The inspector got to his feet. "Very well, then. I suppose that's all for now. But I shall need to speak to your brother, the duke, you know. How can I reach him in Scotland?"

I didn't want the police talking to Binky before I had a chance for my own little chat with him. "As I said, I'm not quite sure where he is at present. You could always try his club, in case he hasn't left London."

"I thought you just said he was in Scotland."

"I said I wasn't sure of his whereabouts and assumed he'd gone home. If you like, I'll try friends and family in Scotland for you, although the telephone is not in the widest use up there. It is rather remote."

"Don't worry, miss. We'll find him, all right."

Belinda took my arm. "Inspector, we really should let Lady Georgiana have a cup of tea. She's obviously in shock. I mean, who wouldn't be if they found a dead man in their house?"

He nodded. "I suppose you've both had a bit of a shock. Off you go and have a cup of tea and a lie-down then. I know where to find you if I need you. And in the meantime if that brother of yours turns up, tell him we need to speak to him right away. Is that clear?"

"Oh, absolutely, Inspector," I said.

"Off you go, then. I'll have men working at the house for some time, I expect." He tried to chivvy us to the front door.

"It will be well supervised, I hope," I said. "There are many valuable objects in this house. I wouldn't want to risk their getting stolen or damaged."

"Don't worry, miss. Your house will be in good hands. There will be a constable on guard outside until this little matter is cleared up. Now off you go."

"Her ladyship needs to collect some belongings before she goes. She can't leave without so much as a toothbrush."

"Very well," he said. "Rogers, go with the young lady and keep an eye on her. We don't want her mucking about with valuable evidence."

I stomped up the stairs, fuming with indignation, threw various illogical articles into a bag, and then realized something. "My toothbrush, soap, and flannel are in that bathroom," I said.

"I don't think you can touch anything in there," the constable said, looking worried.

"I don't think I'd want to use any of them again after this," I replied.

"Darling, I'm sure we can go to my chemist and buy you a new toothbrush," Belinda soothed. "Let's just go. This place is beginning to depress me."

"Got what you need, then?" The inspector halfheartedly raised his hat as we left.

"What a horrid man," Belinda said as soon as the door closed. "I wouldn't mind seeing him floating in a bathtub."

Chapter 15

***Belinda Warburton-Stoke's
mews cottage
3 Seville Mews
Knightsbridge
London
Still Friday***

As soon as we reached Belinda's mews cottage, I asked to use her telephone and called Castle Rannoch. The call was answered, as usual, by Hamilton, the butler.

"Hello? Castle Rannoch here. His Grace's butler speaking." Our elderly butler has never learned to be comfortable with telephones.

"Hello, Hamilton, this is Lady Georgiana," I shouted, because the line was particularly bad and Hamilton has been growing increasingly deaf.

"I'm afraid her ladyship is not in residence at the moment," came the soft Scottish voice.

"Hamilton, this is Lady Georgiana. I am telephoning from London," I positively shouted into the phone. "I wish to leave a message for His Grace."

"I believe His Grace is somewhere out on the estate at the moment," he replied in his calm Scottish voice.

"Don't be ridiculous, Hamilton. You know perfectly well that he's not on the estate. He could not possibly be in Scotland yet unless he has developed wings. Please tell him to telephone me the moment he gets home. It is vitally important and he will be in serious trouble if he doesn't do so. Now let me give you the number at which I can be reached."

It took a good deal of yelling and spelling before he had successfully noted the number. I put down the phone in annoyance. "He's already persuaded our butler to lie for him."

"My dear, I think you should consider the fact that your brother may well be guilty," Belinda said. "Come and have a cup of tea. You'll feel better."

When I took the teacup I found, to my horror, that my hand was shaking. This had been a most vexing day.

A troubled night on Belinda's sofa followed. Belinda herself disappeared to yet another party. She generously invited me to come with her but I was in no mood for parties and had nothing to wear. Also I was waiting for Binky's phone call. The maid went home for the night and I tried to sleep. The sofa was modern, streamlined, and devilishly uncomfortable. So I lay awake, staring into the darkness, feeling scared and empty. I couldn't believe that Binky was guilty, but I also couldn't imagine how a stranger could end up in our bathtub dead unless Binky had had a hand in it. I couldn't wait to speak to him, to know he was all right and not guilty. If only he could have left me some kind of note before he disappeared. If only . . .

I sat up, now horribly wide awake. A note. I had left a note for Binky on his bed, a note in which I had mentioned the corpse in the bath and told him not to telephone the police. I could hardly have left anything more incriminating and the police must have found it by now. I wondered if the constable was stationed outside Rannoch House all night, or if I had any hope of sneaking in to retrieve it, on the unlikely chance that it hadn't yet been discovered. I realized that it would possibly make the police even more suspicious of me if I was caught breaking into my house at night, but it was a risk I had to take. There was just a chance they hadn't done a thorough search yet and the note was still there. I got up and put on my dress and coat over my pajamas, then I stuck some paper into the latch to make sure it would open again (one of the few useful pieces of education I had acquired at Les Oiseaux) and crept out into the night.

The city streets were deserted, apart from a constable on his beat, who eyed me suspiciously.

"Are you all right, miss?" he asked.

"Oh, yes, thank you," I replied. "Just going home from a party."

"You shouldn't be out this late alone," he said.

"I only live around the corner," I lied. He let me go on my way, but I could tell he wasn't happy about it. The farther I went, the more I agreed with him. I heard the sound of Big Ben striking midnight, borne across the city on the breeze. It was cold and I wrapped my coat around me. Belgrave Square slumbered in darkness; so did Rannoch House. No sign of a constable. I went up the steps and put my key in the lock. The front door swung open. I stepped inside, fumbling for the light switch. The hall light threw long shadows up the staircase and I considered, for the first time, that the body might still be lying in the bathtub. I usually pride myself on my sangfroid: when I was three my brother and some friends home for the school holidays had lowered me into the disused well in the courtyard at Castle Rannoch in an attempt to discover whether it was bottomless, as reputed. Fortunately for me, it was not. And once I had sat on the battlements all night in the hope of seeing my grandfather's ghost playing the bagpipes. But the thought of de Mauxville rising from the bathtub to exact revenge was so overwhelmingly disgusting that I could hardly make my feet go up the stairs.

I reached the first landing, then turned on the light and started up the second flight. I let out a little squeak and almost lost my footing as an ominous shadow reared over me, arm raised. It took my heart a couple of minutes to start beating again, before I realized that it was only the statue of an avenging angel that had been banished to the second-floor landing after Binky had chipped its nose with a cricket bat. I felt very foolish and chided myself as I continued up the stairs. Someone had cleaned the water from the floor. The bathroom door was shut. I tiptoed across the landing to Binky's bedroom at the front of the house. The note was no longer on the bed. I hoped that it might have fallen onto the floor and knelt down to look under the bed. I recoiled in horror as my knee touched a wet patch, and stood up again, my heart beating wildly. I made myself kneel and examine the patch and decided that it was nothing more than water. That could be easily enough explained—Binky had come into his room dripping wet from his bath and left a wet towel on the floor. I went carefully around the room, looking for clues, but found nothing.

I was just about to leave when I was sure I heard a heavy tread on the stairs. I couldn't help remembering that someone had committed a murder in this house earlier today. If Binky had indeed had nothing to do with the crime, then a perfect stranger had found a way into our house and lured de Mauxville to his death. Maybe he had returned. I looked around the room, wondering if I should try to hide in a wardrobe. Then I decided that nothing would be worse than waiting to be discovered and helplessly trapped. At least this way I had an element of surprise and might be able to push past him down the stairs. I went out onto the landing, then gave a gasp of horror as a tall figure loomed ahead of me.

The tall figure gave a similar gasp and almost fell back down the stairs. As he did so, I noticed the blue uniform.

"Are you all right, Constable?" I ran to assist him.

"Lawks, miss, you didn't half give me a turn," he said, recovering himself enough to put his hand to his heart. "I didn't think no one was in the place. What on earth are you doing here?"

"I live here, Constable. It's my home," I said.

"But there's been a crime committed. There didn't ought to be nobody in the house."

"I realize that. I'm spending the night with friends but I remembered that I had left my headache powders at home, and I can't sleep when I have one of my headaches." I was rather pleased with the brilliance of this spur-of-the-moment explanation.

"And so you come back on your own at night?" he asked incredulously. "Didn't your host have no aspirins in the house?"

"My doctor makes me up very special headache powders," I said. "They are the only thing that will work, I'm afraid, and I simply couldn't face a sleepless night after what I'd been through today."

He nodded. "So have you found them?"

I realized the light in Binky's room was shining out across the landing. "I thought I must have lent them to my brother when he was here last," I said, "but they don't seem to be in his room."

"They might have been removed as evidence," he said knowingly.

"Evidence? The man was drowned."

"Ah, but what's to say he wasn't rendered unconscious with a drug first and then put in the bathtub?" He looked rather smug, I thought.

"I can assure you that my mild headache powders wouldn't kill a mouse. Now, if you don't mind, I'm going back to bed. It will have to be aspirin after all. I presume you will be staying here and keeping an eye on things? I was quite surprised to find the house unattended when I arrived."

I had obviously hit a nerve. He flushed. "Sorry, miss. Just had to pop to the nearest police station to relieve the call of nature."

I almost said, "Well, don't let it happen again." My look implied it as I made a majestic descent, worthy of my great-grandmother, down the staircase.

I hurried back to Belinda's, let myself in, and tried to sleep. I wasn't any more successful than I had been before. The police had the note I had left for Binky. They had presumably felt the wet patch on his floor and might well have decided that he had soaked his clothing in trying to drown the victim. And another thought crept into my mind: the murderer hadn't just wanted to kill de Mauxville. He had wanted to punish us as well.

At last I suppose I must have drifted off to sleep because I shot awake at the sound of a door closing. Belinda was making a poor attempt to tiptoe quietly across the parquet floor. She looked across at me and noticed my eyes were open.

"Oh, you're awake," she said. "Sorry. There's no way to close that door quietly."

She came across and perched on the sofa beside me. "God, what a night. I swear every new cocktail is more lethal than the one before. They were making something called Black Stallions—I don't know what was in them but, God, did they pack a punch. I'm going to have a frightful hangover in the morning."

"Do you want me to help you make some black coffee now?" I asked, having no clue how one made black coffee.

"No, thank you. Bed is what I need. Bed alone, I mean. I was offered plenty of the accompanied kind, but turned them all down. I didn't want you to wake up all alone."

"That's very kind of you," I said. "Almost beyond the call of duty."

"To be honest, they weren't that desirable," she admitted with a grin. "I could tell they were going to be the 'fancy a spot of the old rumpy-pumpy?' kind. You know, a quick poke and over in five seconds. Honestly, public schools are doing Englishmen a great disservice by not providing elementary lessons in lovemaking. If I were in charge, I'd have employed a school prostitute, preferably French, to teach the boys how to do it properly."

"Belinda, you are terrible." I couldn't help laughing. "And what about a male equivalent for the girls' schools?"

"We had it, darling. Those delicious ski instructors we used to meet at the inn."

"They didn't, did they? All I got was a quick kiss behind the woodshed. Not even so much as a grope."

"Primrose Asquey d'Asquey reputedly used to have it on a regular basis with Stefan. Remember the big blond one?"

"The same Primrose who was wearing white for her wedding the other day?"

Belinda laughed. "Darling, if only true virgins were allowed a white wedding, church organists would die of starvation. I must see if I can line up a suitable foreigner for you. A Frenchman would be ideal. I gather they can keep one in ecstacy for hours."

"At the moment I don't think I'd be anxious to meet any more Frenchmen," I said. "The dead one in my bathtub is bad enough."

"Oh, and speaking of the dead one, I asked a few discreet questions on your behalf. And several people had come across your horrid de Mauxville in Monte Carlo. Nobody had anything good to say about him. Apparently he's one of those fringe dwellers, one gathers—seemed to have connections, but nobody was sure to whom. Always playing at the high-stakes tables—oh, and one person suggested that he was not above a spot of blackmail."

"Blackmail?"

She nodded.

I sat up now. "If that were true, and somebody had had enough of being blackmailed, then killing him would be the answer."

"Exactly what I thought."

"But why in our bathtub?"

"Two reasons: one, because it would not make the murderer the obvious suspect; and two, because somebody had a grudge against you or your brother."

"That's ridiculous," I said. "Nobody knows me, and who could have a grudge against Binky? He's the most inoffensive chap in the world. Not a mean bone in his body."

"Against your family, then? A feud of long standing? Even someone who was antiroyal and thinks that by striking at you they are somehow harming the royal family?"

"That's also ridiculous," I said. "We are so far removed from the line of succession that nobody would care if we were all wiped out in a Scottish avalanche."

Belinda shrugged. "I can't wait to hear what your brother has to say on this. I'm afraid he still has by far the best motive."

"I agree. He does. I hope he's really on his way home to Scotland and that the murderer hasn't disposed of him too."

Belinda yawned. "Sorry, old thing, but I simply have to go to bed. My legs won't hold me up for another second." She patted my hand. "I'm sure everything will be all right, you know. This is England, home of fair play and justice for all—or is that America?" She shrugged and then tottered gamely up the stairs.

I tried to get back to sleep again, but only succeeded in dozing fitfully. I was woken by the shrill ring of the telephone at first light. I leaped up, trying to grab it before it woke Belinda.

"Trunk call from Scotland for Lady Georgiana Rannoch," came the woman's voice on the line, with much crackling.

"Binky?" I demanded.

"Oh, hello there, Georgie, old thing. I hope I didn't wake you." He sounded positively cheerful.

"I was waiting for you to ring me last night, Binky. I stayed awake."

"Didn't get in until midnight. Didn't think I should disturb you at that hour."

He sounded so normal, not at all worried, that my anxiety exploded. "You are absolutely impossible! You run away and leave me here alone and now you are talking to me as if you haven't a care in the world. I take it you did see the body in the bathtub before you made your rapid departure?"

"Careful, old thing. *Pas devant la opérateur.*" (His French always was abysmal. She was feminine.)

"What? Oh, I see, yes. You did see a certain object, in the *salle de bain*? And you recognized it?"

"Of course I did. Why do you think I decided to clear out in a hurry?"

"And left me to face the music alone?"

"Don't be silly. Nobody would suspect you. There's no way a slip of a girl like you could lug a *grand homme* into *le bain*."

"And how do you think it will make you look if they find out? It's just not on, Binky," I snapped, feeling close to tears. "It's not how a Rannoch behaves. Think of your ancestor who rode fearlessly into the guns at the charge of the Light Brigade. He didn't even consider running away, with cannons to the right of him, cannons to the left of him. I will not allow you to let down the family name in this way. I expect you back in London immediately. If you hurry you can catch the ten o'clock from Edinburgh."

"Oh, look here—couldn't you just say that—"

"No, I certainly couldn't," I shouted down the hollow crackling line with my own voice echoing back at me. "And what's more, if you don't come back right away, I'll tell them you did it."

I put the phone down with a certain amount of satisfaction. At least I was learning to assert myself. Good practice for saying no to the queen and Prince Siegfried.

Chapter 16

The sofa in Belinda Warburton-Stoke's living room
Saturday, April 30, 1932

Now that Binky was presumably wending his way back to London, I felt a little better. Belinda's maid arrived about seven and bustled about making so much noise that I had to get up in self-defense. Belinda herself did not appear until after ten, looking pale and wan in her silk kimono.

"No more Black Stallions ever," she groaned, feeling her way to the table and reaching out for the cup of tea the maid placed in front of her. "I seem to remember hearing the telephone. Was that your brother?"

"Yes, and I've told him to come back to London immediately," I said. "I was very firm."

"Good for you. But in the meantime we should start our sleuthing."

"Should we? Doing what?"

"Darling, if your brother didn't drown de Mauxville, then somebody else did. We need to find out who."

"Won't the police be doing that?"

"Policemen are notoriously dense. That inspector has probably leaped to the conclusion that your brother is guilty and thus will look no further."

"But that's awful."

"So it will be up to you, Georgie."

"But what can I do?"

Belinda shrugged. "Start by asking people around the square. Someone might have noticed de Mauxville arriving, possibly with a stranger. Or a stranger trying to get into your house."

"That's true."

"And we could ring up Claridge's and ask them who left messages for de Mauxville or visited him."

"They are not likely to tell me that," I said.

"Pretend to be a relative from France. Distraught. Desperate to find him. Family crisis, you know. Use your feminine wiles."

"I suppose so," I said hesitantly.

"Do it now. Go on." She pointed to the telephone. "With any luck the police haven't grilled everybody yet."

"All right." I got up and went over to the instrument, picking it up gingerly.

"'Allo," I said in pseudo-French when I was connected to the Claridge's operator. "Zis is Mademoiselle de Mauxville. I believe zat my bruzzer stay wiz you, *n'est-ce pas*? De Mauxville?"

"Yes, that's right. Monsieur de Mauxville has been staying with us."

"Would you please put me through to him?" I asked, the French accent already slipping.

"I'm afraid that—that is, he was not in his room last night, Mademoiselle de Mauxville."

"Ooh la la. Terrible. Out on zee town again, I fear. Could you tell me, please, has he had any messages?" (I made it rhyme with "massages.") "Did somebody give 'im zee message from me yesterday? I am desperate to contact 'im and he doesn't call me."

"A message was delivered to his room yesterday, but I couldn't say who it was from. I show no message from you, mademoiselle."

"'Ow is zis possible?" I demanded. "I telephone from Paris in zee morning."

"Maybe your message was passed along verbally," the switchboard girl suggested.

"And has he had any visitors? I need to know if my cousin has encountered him on a matter of family business."

"I'm afraid I don't know that. You'd have to ask at reception and I don't think they'd be at liberty to tell you. Now, if you'd give me your address and telephone number, mademoiselle, someone will probably want to contact you about your brother in the near future."

"My address?" My brain raced. "I am unfortunately touring wiz friends at zee moment. I will telephone you again tomorrow and in the meantime, please tell my bruzzer zat I must speak wiz him."

I put down the phone. "I think they must know," I said. "She wanted my address in France. But a message was delivered to him yesterday, and he may have had a visitor."

"Did she describe the visitor?"

"She wouldn't say."

"You may have to go there and question the staff. They'd probably tell you."

Telephoning was one thing. Grilling the staff at Claridge's was quite another. Besides, my picture was well enough known that I was likely to be recognized, which would only make things worse for Binky and me.

"I suppose I could go and question people around the square," I said. "Will you come with me?"

"It does sound like fun," she said, "but I have a client coming to my dress salon at two. Tell you what—I'll do your sleuthing with you if you'll come to my salon with me and model clothes for the client."

"Me? Model clothes?" I started to laugh.

"Oh, be a brick, Georgie. Usually I have to model them myself and it would be so much easier, and so much better for my prestige, if I could just sit there chatting with the client while someone else modeled them. It's what they do at all the big houses—and I really need this sale. I think this one might actually pay cash for once."

"But, Belinda, I fear I'd be more of a hindrance than a help," I said. "Remember the debutante disaster. Remember when I was

Juliet in the school play and I fell off the balcony. I am not known for my grace."

"It's not as if you have to walk down a runway, darling. Just open the curtains and stand there. Anyone could do it, and you are tall and slim. And your red hair will go so nicely with the purple."

"Oh, dear. All right," I said.

It took Belinda a good two hours to breakfast, bathe, and get dressed, so that it was noon by the time we made our way back to Belgrave Square. This time there were two police cars parked outside Rannoch House, a constable standing on guard, and—horror of horrors—gentlemen of the press, complete with cameras. I grabbed Belinda's arm.

"I can't be seen here. My picture would be in all the papers."

"You're quite right," Belinda said. "You go back to my place and I'll have to do it for you."

"But they might accost you," I said.

"I'll take that risk," she said with an enigmatic smile. "Brave dress designer fights to clear chum's name." The grin broadened. "A little publicity might be just what my business needs."

"Belinda, you will be careful, won't you? Don't say anything about our knowing de Mauxville, or that you're asking questions to try and prove our innocence."

"My dear, I shall be the soul of discretion, as always," she said. "See you in a jiffy."

Reluctantly I left her to her task—as I now remembered that she hadn't always been the soul of discretion at school—and went back to wait nervously at her mews cottage. Time ticked by and finally she arrived back at one thirty, looking smug. "I was only accosted by one reporter. I pretended I had just heard the news and come to hold your hand through the crisis. I was absolutely devastated to find you weren't there. I was awfully good."

"But did you find out anything?"

"One of the gardeners in the square saw your brother arrive on foot and then depart in a taxi. He couldn't tell what time but around the lunch hour, as he was sitting down with his cheese and pickle sandwiches at the time. A chauffeur at the corner house saw a dark-haired man in an overcoat going up the steps of Rannoch House."

"That would be de Mauxville. So he was alone?"

"One gathers so."

"So we now know that my brother and de Mauxville did not arrive together, also that de Mauxville didn't arrive at the same time as anyone else. That must mean that someone was there to let him into the house. Anything else?"

"The only other people the chauffeur remembered seeing were the window cleaners, working their way around the square."

"Window cleaners!" I said excitedly. "Absolutely perfect. A window cleaner could slip into the house through an open window, slip out again, and it wouldn't matter if he looked wet and bedraggled."

Belinda nodded. "You don't happen to know what firm of window cleaners is employed on the square, do you?"

"I don't. One doesn't notice window cleaners, unless they peer in one's bedroom when one is still in bed."

"I'll slip back to the square on our way to my salon. I'm sure to encounter a servant who will know. Then we can ring them up and find out who was working this morning."

"Good idea." I was feeling positively hopeful.

But by the time we reached the square, more press had arrived and there was not a servant to be seen. Reluctantly we had to continue to Belinda's salon. She glanced at her watch as we came to Hyde Park Corner.

"Damn, we're going to be late if we don't hurry."

"Should we hail a cab?" I asked.

"No need. It's just off Curzon Street."

"Mayfair? You pay to have your workshop in Mayfair?"

"Well, it's not exactly a workshop," Belinda threw back at me as she dodged between a bus, a taxi, and an elderly Rolls. "I have a little woman in Whitechapel who does the actual sewing for me, but Mayfair is where I meet my clients."

"Isn't the rent frightfully expensive?"

"Darling, the right sort of people wouldn't come if it was in Fulham or Putney," she said breezily. "Besides, my uncle owns practically the whole block. It's a dinky little place but just big enough for little *moi*. You'll love it."

Belinda had not been exaggerating. The

place consisted of one room, carpeted, with a sofa and low glass table. A big gilt mirror had pride of place. Pictures of Belinda's creations and famous people wearing them hung on the walls. A couple of lovely bolts of silk were flung carelessly in a corner and the far end was blocked off by velvet curtains.

"You pop behind the curtains, darling, and change into the purple evening dress. It's an American lady and you know how impressed they are by royalty and it has that lovely coronationy feel. What's more, I'm sure I can make her come up with the cash in advance. I just hope she's not too large— that dress would make a large person look like a beached whale."

I pulled back the curtains and found a long purple dress hanging there.

"I've seen this dress before, surely," I said. "Didn't Marisa wear it at Primrose's wedding?"

"Similar, but not the same," Belinda said frostily. "I saw the idea and copied it. I expect Marisa paid a fortune for hers in Paris. I'm not above stealing other designers' ideas."

"Belinda!"

"Nobody need know," she said. "The wedding is over. The dresses will never be worn again and I'm sure no American ladies were present."

"Maybe they gate-crashed like us," I suggested.

"If they did, they can't afford my creations," Belinda said smugly. "Hurry up, she'll be here in a second."

I retreated behind the curtains and started to get undressed. It was dark and cramped with hardly enough room to move my arms. I heard a tap on the door when I was standing in my underclothes, wondering whether to put the dress on over my head or to step into it. I hastily stepped into it as I heard strident American tones echoing through the small room.

"People have been mentioning your name and I thought I'd just pop by, as I need something stunning for some upcoming functions. It has to be the very height of fashion, mind you. Important people will be present."

"I think I have something you're going to love," Belinda said at her most condescendingly British. "I have to tell you that royalty have worn my creations."

"Oh, my dear, I won't hold that against you, but please never use that as a selling point again. I immediately picture the dowdy duchess, looking like a Christmas pudding with a tiara on top, or that awful straight-backed queen of yours, looking as if her corset were made of reinforced steel and two sizes too tight."

It was all I could do to stay behind the curtain. The dowdy duchess she was referring to had to be Elizabeth of York, who was delightful, amusing, a fellow Scot whom I absolutely adored, and the queen was— well, she was the queen. Enough said.

"I'll tell you what I want, honey," the American woman went on. "I want an outfit suitable to be worn for cocktails at a smart nightclub—maybe for dancing afterward. Something avant-garde that will make all heads turn in my direction."

"I have the very thing," Belinda said. "One moment while I get my girl to model it for you."

She darted behind the curtain. "Quick. Out of the purple and into that black and white." She almost flung it at me, and disappeared again. I wriggled out of the purple, then tried to put on the black and white creation. In that confined darkness it was hard to see which way to attack it. Tentatively I stepped into it and started to wriggle it upward.

"Hurry up in there. We can't keep the customer waiting," Belinda called.

I struggled manfully. It was black satin with a long, very tight skirt, so tight I could hardly pull it over my thighs and hips. The upper part of the dress had something resembling a white waiter's dicky in the front that buttoned around the throat, and a low back.

"Aren't you ready yet?" Belinda called.

I left one button at the neck undone, hoping that wisps of hair would cover it, and came out. I could hardly walk and had to take teeny, tottering steps. Surely this wouldn't be practical for dancing and nightclubs. She'd never make it down the steps, for one thing. As I walked I noticed something flapping beside me, like a train, but at the side, not behind. Really, it was the strangest garment I had ever seen. The customer obviously thought so too.

"What in heaven's name?" she declared. "Honey, I have more derriere than she does. I'd never fit into something like that. And she looks as if she's about to fall over any second." This as I made a grab for the curtain and almost knocked over the potted palm.

Belinda had leaped up. "Wait, that's not right," she said. Then she shrieked. "It's supposed to be trousers, Georgie. You've got two legs crammed into one."

The American woman gave a shrill laugh. "What a dope," she said. "What you need is a new model, preferably French."

She had risen to her feet. Belinda leaped to her side. "You see, I didn't warn her. She'd never seen—"

The woman cut her off. "If you can't even get good help, honey, I don't hold out much hope for the end product." And she swept out, slamming the door behind her.

"What a rude woman," I said. "Do you have to put up with that sort of thing all the time?"

Belinda nodded. "It's the price one pays," she said. "But honestly, Georgie—who else but you would have tried to cram yourself into one trouser leg?"

"I had no time," I said. "And I warned you I was accident-prone."

She started to laugh. "You did, and you

are. Oh, my poor sweet, take a look at yourself. I must say you look absolutely ridiculous."

I laughed for the first time in days.

Chapter 17

Belinda Warburton-Stoke's shop
Mayfair
London
Saturday, April 30, 1932

It took quite a while to extract me from the trouser leg without ripping the seams.

"She'd have looked stupid in it anyway," Belinda said, glancing in the direction of the door. "Too old and too short."

"Who was she anyway?" I asked.

"The name's Simpson, I believe."

"Mrs. Simpson?"

"You know her?"

"My dear, she's the Prince of Wales's latest flame, the one I have to spy on at the house party next weekend."

"Spy? For whom?"

"The queen. She thinks David is becoming too interested in this Simpson person."

"Is she divorced, then? I gathered there was still a husband in tow."

"There is. Poor chap is dragged around for respectability's sake."

"I must say your family does exhibit awful taste in women," she commented. "Look at the old king and then your mother probably wasn't a suitable choice either."

"My mother was a darned sight more suitable than that woman," I said. "I nearly burst out from behind the curtains and bopped her when she started insulting the family." I glanced up at the clock across the street. "Oh, Lord, is that the time? I have to go to the station to meet Binky. I want to make sure I speak to him before the police quiz him."

"All right then, off you go," Belinda said. "I'll tidy up in here, then I've another party tonight. I presume you'd like to stay with me again?"

"It's very kind of you. But if Binky wants to stay at the house and we are allowed to, I should keep him company there. I don't want him to feel all alone."

We parted ways. I paused for a cup of tea and a toasted tea cake, then had to fight the rush hour traffic when I made my way to

King's Cross in time to meet Binky's train. I came out of the tube to hear the newsboys shouting, "Read all about it. Body in duke's bath."

Heavens, Binky would have a fit. I'd have to try and whisk him through the station without his noticing any of this. The express pulled in on time at five forty-five. I stood behind the barrier, watching anxiously. For a moment I thought he hadn't caught the train, but then I saw him, striding out in front of a porter who carried his ridiculously small overnight bag with some distaste.

"Quick, let's get a taxi." I grabbed his arm as he stepped through the barrier.

"Georgie, stop grabbing me. What's the rush?"

Suddenly a voice shouted, "There he is. That's the duke. He's the one," and people began to congregate around us. A flashbulb went off. Binky looked at me with utter panic in his eyes. I grabbed the overnight case from the porter, took Binky's hand and dragged him through the crowd, then shoved him into an arriving taxi, much to the annoyance of those waiting patiently in line.

"What on earth was that?" Binky asked,

wiping the sweat from his brow with a monogrammed handkerchief.

"That, dear brother, is the London press. They've found out about the body. They've been camped outside the house all day."

"Oh, Lord. Well, that settles it. I'm going to my club. I'll not put up with that kind of rubbish." He tapped the glass. "Take us to Brooks, driver."

"What about me?" I demanded. "Did it occur to you that I can't go to your club?"

"What? Well, of course you can't. No women allowed."

"I'm currently sleeping on a friend's sofa, but it's dashed uncomfortable," I said.

"Look, Georgie, maybe you should go on home."

"I've told you, there are reporters camped out in the square."

"No, I meant home to Scotland, out of the way of all this unpleasantness," he said. "It would be the safest thing to do. Book a sleeper on tonight's Flying Scotsman."

"I'm not leaving you in the lurch," I said, thinking that any amount of policemen was preferable to being marooned alone with Fig. "And I think the police would be highly suspicious if I suddenly vanished, the way they are currently suspicious about your vanishing act."

"Oh, dear, are they? When I realized who was floating there, I thought they'd immediately assume that I did it, and then I thought if I'm up in Scotland, they can't suspect me, so I made a beeline for King's Cross and off I went."

"And left me to be their number one suspect!" I said indignantly.

"Don't be silly. They can't possibly suspect you. You're a mere slip of a girl. You wouldn't have the strength to drown a big chap like de Mauxville."

"Not alone. I could have had an accomplice."

"Oh, I suppose so. Didn't think of that. I must admit it did cross my mind that you might have arranged to do him in. After all, you were the one who talked about pushing him off the crag." He paused, then asked, "You didn't tell the police anything, did you?"

"I have nothing to tell them, Binky. I don't know what happened. All I know is that you were there in the morning and when I came back in the afternoon there was a body in our bathtub and you had vanished. In fact, since I seem to be involved in this, whether I like it or not, I wouldn't mind knowing the truth."

"I'm completely in the dark myself, old bean," he said.

"So you didn't arrange to meet with de Mauxville at the house?"

"Certainly not. Actually, it was the rummest thing—my club telephoned to say that some chap wanted to meet me there, right away. I went to the club but nobody there seemed to have any interest in me at all. I came home, went upstairs, wondered where I had left my comb, wandered into the bathroom, and saw someone lying in the bathtub. I tried to get him out; got rather wet and realized he was dead. I also realized who he was and I might not be the brightest chap in the world, but I realized the ramifications."

"So somebody lured you out of the house, brought de Mauxville there, and killed him," I said.

"Must have done."

"What did the person sound like?"

"I don't know. A bit muffled actually. He said it was the club calling and I assumed it was one of the hall porters. They've only got half their teeth and they are not always easy to understand."

"So it was an English voice?"

"What? Oh, definitely English, yes. Oh, I see. You're saying that it wasn't actually a club employee who called me. It was an imposter. What a perfectly despicable thing to do. So someone else must have wanted de Mauxville dead—but why arrange it at our house?"

"To implicate you, or us."

"Who on earth would want to do that?" He stared out of the cab window as we waited on the corner of Baker Street. I looked across at the place where 221B should have been, and wished it had been real. A good detective was exactly what I needed at this moment.

"Do you think they've discovered the letter yet?" Binky asked in a small voice.

"I happen to have destroyed the original. It was the first thing I thought of. I went through his pockets, found it, and flushed it down the lav."

"Georgie, you're brilliant!"

"Not quite brilliant enough. I'd forgotten that our solicitors still have a copy and there may be other copies lying around."

"Oh, cripes. Hadn't thought of that. It won't look too good for us if the police find a copy, will it?"

"It won't look too good for you, Binky. You're the one who fled the scene of the crime. You're the one who possesses the strength to have drowned him."

"Oh, come on, old bean. You know I don't go around drowning people, not even rotters like de Mauxville. You don't think you could tell the police that I left town before all this happened?"

"No, I couldn't. I'm not lying for you, Binky. And besides, all sorts of people will know exactly when you left—porters and taxi drivers and ticket collectors. People do notice when a duke travels, you know."

"Do they? Oh, blast. What do you think I should do?"

"Unfortunately you were seen coming back to Rannoch House and then departing again in a taxi, so you can't claim that you'd been at your club or already left. I suppose you could say that you never went up-stairs—you were catching the midday train for Scotland—you came home only to pick up your suitcase in the front hall. That might work."

"They won't believe it, will they?" He sighed. "And they'd find out about the letter and I'll be doomed."

I patted his hand. "We'll sort this thing out one way or another. Everyone who knows you can testify that you're not the violent type."

"Too bad it's Saturday. We'll have to wait until Monday to go to our solicitors'."

"Do you think we can persuade them not to mention the letter?"

"I've no idea." Binky ran his hands through his unruly mop of hair. "This is a nightmare, Georgie. I don't see any way out of it."

"We'll have to find out who really did it," I said. "Now think, Binky. When you left the house, did you lock the door after you?"

"Not sure. I'm not very good at locking doors, because there are always servants around."

"So the murderer could have walked up the front steps and entered the house with no problem. Did you notice anybody in the square when you left?"

"Can't say I did. The usual—chauffeurs hanging around, nannies pushing prams. I believe I said good morning to that old colonel from the corner house."

"What about window cleaners?" I asked. "Were the windows being cleaned when you were there?"

"I don't notice window cleaners. I mean, one doesn't, does one."

"Do you happen to know what firm we employ?"

"No idea. Mrs. McGregor is the one who pays the bills. She'd have it in her house-keeping journal, but that's probably with her in Scotland."

"We must find out," I said. "It may be important."

"Window cleaners? Do you think they saw something?"

"I mean that the murderer could have disguised himself as a window cleaner to gain access to the house."

"Oh, I see. You know, you're dashed clever, Georgie. What a pity you're the one with the brains. I'm sure you'd have made a splendid go of Castle Rannoch."

"I'm afraid I'll need every ounce of brainpower that I possess to get us out of this mess."

He nodded gloomy agreement.

The taxi pulled up outside the imposing entrance of Brooks's. The doddering porter hobbled down the steps to take Binky's bag.

"Welcome back, your lordship," he said. "May I offer my commiserations in such a distressing time. We have been gravely concerned for your safety. The police have been here asking for you more than once."

"Thank you, Tomlinson. Don't worry. It will all soon be sorted out." He gave me a valiant smile and followed the old man into the building. I was left standing on the pavement alone.

Chapter 18

Yet again Belinda
Warburton-Stoke's sofa
Yet again Saturday, April 30, 1932

I waited for Binky to reappear but he didn't. Really, men are too hopeless. Wrapped up in themselves from the day they are born. I put it down to a public school education. It would serve him right if he was arrested, I thought, then immediately regretted it. Anyone who had gone straight from the rigors of Gairlachan school to Brooks club couldn't be expected to know any better.

I stood on the pavement outside Brooks, watching a parade of taxies and Rolls-Royces go past as the fashionable set headed out to evening functions, and I wondered what to do next. Belinda was going out for the evening. Rannoch House was teeming with police and reporters. I was beginning to feel rather lost and abandoned, when there was the sound of a siren and a police car pulled up beside me. Out of it stepped Inspector Sugg. He tipped his hat to me.

"Evening, miss. I understand that your brother has just arrived back in town."

"That's correct, Inspector. He's just gone into his club."

"I'd like a word with him, if I may, before he settles down for the evening," he said and strode up to the front door.

Good luck, I thought, and expected him to be repelled from that bastion as I had been. But in no time at all Binky appeared, with Inspector Sugg following on his heels.

"We're just on our way to Scotland Yard for a little chat," the inspector said. "This way, if you please, sir."

"It's 'Your Grace,'" Binky said.

"What?"

"One addresses a duke as 'Your Grace.'"

"Does one?" Inspector Sugg was clearly not impressed. "I haven't had the pleasure of arresting too many dukes in my career. Into the backseat, if you don't mind."

Binky shot me a frightened glance. "Aren't you coming along too?"

"I didn't think you needed me," I said, still rankled by his lack of sensibility.

"Good Lord, yes. Of course I need you."

"It might be useful to have you there too, miss," Sugg said. "Certain facts have come to light . . ."

He knows about the letter, I thought.

Binky stood aside to help me into the car. "Oh, and for the record, Sergeant, my sister is 'her ladyship.'"

"Is she, now? And I'm 'Inspector,' not 'Sergeant.'"

"Are you really?" Binky gave the smallest of smiles. "Fancy that."

Sometimes I think he's not as dense as he makes himself out to be.

We set off, mercifully without the bell ringing. But it was an odd feeling when we passed through the gate of New Scotland Yard. Visions of my ancestors going to the Tower flashed through my mind, even though I knew that Scotland Yard had no dungeons and no chopping block. We were escorted up a flight of stairs and into a drab little room that looked out onto a courtyard and smelled of stale smoke. The inspector pulled out a chair for me on the far side of a desk. I sat. Binky sat. The inspector sur-

veyed us, looking rather pleased with himself, I thought.

"We've been searching for you, Your
Grace," he said, stressing the last two
words. "Looking all over."

"Nothing hard about finding me," Binky
said. "I was at home in Scotland. I went
back yesterday and it's damned inconvenient to have to turn around because some
fellow drowned himself in my bathtub."

"Not drowned himself, sir. I imagine that
someone helped him. So was he a friend of
yours?"

"I really can't tell you that, Inspector,
since I haven't had a chance to look at the
blighter."

I glanced at Binky. That good old Rannoch and royal blood certainly comes
through in moments of crisis. He sounded
quite "we are not amused."

"You mean to tell me you didn't see the
body in your bathtub?"

"Absolutely. Rather. That's precisely what
I mean."

I glanced at him. He was sounding a little
too emphatic.

The policeman obviously thought so too.

"If you hadn't seen him in the bathtub, sir, how did you know he was a blighter?"

"Anyone who has the nerve to die in my bath without my permission has to be a blighter, Inspector," Binky said. "If you must know, the first I knew about it was when my sister telephoned me with the news."

"If I tell you the gentleman's name was Gaston de Mauxville, does that ring a bell?"

"De Mauxville? Yes. I know that name." Again he was sounding too hearty.

"I believe he was an acquaintance of our late father, wasn't he?" I cut in.

"De Mauxville. Yes. I met him once or twice."

"Recently?"

"Not that recently."

"I see. So would it surprise you to know that a note was found in that gentleman's hotel room inviting him to speak with you on a matter of great urgency at eleven o'clock yesterday at your London address?"

"Not only would it surprise me but I can tell you that I wrote no such note," Binky said in his best ducal tones. Again our great-grandmother would have been proud.

"I happen to have the note here." The inspector opened a folder and pushed a sheet of paper in front of us. "This was delivered by hand to Claridge's yesterday morning and taken up to Monsieur" (he pronounced it "Mon-sewer") "de Mauxville's room."

Binky and I looked at it.

"Certainly a forgery," Binky said.

"And how can you tell that, sir?"

"For one thing, I only write on paper embossed with my crest. This is cheap stuff that one would buy in Woolworths."

"And for another," I said, "it's signed 'Hamish, Duke of Rannoch.' My brother signs letters just plain 'Rannoch' to social equals, and if he were to include his full title, it would be 'Duke of Glen Garry and Rannoch.'"

"And what's more, it's not my handwriting," Binky said. "Close, I'll agree. Someone has tried to imitate my style, but I cross my *t*s differently."

"So you are maintaining that this note was not sent by you."

"Precisely."

"So what happened when the gentleman showed up on your front doorstep?"

"I have no idea. I wasn't home. Let me see. Where was I?"

"You were planning to go home to Scotland, Binky," I reminded him.

"That's right. I had packed my bags ready to leave when I received a telephone call asking me to come to my club on a matter of urgency. Naturally I went straight away and found that no such message had been sent. I chewed the fat with a couple of friends and then came back to Rannoch House in time to pick up my bag from the front hall and take a taxi to the station." It did rather sound as if he were rattling off his lines, the way one does in a school play.

"How very convenient, sir."

"It's 'Your Grace.'"

"As you say, sir." He looked from my brother to me. "You know what I think? I think the two of you are in this together. Why would a duke and his sister come to London alone, leaving all their servants behind, if it was not for something underhanded?"

"I've already told you that I left my maid behind and hadn't had enough time to hire a new one," I said, "and my brother was only down on business for a couple of days. He took his meals at his club."

"But who dressed him?" The inspector

was smirking now. "Don't you upper-class folks all need valets to help you dress?"

"When one has been to a school like Gairlachan one has learned to stand on one's own feet," Binky said frostily.

"Besides," I said, "what possible motive could the duke and I have in wanting to kill a strange Frenchman?"

"Plenty of motives come to mind, your ladyship." These last words dripped with sarcasm. "This man was known to be a gambler. He was seen in one of the city's most notorious gambling haunts this week. Maybe your brother had run up gambling debts that he couldn't afford to repay. . . ."

"My dear man," Binky spluttered, rising to his feet. "I can barely afford to keep my place in Scotland running. It takes every penny of my meager income to feed my cattle and my staff. We don't heat the place. We live with incredible frugality. I assure you I have never gambled in my life!"

"All right, sir. As yet nobody has accused you of anything. We're merely putting together pieces of the puzzle. I think that's all for now. But I expect we'll want to speak to you again. Will you be staying at your house—without servants?"

"I'll be at my club," Binky said, "and Lady Georgiana, I believe, is staying with friends."

"We'll be in touch, sir." The inspector got to his feet. "Thank you both for coming in."

The interview was at an end.

"I thought that went rather well, don't you?" Binky said as we came out of Scotland Yard.

Rather well? This was rather like our ancestor, Bonnie Prince Charlie, saying that he thought the battle of Culloden went rather well. I wondered whether the men of our family line were unbridled optimists or just plain thick.

The next morning I awoke, with a definite crick in my neck, to see Belinda tiptoeing across the room.

"You're up early," I said drowsily.

"Darling, I haven't been to bed yet—or should one correct that to I haven't been to my own bed yet."

"So I take it the selection of males was preferable to last night's?"

"Absolutely, darling."

"Are you going to elaborate?"

"That would not be discreet. Suffice it to say that it was heavenly."

"And will you be seeing him again?"

"One never knows." Again a dreamy smile as she made for the stairs. "I am now going to sleep. Please do not wake me, even if a body turns up in my own bathtub."

She reached the bottom step then turned back to me. "There's going to be a fabulous party on a boat this evening. A real boat with a motor this time. We're going to take a picnic down the Thames to Greenwich, and you're invited, of course."

"Oh, I don't think—" I began but she cut me off.

"Georgie, after what you've been through, you need some fun. Let your hair down. Besides, there are certain people who will be most disappointed if you don't show up."

"What people?"

A beatific smile. She put a red-nailed finger to her lips. "Ah, that would be telling. We'll be taking a cab at five. See you then. Night night."

And she was gone, leaving me wondering which people hoped to see me. Probably thrill-seekers wanting to get the gory details on a murder story, I thought angrily. I wouldn't go. But then a ride down the Thames and a picnic in a park did sound heavenly. How long had it been since I'd truly had fun?

Until then I had already decided what I was going to do: I was going to ask help of the only person who could be of use to me—my grandfather. It was a glorious May Day with the sun shining down, the trees in blossom, the birds chirping madly, and pigeons whirling in flocks. The sort of day when one is glad to be alive, in fact. I caught the train to Upminster Bridge and walked back up the hill to Granddad's house. He looked half pleased, half startled when he opened the door and saw me standing there.

"Well, blow me down," he said. "'Ello, my love. I've been worried sick about you. I read it in the papers this morning. I was thinking of going to the telephone kiosk and ringing you up."

"It wouldn't have done any good. I'm not at Rannoch House at the moment. It's swarming with police and reporters."

"Of course, it would be. It would be," he said. "Well, don't just stand there. Come in.

Come in. What a terrible thing to have happened. What was it? He'd drunk too much?"

"No, I'm afraid he was murdered," I said. "But neither Binky nor I has a clue as to who could have done it. That's why I came down to see you. You used to be in the police force."

"Ah, yes, but just on the beat, ducks. 'Umble copper plodding his beat, that's what I was."

"But you must have been part of criminal investigations. You know how these things work."

He shrugged. "I don't see what I can do. Nice cup of Rosie Lee?" he asked, using the Cockney tradition of rhyming slang.

"Yes, please." I sat at his tiny kitchen table. "Granddad, I'm worried about Binky. He's the obvious suspect and the fact that he fled to Scotland on discovering the body won't help him."

"Does your brother have close ties with the murdered man?"

"Unfortunately one close tie." And I told him about the letter.

"Oh, dear me. Dearie me. That's not

good, is it?" he said. "And you're sure your brother is telling you the truth?"

"Positive. I know Binky. When he lies his ears turn red."

Granddad picked up the shrieking kettle and poured the water into the teapot. "It seems to me you need to find out who else knew this chap was coming over to London. Who else he planned to meet while he was here."

"How would we do that?"

"Where was he staying?"

"Claridge's."

"Well, that makes it easier than a private house. Good hotels know everything about their guests—who visits them, where they ask a taxi to take them. We can go to Claridge's and ask a few questions. We can also take a look at his room."

"What would be the point of that? Wouldn't the police have searched it thoroughly?"

"You'd be surprised at what the police don't consider important."

"But it's two days now since he was murdered. Won't they have removed his things and cleaned out his room?"

"Possibly, but in my experience they

don't rush these things, especially over the weekend. They'll want to make sure they haven't missed anything. And after the police have released his effects, they'd have to be stored somewhere until they have orders to ship them to a next of kin."

I shook my head, feeling as if I were about to face a horrible exam. "Even if his things are still in his room, who would let us in? They'd think it highly suspicious if I asked to go in there."

He looked at me, head tilted to one side in the cheeky Cockney way. "Who said anything about asking?"

"You mean break into his room?"

"Or find a way to get in. . . ."

"I can get my hands on a maid's uniform," I said, cautiously. "Nobody ever notices maids, do they?"

"That's the ticket."

"But, Granddad, it's still breaking and entering."

"Better than swinging on the end of a rope, my dear. As an ex-member of the force I shouldn't be encouraging this sort of thing, but it seems to me that you and your brother are in big trouble and desperate means are called for. I'll come along and have a little chat with the doorman and the bellboys. Some of them may still remember me from the time when I was on the beat."

"That would be brilliant," I said. "And another thing. I need to find out if real window cleaners were working in the square on Friday, and if so, who they were. I'd ask myself, but with all those reporters . . ."

"Think no more about it, my love. That much I can do for you. And I'd ask you to stay for lunch but I promised I'd go over to the widow next door. She kept on inviting me and I kept on refusing, and then I thought, Why not? What's wrong with a bit of company?"

"What's wrong indeed," I said. I reached across the table and took his hand. "Can she cook?"

"Not as good as your grandma, but she ain't bad. She ain't bad at all."

"Enjoy your lunch, Granddad."

He looked almost bashful. "She can't be after my money," he said with a wheezy laugh, "so it must be my good looks. Shall I meet you tomorrow, then? I'll find out about your window cleaners and then we'll go to Claridge's."

"All right," I said, feeling my stomach

twisting itself into a knot. Posing as a maid to get into a person's room was serious business. If I was caught, I might well harm Binky's cause rather than help it.

Chapter 19

Belinda's mews and later
Rannoch House
Sunday, May 1, 1932

Belinda roused herself shortly before five o'clock and came downstairs looking stunning in red trousers and a black riding jacket. This immediately reminded me that I had nothing to wear, even if I could get into Rannoch House, which didn't seem likely. I lamented this to Belinda, who immediately opened up her wardrobe and fixed me up with a spiffing yachting outfit consisting of white skirt and blue blazer with white trim. It even came with a jaunty little sailor's cap. The result, when I looked in the mirror, was quite satisfying.

"Are you sure you don't want to wear this?" I asked Belinda.

"Good Lord, no. It's not exactly the height of fashion, darling. You can get away with it, of course, but if I were to be seen in it at Cowes, bang would go my reputation."

I thought privately that her reputation had probably gone bang already.

"Off we go, then," she said, slipping her arm through mine.

"Belinda, I'm very grateful for everything you're doing for me," I said.

"Darling, think nothing of it. I would have been expelled from Les Oiseaux many times over if you hadn't rescued me. And you are certainly in need of a friend at the moment."

I couldn't have agreed more. We took a taxi to the boat dock at Westminster pier, even though I suspect that neither of us had money to waste on taxies. But one had to arrive properly, as Belinda put it, and so we did.

The boat/ship/yacht currently tied up at the pier was large and sleek, bigger than any cabin cruiser I had seen—a sort of junior transatlantic liner. An awning had been erected on the rear deck (Is that called the poop? I'm not up in nautical terms). A gramophone was playing and couples were already dancing some kind of hop. I was so enthralled with the scene on board that I almost caught my foot in a rope lying across the top of the steps and would have sprawled forward if Belinda hadn't caught me.

"Careful," she said. "You don't want to arrive headfirst. Now go down the ladder backward and watch your footing. I really don't want to have to fish you out of the Thames."

"I'll try hard," I said. "Do you think I'll ever outgrow my clumsiness?"

"Probably not," Belinda replied with a grin. "If deportment classes, gym at Les Oiseaux, and climbing those crags in Scotland haven't cured you, I'd say you were destined to be clumsy for life."

I lowered myself down the ladder carefully. I hadn't reached the bottom step when hands came around my waist and lifted me to the deck.

"Well, look who's here," said a familiar voice and there was Darcy, looking devastating in a white open-necked shirt and rolled up sailor's trousers. "I'm glad Belinda persuaded you to come."

"So am I," I stammered, because his hands were still around my waist. To my annoyance I found myself blushing.

"Aren't you going to give me a hand, Darcy?" Belinda asked. Darcy let go of me.

"If you wish, although I thought you were capable of doing most things remarkably well."

There was something in the quick glance that passed between them that I couldn't interpret. It did cross my mind that his might have been the bed she shared last night. I was surprised at the rush of jealousy I felt. But then, I reasoned, why would she have insisted that I come this afternoon if she wanted him for herself?

"Come and meet our host," Belinda said, dragging me away. "Eduardo, this is my good friend Georgiana Rannoch. Georgie, may I present Eduardo Carrera from Argentina."

I found myself looking at a most suave gentleman, maybe in his late twenties, dark sleek hair, Ronald Coleman mustache, dressed impeccably in blazer and flannels.

"Señor Carrera." I held out my hand and he brought it to his lips.

"Delighted to welcome you on board my little tub, Lady Georgiana," he said in perfect English without trace of a foreign accent.

"Little tub!" I laughed. "Did you sail it all the way from Argentina?"

"No, I regret it was just from the Isle of Wight. Although she is supposed to be up to an Atlantic crossing. I have not been back to Argentina since my parents sent me to Eton. Obviously I'll have to go back sometime to take over the family business, but until then I make the most of the delights Europe has to offer." He let his gaze linger first on me then on Belinda in a most suggestive way. "Let me find you some champagne."

Belinda nudged me as he moved off. "See what I mean about charming foreigners? Any Englishman you meet would say, 'What-ho, old thing,' and start talking about the cricket or at most the hunting."

"He is rather dashing," I said.

"His mother's Argentine English. Between the two families they own half of Argentina. Not a bad catch at all."

"Are you angling yourself or are you telling me to cast my line?" I whispered.

She smiled. "Haven't decided yet, so feel free. My theory is always that all is fair in love and war." Again I wondered if she was referring to Darcy.

"So where did you meet Darcy?" I couldn't help asking. "Was it at the party last night?"

"What?" she appeared distracted. "Darcy? Oh, yes. He was there. He may be a little too wicked for you, Georgie, but I can tell you that he's certainly still interested. He asked a million questions."

"About what?"

"Oh, this and that. Of course everyone was speculating about the murder. They were all on your side, by the way. Nobody in the room could believe that Binky could drown anyone in a bathtub."

"Did they have any theories on who might have done the drowning?"

"None at all. But I can tell you that de Mauxville was not the most popular man in the world. Everyone agreed that he cheated at cards and did not behave like a gentleman. So I think it's safe to say he had his share of enemies."

"No suggestion as to who they might be?"

"If you mean did anyone own up to the murder, the answer is no. The murderer could be quite outside of our set. If de

Mauxville has criminal connections it could be a falling-out of thieves."

"Goodness, I hadn't thought of that," I said. "But we'd have no way of checking up on criminals."

"Everyone got a glass in their hands?" Eduardo called. "Right-o. Take a seat and hold on tight so that we can cast off."

"Let's sit here, on the side, so that we'll get the heavenly breeze in our faces," Belinda said, hoisting herself up onto the rim of the boat with her feet on the teak seat. I followed suit. "I'm sure we'll be going very fast, if I know Eduardo. He also drives racing cars, and he flies."

"Like Peter Pan?"

She laughed. "A plane, darling. A dear, dinky little plane. He's promised to take me up sometime."

As if on cue a motor roared to life, making the whole boat throb with power.

"Ready to cast off," Eduardo shouted as someone rushed to release the ropes that held the ship fast to the jetty. Suddenly we took off with such force that I was thrown backward. I made a futile grab at the smooth side of the boat as I went flying off into the ice cold water. Around me the water was churning madly and the thrashing of propellers boomed through my ears. Gasping, I fought my way to the surface. I'm a strong swimmer and wasn't particularly scared until I realized I was being dragged along. Something was wound tightly around my ankle and I couldn't reach it because of the speed at which I was being dragged. I fought to keep my head above water long enough to scream, but I couldn't without getting a mouthful of water. Surely someone must have seen what had happened. I had been surrounded by people. Belinda had been sitting right beside me. I waved my arms frantically. Then there was a splash, strong arms came around me, and the motor was mercifully cut. I was dragged back to the ship and hauled back on board. Everyone was making a big fuss of me, while I sat there, gasping and coughing like a landed fish.

"Are you all right?" Darcy asked, and I saw from his wet state that he had been one of those who dived in to save me.

"I think so," I said. "More shocked than anything."

"You're lucky you didn't bash your head on the side as you went in," another voice said and I looked up to see the stiff, upright form of Whiffy Featherstonehaugh. "Because then you'd just have gone under and we might never have noticed you."

I shivered. Whiffy patted my shoulder awkwardly. "Anyway, my dear Georgie, I regret to inform you that there are no fish big enough in the Thames to warrant using you as bait," he said. The typical Englishman's way of offering sympathy. I noticed he was not wet.

Eduardo appeared with a blanket in one hand and a brandy in the other. "I'm so frightfully sorry," he said. "I can't think how that happened."

"It's just Georgie," Belinda said, helping to put the blanket around my shoulders. "Things seem to happen to her. Accident-prone, you know."

"Then I'll watch out for albatrosses on the voyage," Eduardo said. "Come down to the cabin and I'll find some dry clothes for you."

"So you have to almost drown a girl before you can lure her to your cabin these days, eh, Eduardo?" someone asked.

Everyone was making light of the episode, the way people do after they have had a fright. Belinda went down below with me and helped me into Eduardo's striped fisherman's jersey and a pair of baggy trousers about five sizes too big for me.

"Honestly, Georgie," she said, laughing and looking worried at the same time, "who else but you could fall off a boat with her foot tangled in a rope?"

"I can't imagine how it happened," I said. "The beastly thing was absolutely knotted fast around my ankle. I tried to get it off but I couldn't."

"I'm going to watch over you like a hawk for the rest of the trip," she said. "Now come back on deck and let's see if we can dry out your clothes."

"They are your clothes and I'm afraid they are rather the worse for being in Thames water," I said. "It tasted foul."

Darcy was waiting as I came out of the cabin. "Are you sure you're all right?" he said. "My God, you look like a drowned rat. Are you sure you wouldn't rather I took you home?"

I had to admit that I wasn't feeling too well. I must have swallowed gallons of Thames water and I was still shivering, probably with delayed shock.

"If you really don't mind," I said. "It might

be best. But I don't want to spoil your afternoon."

"I am also, as you might notice, pretty
darned wet," he said, "and Eduardo didn't
offer to take me to his cabin and dry me
off."

I laughed.

"That's better," he said. "You looked as if
you were about to pass out a minute ago.
Come on, let's see if Eduardo knows how to
back this thing up."

A few minutes later we were moored,
once again, at the jetty.

"Watch out for ropes this time," Belinda
called after me. "See you tonight."

Darcy hailed a taxi.

"Belgrave Square, isn't it? What's the
number?" he asked.

"I can't go home," I said dismally. "The
police may still be there and anyway the
house is surrounded by reporters and the
morbidly curious."

"Then where are we going?"

"I've been sleeping on Belinda's sofa," I
said. "I do have a change of clothes there
and I can wash out the clothes she lent me
before they are stained forever with this
Thames water."

"You want to go back to Belinda's place?"

"I can't think where else to go right now," I said, and my voice wobbled. "The problem is that it's her maid's day off and I only know how to cook baked beans and I was so looking forward to a lovely picnic."

"I tell you what," Darcy said. "Why don't we go back to my place? Don't look like that. I promise to behave like a gentleman and there is good wine in the cellar and I know a great place to have a picnic. And I am about to catch pneumonia myself and you wouldn't want that, would you, especially after I dived into that awful water to rescue you."

"How can I refuse," I said. "And it does sound a lot better than baked beans."

The taxi now whisked us in the direction of Chelsea and stopped outside a pretty little blue and white shuttered house. "Here we are," he said.

Darcy opened the front door and ushered me through to a tiny living room. No heads or shields on the walls, no portraits of ancestors, just a couple of good modern paintings and comfortable sofas. This is how ordinary people live, I thought with a pang of envy, and I pictured myself living in a house like this with Darcy, doing the cooking and cleaning myself, and . . .

"Give me a second to go and change," he said. "If you want to rinse out those wet clothes there's a sink in the scullery."

Thanks to living alone at Rannoch House, I now knew where a scullery was to be found and went through a small, neat kitchen to the room beyond. Here I ran the sink full of water (hot water, oh, the bliss of it; I almost jumped in with the clothes) and plunged the clothes into it. When they came out, I did notice that the white skirt had now become light blue, but hoped it might go away when the garment dried. I opened the door to find a place to hang them and found myself beside the Thames. I was in a small, pretty garden with a tiny lawn and a tree that had just burst into leaf. Beyond was a jetty. I stood there entranced until I was found by Darcy.

"Now you've seen how the plebs live," he said. "Not bad, eh?"

"It's lovely," I said, "but didn't you say you were borrowing it?"

"Absolutely. I can't afford this kind of place. It belongs to a distant cousin of mine who chooses to spend his summers on the

Med in his yacht. Fortunately I have cousins all over Europe, thanks to the Catholics' view on birth control. Stay here and I'll bring out the wine and whatever food I can rustle up."

Soon we were sitting on deck chairs in that little garden with cold white wine, ripe cheeses, crusty bread, and grapes. It was a warm evening and the setting sun glowed on the old brick of the walls. For a while I ate and drank in silence.

"This is heaven," I said. "Hooray for all your cousins."

"Speaking of cousins," Darcy said, "I gather that poor old Hubert Anstruther is not expected to last much longer. In a coma, so they say."

"Do you know him?"

"Went climbing a couple of times with him in the Alps. Didn't strike me as the kind of fellow that would let himself be swept away by an avalanche."

"Tristram is devastated," I said. "Sir Hubert was his guardian, you know."

"Hmph," was all he said to this.

"And neither Sir Hubert nor Tristram is my relative," I added. "My mother was married to Sir Hubert many husbands ago, which made Tristram and me almost related once, that's all."

"I see." There was a long pause while Darcy poured us another glass of wine. "So are you seeing much of that blighter Hautbois?"

"Darcy, I do believe you're jealous."

"Just keeping a protective eye on you, that's all."

I decided to strike back. "So I gather you were at a party with Belinda last night."

"Belinda? Yes, she was at the party. What a grand girl she is—heaps of fun. Not an inhibition in sight."

"She told me you might be too wild for me." I paused. "I wondered how she knew that."

"Did you, now? That would be telling."

He grinned at my obvious discomfort, then he leaned closer to me. "Are you going to let me kiss you tonight? Even though I'm wild?"

"You did promise to behave like a gentleman, remember."

"So I did. Here, let me fill that wineglass for you."

"Are you attempting to get me drunk so that you can have your way with me?" I asked, my own inhibitions miraculously melting with the first glasses of wine.

"I don't believe in that approach myself. I like my women to be fully aware of what they are doing so that they get the maximum enjoyment from it." His eyes, over his raised wineglass, were flirting with me. I was very conscious of those melting inhibitions.

I made an attempt to stand up. "It's getting rather cold out here, isn't it? Don't you think we should go inside?"

"Good idea." He picked up our glasses and the wine bottle, which was now miraculously empty, and went ahead of me into the house. I followed with the remains of the food. I was just setting it down in the kitchen when his arms came around my waist.

"Darcy!"

"I always think it's better to take 'em by surprise," he whispered, and started kissing the side of my neck in a way that made me go weak at the knees. I turned to face him and his lips moved to meet mine. I had been kissed plenty of times before, behind the potted palms at deb balls, in the backseats of taxies on the way home. There had even been a bit of groping thrown in, but nothing had made me feel like this. My arms came around his neck and I was kissing him back. Somehow my body seemed to know how to respond. I felt giddy with desire.

"Ow," I said as I was somehow backed into a cooker knob.

"Kitchens are damned uncomfortable places, aren't they?" He was laughing. "Come on, let's go and take in the sunset from upstairs. It's the most glorious view across the Thames."

He took my hand and started to lead me up the stairs. I floated behind him, half in a dream. The bedroom was bathed in a glorious rosy sunset and the waters of the Thames below sparkled like magic. Swans were swimming past, their white feathers tinged with pink.

"This is heavenly," I said again.

"I promise you it will be even more heavenly," he said and started kissing me again. Somehow we seemed to be sitting on the bed. But that was when the little alarm bells started going off in my head. I hardly knew him, after all. And it was just possible that he had spent last night with Belinda. Was that what I wanted for myself—a man who flitted from girl to girl, from one encounter to the next? And another thought alarmed me even more. Was I following in my mother's footsteps? Would I be starting down that long road that she took, moving from one man to the next with no home, no stability?

I sat up and took hold of Darcy's hands. "No, Darcy. I'm not ready for this," I said. "I'm not another Belinda."

"But I promise you'd like it," he said. The way he was looking at me almost melted my resolve again. I rather thought I might like it myself.

"I'm sure I would, but I'd regret it afterward. And with all that's going on in my life right now, this would not be the right time. Besides, I want to wait for a man who really loves me."

"How do you know I don't love you?"

"Today, maybe, but can you guarantee tomorrow?"

"Oh, come on, Georgie. Let go of that awful royal training. Life's for having fun. And who knows how it might turn out."

"I'm sorry," I said. "I should never have led you on. You did promise to behave like a gentleman."

"As for that"—he had such a wicked

grin—"your relative King Edward was a per-fect gentleman but by God he bedded half the females in his kingdom."

He took a look at my face and stood up with a sigh. "All right, then. Come on. I'll call a cab to take you home."

Chapter 20

Belinda Warburton-Stoke's
sofa yet again
Monday, May 2, 1932

When I arrived back at Belinda's place that
night, with more than a modicum of regret, I
found a note from Binky, instructing me to
meet him at our solicitors' office at ten
o'clock. This could prove to be awkward if it
went on too long, as I had arranged to meet
my grandfather at lunchtime. To be on the
safe side, I went into Rannoch House early
in the morning to pick up the maid's uniform. This was a wise move as there was no
sign of either police or journalists outside at
that hour. The house felt very strange and
horribly cold, although all traces of the body
had been removed from the bath. But I
found myself tiptoeing past the bathroom
door under the watchful eye of that avenging statue.

As I took the maid's uniform out of my wardrobe, I heard something chink. I put my hand into the apron pocket and there was the figurine I had broken at the Featherstonehaughs'. So much had happened since, that I had completely forgotten about it. Oh, dear. Now I'd have to think of a way to have it mended and sneak it back. I just hoped they hadn't noticed it was missing among all those swords and gods and whatnots. I shoved it into the top drawer of my dressing table and put the maid's uniform into a carrier bag. I'd have to find a loo to change in somewhere along the way.

I was just leaving the house when the telephone rang.

"Georgie?" a male voice asked.

For a second I thought it was Binky, but before I could answer he went on to say, "It's Tristram. Sorry to ring you at this hour. Did I wake you?"

"Wake me? Tristram, I've been up for hours. Actually I'm staying with a friend and I just stopped at Rannoch House to pick up some things before I have to meet my brother at the solicitors'. You've heard the news presumably?"

"I saw it in the papers. I couldn't believe

my eyes. What a rum do. Your brother's not the sort who goes around bumping off people, is he?"

"Absolutely not."

"So who could it have been? I was talking to Whiffy on the phone last night and we just couldn't imagine why someone would leave a body at Rannoch House. Do you think it was a poor sort of joke?"

"I've no idea, Tristram," I said.

"Rotten luck on you, anyway."

"Yes. It has been pretty rotten."

"And Whiffy tells me that you had a nasty accident yesterday. Fell off a boat and nearly drowned, so he says."

"Yes, things don't seem to be going too swimmingly at the moment," I said, trying to think how I could end this conversation politely.

"And Whiffy said you went off with that O'Mara fellow."

"Yes, Darcy was kind enough to escort me home," I said.

"I ballywell hope he behaved like a gentleman," Tristram said.

A smile twitched across my lips. "Tristram, I believe you're jealous of Darcy."

"Jealous. Good Lord, no. I'm just worried

about you, old thing. And I make no bones about it: I don't trust that O'Mara. Nothing good ever came out of Ireland."

"Whiskey," I said, "and Guinness."

"What? Oh, rather. But you know what I mean."

"Tristram, Darcy is a peer of the realm and he behaved like one," I said firmly, thinking of the extraordinary ways I had known peers to behave. Before he could answer this I said briskly, "But I really have to run. I'm going to be late."

"Oh, right. I just wanted to offer my services, you know. See if there's anything I can do."

"It's sweet of you, but there's nothing, really."

"I suppose your brother is taking good care of you."

"My brother is at his club."

"Weally? If you wanted me to come and stand guard at night, I'd be happy to."

I had to chuckle at the thought of Tristram standing guard. "Thank you, but I'll probably continue to stay with my friend for a while."

"Good idea. Quite a relief to have someone keep an eye on you. I don't suppose you'd like to meet me later, so that I can take you for a bite to eat and cheer you up?"

"Thank you. You're very kind, but I don't think I'm in the mood for eating and I've no idea how long this will take."

"Right-o, then. I'll check in from time to time and see how you're getting along. Whiffy and I both want to help if we can. Toodle-oo, then. Keep your pecker up, old thing."

I hung up and hurried out to meet Binky. I was rather intrigued to know whether we might see Old Mr. Prendergast today and how he might look, until I was informed that he had been dead for ten years. Young Mr. Prendergast tut-tutted and sighed as he sat surveying us. "A bad business, Your Grace. A nasty business indeed."

"I give you my word my sister and I had nothing to do with it," Binky said.

"My firm has handled the legal affairs of your family for generations," the old man said. "Your word is enough for me."

"But you can see how bad it looks for us."

"I can indeed. Most unfortunate."

"We were wondering," Binky said, "whether you would have to tell the police about the letter—if they haven't yet found out about it. Because, I mean to say, that would really put the cat among the pigeons, so to speak."

"That is indeed a difficult ethical decision, Your Grace. Our loyalty to our clients versus withholding information in a criminal case. I should, of course, be obliged to answer any question truthfully, should the police choose to question me. That would include revealing the document. However, as to whether I feel it incumbent upon myself to volunteer information to the police that might incriminate my client—a client who has given me his word that he is innocent—then I think that I feel no such obligation."

Binky got to his feet and shook the old man's hand. I could hear the bones creaking.

"I think that went rather well," Binky exclaimed as we came out. "Care to go for a spot of lunch with me somewhere? Claridge's, maybe?"

"Claridge's?" It came out as a squeak. "I'd love to, but unfortunately I'm meeting my grandfather today. Remember he was in the police once. I'm hoping he'll have some advice for us and maybe still know some men at Scotland Yard."

"Spiffing. Super idea."

"And anyway I hear the food's not up to much at Claridge's these days," I added for good measure, just in case he decided he was going to take his luncheon there without me.

"You don't say? I always thought Claridge's was the tops," Binky said. "Oh, well. Might as well eat at the club and save money, then. Where will I find you, Georgie? And how long do you think I'm supposed to hang around down here? It's costing a fortune to stay at the club, you know. Those whiskey and sodas don't come cheap."

"You'll have to ask the police when it's all right for you to go home," I said. "And as to where you can find me, I'm thinking of moving back into the house. I was there this morning and the police have gone. So has the body."

"That's dashed brave of you, old bean. I don't think I could stomach it, somehow. And they do make one so blinking comfortable at the club."

With that we parted company, he into a taxicab and me down the steps of the underground at Holborn Station. I went one stop, then changed at Tottenham Court

Road. I suppose I could have walked to the Strand and Claridge's, but it had started to rain and I had no wish to appear like a drowned rat.

I had ridden the underground so seldom in my life that I was always somewhat bewildered by the various passages and escalators leading from one line to the next. Tottenham Court Road was a hub of activity, with people running in all directions. Everybody seemed to be in a frightful hurry. I took the escalator down to the Northern Line, getting buffeted by people trying to push past me on the right. At last I found the right platform and stood at the front, waiting for the train. More and more people streamed onto the platform behind me. At last there came the rumbling of an approaching train. A wind came rushing ahead of it from the tunnel. Just as it appeared I was shoved hard from behind in the middle of my back. I lost my footing and went pitching forward toward the electric rails. It all happened so quickly. I hadn't even time to scream. Hands reached out and grabbed me and I was yanked back onto the platform again, just as the train thundered past me.

"Phew, that was a close one, miss," a

large laborer said, as he stood me on my feet again. "I thought you was a goner then." He looked positively green.

"So did I," I said. "Someone pushed me."

I looked around. People were already streaming past us onto the train as if we didn't exist.

"They're always in so much of a bloomin' hurry, I'm surprised there aren't more accidents," my workman friend said. "There's too many people in London these days. That's the trouble. And those what's got motorcars can't afford to run them no more, what with the price of petrol."

"You saved my life. Thank you very much," I said.

"Don't mention it, miss. Probably wise not to stand too near the edge next time," he said. "You've only got to have one person stumble or shove behind you and you're off the edge, under a train."

"You're right," I said. "I'll be more careful."

I completed the journey, glad for once that Belinda wasn't with me. She'd definitely have something to say about my clumsiness getting out of hand. Although this time it hadn't been my clumsiness. I had been at the wrong place at the wrong time.

My fingers still trembled as I changed into my maid's uniform in the lady's lavatory at Charing Cross Station, but by the time I reached Claridge's, I had calmed down. It was lucky it was raining, as I could conceal my uniform under my mackintosh. As I approached Claridge's, I saw my grandfather's familiar form waiting for me.

"Hello, my ducks. How are you holding up, then?"

"All right," I said. "Apart from nearly being pushed under a train."

I saw the worried look cross his face. "When was this?"

"On my way from my solicitors'. I was at the front of a crowded platform and the crowd must have surged forward at the approach of a train. I was almost pushed in front of it."

"You want to be more careful, my love. London's a dangerous place," he said.

"I will be in future."

He looked at me for a moment, head cocked on one side, then he said, "Oh, well, I suppose we had better get on with what we came to do."

"Have you had a chance to speak to anybody yet?"

He touched the side of his nose. "Hasn't lost his touch, your old granddad. Still got what it takes. Knows how to butter 'em up. I went to your posh square first and I can tell you that there weren't no window cleaners working that day."

"So if somebody saw a window cleaner . . ."

"It was someone up to no good."

"Exactly what I thought. I wonder if they could describe him, or them?"

"Nobody notices tradesmen, my love."

"The same as nobody notices maids," I said. "I'm wearing my maid's uniform, but I have to find out which room and I have no idea how I can possibly get into it."

"As for that, it was room 317. And what's more, it ain't been cleaned out yet. Seems that the gentleman paid a week in advance and so they didn't like to shift his things without instructions."

"How did you manage to find out all that?"

He grinned. "Alf the doorman still remembered me."

"Granddad, you're a genius."

"See, your old granddad does still have his uses." He beamed at me.

"Anything else you can tell me?"

"Your Monsieur de Mauxville went out every night gambling—to Crockford's and to other places less savory. And he had a visitor. A dark-haired young man. Posh."

"Anything else?"

"Not yet. I thought I'd have a chat with the bellboys and you could ask the other maids on that floor."

"All right," I said. Now that it was about to happen, I was terrified. Breaking and entering were serious enough, but they would also make me look guilty in the eyes of Inspector Sugg. "How can I possibly get up the stairs without being noticed? People might recognize me."

"Fire escape. There always has to be a safe way out of a hotel."

"Here I go, then. You wouldn't like to come with me, I suppose?"

"I'd do a lot for you, my sweet, but not this. I'm an ex-policeman and a nobody. The law would treat me very differently from you, if we're caught. I've no wish to spend the rest of my days in Wormwood Scrubs."

"I'm not too anxious to do so either," I said and he laughed.

"Wormwood Scrubs is a men's prison.

But they'd let you off, being who you are and knowing you were just trying to help your brother."

I nodded. "I sincerely hope so. Wish me luck, then," I said. "I'll meet you back here in an hour."

I made it up the fire escape staircase with no problem, left my mack rolled up in a corner, put on my maid's cap, and came out onto the third floor. Then, of course, it occurred to me that I had no way to get into the room. I clearly hadn't thought this thing through properly. I wandered down the hall, trying the door handles, until a voice behind me made me jump out of my skin.

"Hey, you, what are you doing?"

I turned around to see a fresh-faced Irish girl in a maid's uniform quite unlike my own. I decided to change my story rather rapidly.

"My mistress was staying here last night and her diamond earring must have fallen off while she was asleep. She doesn't usually go to bed with earrings on, but she got in so late. So she's asked me to retrieve it. But nobody answers the door so the master must have also left by now."

"What room was it?"

"Three seventeen."

She looked at me queerly. "Three seven-teen was that French gentleman who was murdered," she said.

"Murdered? Here?"

"Don't you ever read the papers? Not here. In some duke's bathtub. Anyway, the police came and gave his room a good go-ing-over."

"Did they find anything?"

"How would I know? They'd not have told me, would they?"

"So did you have to pack up all his things?"

"Not yet. They're still in there, as far as I know, and the police have given orders that no one is to go in."

"How terrible that he got killed. Was he a nice man?"

"Quite the opposite. Rude and ungrateful, from what I saw. He snapped his fingers and shouted at me because I'd moved the papers on his desk."

"What kind of papers?"

"Nothing special. Just some magazines he'd been reading. You'd have thought I'd been snooping." She brushed down her uniform. "Anyway, I can't stand here chat-ting. I have to get back to work."

"And I have to find that earring or risk getting my head bitten off. My memory's hopeless. Could it have been 217? Any idea where Lord and Lady . . ." I let the rest of the sentence hang, hoping she'd take the bait. She did.

"Lady Furness? That was 313."

"Oh, thank heavens. I'd never have heard the last of it if I returned home without her earring. Do you think you could let me in?"

"I suppose so, but I really ought to—"

"Look, Lady Furness is lunching with a friend in the restaurant downstairs. Do you want me to go and find her to tell you that it's all right for me to go in there?"

She looked at me long and hard, then she said, "No, I suppose it can't do no harm, can it? But the bed's already been stripped. If it hasn't been found yet, chances are it's not going to be."

"A little diamond could have fallen down the back of the bed and nobody would notice it," I said. "Anyway, I've been commanded to search and search I'd better, or else. You should see her when she gets rattled."

She grinned at me then. "Go on, then, in you go and make sure you shut the door firmly behind you. I don't want to get in trouble for leaving a door open."

"Oh, definitely. I'll make sure I shut it," I said. "I'll even keep it shut while I'm searching."

She opened the door. I went inside and shut it behind me. I wasn't quite sure what use it was being in room 313, but it was better than nothing. I opened the window and saw that there was a broad ledge running around the outside. If the window of 317 was not latched tightly, it was possible I might get in that way. I climbed out gingerly onto the ledge. It was certainly a long way down. I could see the parade of bright red buses passing below me along the Strand. And that broad ledge didn't seem so broad any longer. I didn't have the nerve to stand up. I started to crawl slowly along the ledge. I passed 315 successfully and reached 317. It was hard to get any purchase on the window frame from my precarious position, but at last I felt it give a little.

I managed to raise it, then crawled inside and stood, breathing very hard, on the carpet of the deserted room. As the maid had said, the room had been stripped since de Mauxville left. No sheets, no towels. There were still papers on the desk in a neat pile. I went through them but found only a three-day-old copy of the *Times*, and some sporting magazines. His wastebasket had been emptied. No telltale marks on the blotting paper. I looked under his bed but the floor was spotless. I opened the chest of drawers but they only contained some rather gray undergarments and a pair of socks in need of darning. The handkerchiefs, however, were embroidered with a crest. Then I went through his wardrobe. A dinner suit was hanging there, and a couple of clean white shirts. I tried the pockets of the dinner jacket and found nothing. But when I put it back on the hanger, it just didn't hang correctly. Gentlemen's suits should be tailored to perfection and not droop. I tried pockets again and found that the lining was torn on one inside pocket. I traced down the tear in the lining and brought out a roll of paper. I let out a gasp when I saw what it was: a tight roll of banknotes—five pound notes, hundreds of them—well, maybe not hundreds but a big fat wad of them. I stood there staring at the money. To someone like me, who had been penniless most of her life, it represented a fortune. Who would know if I took it? The words echoed through my head. Ill-gotten gains of a dead man— surely nobody would ever find out. But then my ancestors, both sides of them, triumphed. Death Before Dishonor.

I was about to put them back when I realized I might be handling evidence and I was busily leaving my fingerprints all over them, and all over the room! I couldn't believe my stupidity. I didn't know whether the police could test things like money for fingerprints, but I wasn't going to take a chance. Hastily I wiped the roll with my apron and put it back. Then I went around the room, wiping every surface I had touched.

There was a notepad beside the telephone. It appeared unused, but as the light struck it I could tell that there was an imprint on the top sheet as if the writer had pressed too hard as he wrote. I went over to the window and held the sheet up.

It said, *R—10:30!*

I wondered if the police had torn off that top sheet. Even the least intelligent policeman would be able to deduce that *R* meant "Rannoch." Things didn't look good for Binky unless I could find out where these large sums of money came from.

The room revealed no more secrets and I made my way back onto the ledge, carefully closing the window behind me. I started to crawl back. I had just reached the window of number 315 when I heard voices in the room. I froze. To my horror I heard someone say, "Isn't it stuffy in here?" and there came the sound of the window being opened. I scrambled to my feet and stood to one side of the window, pressing myself against the drainpipe, holding on for dear life. A young sandy-haired man looked out. I heard him say, "There, are you satisfied now?" and he moved away again. Now I had to risk crossing an open window or going back into 317 and risk being seen coming out.

I decided on the latter. As I tried to kneel down again the drainpipe moved with me. It started to come away from the wall. I clawed at the stonework on the building and grabbed on to it. I suppose I must have screamed because a voice behind me asked, "What the devil are you doing?" and it was the young man with the sandy hair peering out of the window.

"Sorry, sir. I dropped my feather duster out onto the ledge when I was shaking it," I said. "And when I climbed out to get it, I couldn't get back in again."

"My dear girl. A feather duster isn't worth risking your life for," he said. "Here. Give me your hand and come inside here." He helped me step down into his room.

"Thank you, sir. You're most kind," I said in what I hoped was an Irish accent.

He reached into his waistcoat pocket and drew out a sovereign. "Here, that should buy you a new feather duster so that you don't get into trouble."

"Oh, no, sir. I couldn't."

"Take it. I've had rather a successful week, as it happens." He forced it into my hand.

"Thank you, sir. Very generous of you."

I nodded to the young woman who appeared from the bathroom and made a hurried exit. There was no sign of the Irish maid.

I hummed to myself as I put on my mack and made my way down the stairs. A sovereign for my pains. Maybe I should think of working in a hotel!

Chapter 21

Rannoch House (minus body)
Monday, May 2, 1932

My grandfather was waiting for me, standing under the awning while the rain came
down. Unfortunately he had nothing much
to report. I told him about the five-pound
notes and suggested that he should call the
police with an anonymous tip about de
Mauxville's gaming. I felt the least I could do
was treat him to lunch, and almost had to
drag him to Lyons Corner House. I tried to
be jolly and bright but he looked worried
and preoccupied the whole time. When we
parted company he looked at me long and
hard. "Take care of yourself, won't you, and
if you'd rather come and stay with me, then
you know you're more than welcome."

I smiled at him. "That's sweet of you,
Granddad, but I have to stay in town to

keep an eye on Binky, and to find out things."

"I suppose so," he said with a sigh. "But watch out for yourself."

"Don't worry about me. I'll be fine," I said with more bravado than I felt. I looked back once and saw him standing there, watching me.

When Belinda did her Lady Macbeth routine down the stairs about two o'clock, I told her of my decision to move back to Rannoch House.

"Georgie, are you sure?" she asked.

"I went back this morning. All traces of the body have been removed and it seems silly to go on sleeping on your sofa when I have a perfectly good bed of my own."

"I think it's awfully brave of you," she said, but I could tell she was relieved.

"I do have one teeny favor to ask," I said. "Do you think you would mind keeping me company tonight? I'm not sure how hard it will be and I'd really appreciate knowing you were there with me for the first night at least."

"You want me to stay at Rannoch House?" I could see she was struggling. Then she said, "Of course. Why not? It's about time I had an early night with no parties. I saw bags starting to form under my eyes when I looked in the mirror."

So that evening, after the press and any gawkers had gone home, we made our way up the steps and into the house.

"This place has always struck me as creepy at the best of times," Belinda said. "It's always so cold and damp."

"Compared to Castle Rannoch it's a furnace," I said, laughing uneasily because I too found it cold and damp. I was about to suggest that we go back to Belinda's comfortable mews again, until I reminded myself that a Rannoch never runs away from danger. We undressed and prepared for bed, then I went downstairs and poured us both a Scotch to bolster our spirits. We sat on my bed, talking about anything rather than turning the light out.

"My dear, I'm dying to hear the details on last night," Belinda said. "I almost woke you when I got home. You did have a lovely smile on your face so I could only conclude that Mr. O'Mara had revealed to you the mysteries of life and love."

"He wanted to."

"But you didn't?"

"It wasn't that I didn't. As a matter of fact I did. Very much."

"Then why didn't you?"

"I just couldn't go through with it. I realized that he wasn't suitable husband material and I had this horrible vision of ending up like my mother."

"But she's had plenty of husbands."

"But I want somebody who's going to love me and stick with me for the rest of my life."

"Darling, how terribly old-fashioned. And someone has to relieve you of this frightful burden you carry. Who better than Darcy?"

"You can recommend him, can you?"

She looked at me and gave a delightful peal of laughter. "Oh, so that was it! You thought that Darcy and I—and you didn't want to tread on my toes. Aren't you sweet."

I didn't like to mention that I didn't want shop-soiled goods.

At that moment a great blast of wind came down the chimney. The storm had been building all day and we looked at each other in alarm.

"You don't think his ghost is lingering

here, wanting vengeance, do you?" Belinda asked.

"Castle Rannoch is full of ghosts. I'm used to them."

"Really? Have you ever actually seen one?"

"Sort of. You know, when you are aware of something out of the corner of your eye."

"Does it really go awfully cold before they appear?"

"You can't tell at Castle Rannoch."

There was a clattering noise on the street below.

"What was that?" Belinda asked nervously.

I went to the window. "I can't see from here," I said.

"It sounded as if it was close. Maybe in your basement area."

"It's probably only a cat or a rubbish bin blown over. But we can go down and see."

"Are you mad? A killer has been in this house."

"Belinda, there are two of us, and we'll take something to hit him with. The house is full of weapons. Take your pick."

"All right." She didn't sound all right at all, but suddenly I felt very angry. My whole life had been turned upside down. My brother was suspected of a crime and I wanted this over. I stamped down the stairs, grabbing an assegai that a family member had brought back from the Boer War.

We made our way down to the kitchen, not turning on the light to warn whoever it was. Halfway across the kitchen floor a shadow of a man outside the window was thrown across the room and we leaped into each other's arms.

"Enough stupid bravery. Call the police," Belinda hissed and I couldn't help but agree with her. We crept to the phone and dialed 999, then waited clinging on to each other as if we were in a storm-tossed ocean. At last I thought I heard shouts and a scuffle and then a thunderous knock at our front door. I opened it a crack and saw with relief two constables standing there.

"We've caught someone snooping around your house, my lady," one of them said. I recognized him as the constable from the other night.

"Good work, Constable. It may be the man who broke in and killed the Frenchman. Where is he?"

"Bring him over here into the light, Tom," my constable instructed.

A fellow constable appeared, forcing in front of him a man in a raincoat.

I looked at him and let out a shout. "Granddad! What are you doing here?"

"You know this man, my lady?"

"It's my grandfather."

He released Granddad. "Sorry, sir, only the young lady called us to say she heard noises outside."

"No offense, Constable. My granddaughter had no idea that I'd be here."

"I'm glad you are here now," I said. The constables departed and Granddad came inside. We all poured ourselves another Scotch to calm our nerves and sat in the morning room.

"What were you doing here?" I asked. "You scared us to death when we saw your shadow outside."

He looked sheepish. "I was worried about you, so I decided to come and keep an eye on you. Just in case."

"You think I'm in danger?"

He nodded. "Listen, my love. I've lived in London all my life and I can only think of one or two accidents on the tube lines. People don't fall off platforms very easily."

"What do you mean?"

"I mean that somebody might be trying to kill you."

"Kill me—why?"

"I've no idea, but it did cross my mind that the person who murdered that Frenchie might have thought he was killing your brother."

"Oh, surely not." Even as I said it I realized that they were about the same build.

"Well, I for one am glad that your grandfather is here," Belinda said, getting up and yawning. "Let's make a bed up for him and we can all get some sleep."

I lay listening to the storm blustering outside, the rain peppering the windows, the wind howling down the chimney. Given the perpetual gales at Castle Rannoch I should have been immune to a mild London storm, but this night I was so tense that I jumped at every noise. I tried to tell myself that, now Belinda was sleeping beside me, now my grandfather was here, everything was all right. But he had injected a new and alarming facet into this nightmare: the suggestion that someone was trying to kill me. Also that someone might have mistaken de Mauxville for Binky. I racked my brains but I had no idea who or why. We weren't the sort of people who had enemies. We were too far from the throne to warrant bumping us off. We were well behaved to the point of being boring.

I relived that moment on the tube platform, trying to remember if I had seen any vaguely familiar face in the crowd, but the whole thing was just one big blur. One thing was very clear, however: but for that giant of a workman standing on the platform beside me, I should be dead by now.

Then I realized something else: the accident on the boat the night before. I sat up in bed, every muscle tense. It had been no accident. I might be clumsy, but how could a rope have wound itself so tightly around my ankle that I couldn't undo the knot, unless somebody had deliberately tied that rope? I realized that I had been sitting on the side of the boat, with loads of other people standing and sitting around me. We'd all been having a good time and truthfully I would probably not have noticed if someone had eased a rope around my ankle and then given me a shove at the right moment. Someone I knew, then. One of my own set. I felt cold all over.

"Belinda," I whispered and nudged the shape beside me.

"Mmmm," she grunted, already deeply asleep.

"Belinda, wake up. I need to know who was on that boat."

"Wha . . . boat?"

"The one I fell off. Belinda, wake up, do. I need to know exactly who was on that boat. You were there the whole time."

She turned over, grunting, and half opened her eyes. "The usual crowd," she said, "and some friends of Eduardo. I didn't know them all."

"Tell me who you did know. People who knew me."

"I really don't know who knew you. Whiffy Featherstonehaugh, for one. And Daffy Potts was there, and Marisa, the girl who got so drunk at the wedding. Apart from that I can't really say. Now can I go back to sleep?" And she did.

I lay listening to her breathing. Whiffy Featherstonehaugh. Wasn't he the one who had helped Eduardo with the ropes, climbing on board at the last minute with a rope in his hand? But what kind of grudge could he possibly have against Binky or me? I did remember that he hadn't been wet when he spoke to me. He had not dived in to save me.

Chapter 22

Rannoch House
Tuesday, May 3, 1932

I woke with a start as a hand touched me.

"It's all right, my love. Only me," came my grandfather's calm voice, "but you're wanted on the telephone."

Sun was streaming in through the window. The storm had blown itself out during the night. I got up and slipped on my dressing gown, then I padded downstairs to the front hall.

"Hello?"

"Georgie, it's me, Binky," came the voice. "I'm at Scotland Yard. They've arrested me."

"Arrested you? They're mad. They have no evidence. They are just clutching at straws. What do you want me to do?"

"For one thing get in touch with Prendergast. I tried phoning but there's nobody in their office yet."

"Don't worry, Binky. I'll come to Scotland Yard immediately and get things sorted out. It's that bumbling Inspector Sugg. He can't see an inch past his face. We'll have you out of there in no time at all."

"I hope so." Binky sounded desperate. "I jolly well hope so. I mean, hell's bells, Georgie. This shouldn't happen to a chap. It's humiliating, that's what it is—being dragged in like a common criminal. They've even taken away my Conway-Stewart fountain pen with the gold nib that I got for my twenty-first. Apparently they thought I might want to stab myself with it. And I shudder to think what Fig will say when she finds out. In fact, hanging sounds rather preferable to facing her."

I had to smile in spite of the gravity of the situation. "Hang on, Binky, and don't say anything until our solicitor is with you. I'm coming over right away."

I rushed upstairs and threw on a smart town suit—the sort of thing I'd use for opening bazaars. One had to look the part today. Then I wrote out a message for Young Mr. Prendergast and asked my grandfather to telephone his office on the stroke of nine thirty. I managed to drink a few sips from the cup of tea Granddad pressed on me then hailed the nearest taxi for Scotland Yard, which I entered like a ship in full sail.

"I am Lady Georgiana Rannoch. I have come to see my brother," I said.

"I'm afraid that's not possible," I was told by a burly sergeant. "He's being interviewed as we speak. If you'd care to take a seat and wait?"

"I wish to speak with Inspector Sugg's superior officer immediately," I said. "It is vitally important."

"I'll see what I can do, your ladyship," the sergeant said.

I sat and waited in a grim hallway. After what seemed like hours I heard the brisk tap of shoes on the floor and a man came toward me. He was wearing a well-tailored suit, crisp white shirt, and a striped tie. I couldn't immediately identify the school but I wasn't going to hold that against him at this point.

"Lady Georgiana?" he said. He sounded as if he'd been to the right sort of school.

I got to my feet. "That's right."

"I'm Chief Inspector Burnall." He held out his hand to me. "Sorry to keep you waiting.

If you'd like to come this way?" He led me up a flight of stairs and into a spartan office.

"Please do take a seat."

"Chief Inspector," I said, "I understand that my brother has been arrested. This is absolutely ridiculous. I do hope you can instruct your junior officers to let him go immediately."

"I'm afraid I can't do that, my lady."

"Why not?"

"Because we have enough evidence in our possession to believe that your brother was the most likely person to have murdered Mr. de Mauxville."

"I have one word for you, Chief Inspector. Balderdash. All you have is a note purporting to come from my brother, which is an obvious forgery. There must be fingerprints on it. You can analyze the handwriting."

"We have done so. There are no fingerprints but de Mauxville's, and it is not at all clear that the handwriting is forged. I agree there are some vital differences from the way your brother forms some of his letters, but that could have been done to make the note appear like a forgery."

"And my brother has already told you that he would never write to anyone on writing paper that did not bear the family crest, unless he was at his club at the time, in which case it would bear the club crest."

"Again he could have deliberately substituted substandard notepaper, to make this very argument."

With the use of the word "notepaper," my opinion of him went down. Not the right sort of school then. "I have to tell you, Chief Inspector, that my brother has never been known for his quick wit or his brainpower. He would never have thought through such complicated details. Besides, what possible motive could he have had for killing a man he hardly knew? Without a motive, surely you have no case."

He looked at me long and hard. He had the most piercing blue eyes and I found it hard to hold his gaze. "We happen to think he had the strongest of motives, my lady. He was fighting to preserve his home."

He must have noticed my face fall.

"Of which I am sure you were fully aware. Or maybe you were in on it too. We'll be looking into that, but you do seem to have an alibi for the day in question, if your friend can be trusted."

"May one ask how you came about this knowledge?" I asked.

"Pure luck. The handwriting expert we took the writing samples to was the same woman who had been asked to verify your father's handwriting. Of course she was delighted to show us her copy of de Mauxville's document. Maybe your brother thought that with his royal connections, he was above the law. But I can assure you that the law is the same for a duke or a pauper. We think he killed Gaston de Mauxville and if he did, then he will hang for it."

"I trust you are still considering other leads, or have you decided that my brother makes a good sitting duck?" I tried to sound calm and in control although my mouth was so dry it was hard to form the words.

"If we find any other credible leads, we will pursue them," he said calmly.

"I have been asking around and I understand that this de Mauxville was a known gambler, also a known blackmailer. Did it occur to you that someone he had been blackmailing had finally had enough?"

He nodded. "Yes, that did occur to us. We found a wad of five-pound notes in his suit pocket. And it did cross our minds that he might also have been blackmailing your brother."

I had to laugh at this. "I'm sorry, Chief Inspector, but one person in the world you couldn't blackmail is my brother. Hamish has led an impeccable life to the point of being utterly boring. No affairs, no debts, no bad habits at all. So find somebody with a more interesting lifestyle, and you'll have your killer."

"I admire your loyalty, Lady Georgiana. I assure you that we will be looking into all possibilities and your brother will get a fair trial."

"Before you hang him," I said bitterly and made a sweeping exit.

I left Scotland Yard in deep gloom. What could I possibly do to save Binky? I hardly knew my own way around London. We would have to rely on a solicitor who should have retired to Worthing or Bournemouth years ago.

As I passed the post office, I realized that I had completely forgotten about my new business enterprise. I hardly felt in the mood to clean houses at the moment, but I would need money if I was to go running around

London in taxies on Binky's behalf. So I went inside and was handed two letters. The first was from a Mrs. Baxter of Dullwich who wanted extra staff for her daughter's twenty-first birthday party. Since I could only supply a staff of one, I thought that assignment highly unlikely.

The next was from Mrs. Asquey d'Asquey, mother of the bride at the Grosvenor House wedding. Her daughter (now Primrose Roly Poley) was due home from her honeymoon in Italy on the seventh and she wanted to surprise her by having her new house opened up, clean and welcoming, with windows open and fresh flowers everywhere. I was tempted to accept. The money was desperately needed, but the risk was just too great. I had no guarantee that Primrose's mother would not be sailing in and out with her arms full of fresh flowers, reorganizing Primrose's furniture, if my suspicions were correct. She might not have noticed me at the wedding, when everyone is in a state of shock, but she'd certainly recognize me if I was dusting her bedroom. Reluctantly I'd have too many prior assignments this week to meet her needs.

I came home to the most heavenly smell

of cooking. My grandfather was making a steak and kidney pudding. What's more, the boiler was now working and the house was delightfully warm in a quite un-Rannoch-like way. Belinda had already escaped to the comfort of her own house, declaring that one night of excitement was all she could take, so Granddad and I sat together, debating what could be done for Binky. Neither of us could come up with any good suggestions.

At four o'clock Fig telephoned. She was coming to London the next day to be at her husband's side. Would I make sure her bedroom and dressing room were ready for her? A fire would be nice as she'd be tired from the journey. She blamed me, she went on to say. How could I possibly let Binky get into such a mess? Now she supposed she'd have to sort it out. For a moment I actually pitied the policemen at Scotland Yard. I couldn't wait to see the meeting between Fig and Harry Sugg. If the situation hadn't been so grim, I would have chuckled.

The next morning I was in the midst of dusting her dressing room when there was a knock at the front door. Granddad, who had now turned himself into butler as well as cook, came back to report that there was a policeman to see me. A Chief Inspector Burnall.

"Show him into the morning room," I said with a sigh and hastily removed the scarf I had been wearing for my cleaning duties.

The chief inspector was looking impeccably groomed and very distinguished and I was horribly aware that I was wearing an old skirt in which the tweed had bottomed over the years. He rose to meet me and greeted me with a polite bow.

"Your ladyship. I'm sorry to disturb you again. I see you now have your butler in residence."

His smug look indicated that we'd had no servants in the house only while we killed de Mauxville.

"That is not our butler. It's my grandfather. He's come to keep an eye on me since he thinks my life might be in danger."

"Your grandfather. Well, I'm damned."

"So what brings you here this morning? Good news, I hope. You've found the real killer?"

"I'm afraid to disappoint you in that, my lady. In fact I come on a quite different matter today. One of great delicacy."

"Really?" I couldn't think what he could be talking about. "I suppose you'd better take a seat."

We sat.

"You are familiar with the home of Sir William Featherstonehaugh on Eaton Place?"

"Of course I am. Roderick Featherstonehaugh was one of my dancing partners when I came out."

"I regret to inform you that several items of considerable value were found to be missing from that house when Lady Featherstonehaugh arrived last weekend."

"How terrible." I could feel my heart thumping and hoped he couldn't actually hear it.

"It transpires that Lady Featherstonehaugh hired a domestic agency to open up the house for her. Coronet Domestics, I believe the name is. And following up on the advertisement in the *Times*, it appears that Coronet Domestics is owned by none other than yourself, Lady Georgiana. Is that correct?"

"That is correct."

"Interesting. May I ask if you have any input in the day-to-day running of this service or are you merely the titular head?"

"No, I am involved."

"I see. So I would be grateful if you would supply me with the names of the staff members who were working at Lady Featherstonehaugh's that day. I trust you have checked all their references thoroughly before you employed them?"

I swallowed hard, trying to think of a plausible lie, but couldn't come up with one.

"This is strictly between ourselves, Chief Inspector," I said. "I'd appreciate it if it didn't go any further than necessary."

"Go on."

"The truth is that I am Coronet Domestics. As yet I have no staff."

He couldn't have looked more shocked if I had told him that I danced naked on the tables at the Pink Pussycat. "You clean other people's houses? Yourself?"

"Strange though that may sound, I do it out of necessity. My allowance has been cut off and I need to survive on my own. This seemed a good way to start."

"I must say, I take my hat off to you," he said. "Right. Well, this should make it much simpler. I am going to read you a description of the objects and maybe you can tell me whether you noticed them while you were doing your domestic duties.

"A Georgian silver coffeepot. A large silver salver. Two miniatures of the Moghul school from India. A small Chinese figurine of the Goddess of Mercy."

"I can answer that one," I said. "I broke an arm off, accidentally. I took it with me, planning to have it repaired and replace it. I didn't think it would be noticed among so many knickknacks."

"Apparently it's eighth century."

"Gosh, is it?" I swallowed hard. "As to the other things. I remember dusting a glass-topped table full of miniatures, but I don't think any were missing, or I'd have noticed the gaps. And I really can't remember seeing a silver coffeepot or a salver."

I noticed he was looking around the room, as if he expected to see the coffeepot hidden behind the ormolu clock.

"You did say you were short of funds, my lady. Maybe the temptation was just too great."

I felt a Great-grandmother impersonation coming on. "Chief Inspector, did you ever steal anything?"

He smiled. "Scrumping apples from a nearby orchard when I was a small boy."

"When I was three I took one of Cook's shortbread biscuits from the rack where they were cooling. They had just come out of the oven and were still hot. I burned my mouth. I have never taken anything since. But you are most welcome to search this house if you choose."

"I take your word for it. Besides, a pawnbroker or jeweler would remember someone like you coming into his shop."

"You're confident the items will show up at a pawnshop or jeweler's?"

"Unless the thief is a pro, then they'd be handed over to a proper fence. But we've got our spies working that aspect as well. One of the items will appear somewhere before long, you'll see."

"You don't think the thief is a professional?"

"Not worth his while. If he gained access to the house, why limit himself to a few items when there was plenty of more valuable stuff there for the taking? This was someone who seized the opportunity to grab a few things. So let me ask you—were you alone in the house the whole time?"

I opened my mouth but no sound would come out. I couldn't tell him about Darcy's visit without getting myself into deep trouble. Because Darcy would say that he had come to visit me and then the Featherstonehaughs would know that I'd been cleaning their house and it would be all around London in two seconds and at the palace in three.

"Not all the time," I said carefully, trying to avoid a complete lie. "The Featherstonehaughs' son came in at one stage with one of his friends."

"And saw you?"

"He didn't recognize me. I was on my hands and knees at the time and I made sure I didn't look up. Besides, nobody looks twice at servants."

"When you left did you lock the front door?"

I considered this. "Yes, I think I heard the latch click behind me. I don't know if Roderick Featherstonehaugh was still in the house when I left. He might have been the one to have left the door open. As my brother said, when one is used to servants in the house, one doesn't think about locking doors."

Burnall rose to his feet. "Sorry to have troubled you again, my lady. If you happen to remember seeing any of those items, do get in touch, won't you? And the little Chinese figure—if you hurry up and get it repaired, I'll take it back to Lady Featherstonehaugh and I'll be suitably vague about where we located it."

"Very kind of you, Chief Inspector."

"The least I could do, my lady."

My grandfather was waiting in the front hall with the inspector's hat. He inclined his head to me and departed. I went upstairs again to finish Fig's room. Having specks of dust pointed out to me would be the last thing I could stand at the moment. In fact I was so wound up I felt as if I might snap. More than anything I was furious with myself for being so naïve. Darcy had just been using me. Why else would he have sought out my company after he found out that I was as penniless as he? I wasn't the sort of fun-loving, nightclubbing girl he liked. I ran downstairs and put on my coat.

"I'm going out," I shouted to my grandfather and took a cab to Chelsea.

Darcy looked as if he had just got out of bed. He was barefoot, in a toweling robe, and he hadn't shaved and his hair was tousled. I tried not to register how very attractive that looked. His eyes lit up when he saw me on the doorstep.

"Well, what a surprise this is. Good morning to you, my lovely. Have you come back to continue from where we left off the other night?"

"I've come back to tell you that you are a despicable rat and I never want to see you again and you're very lucky that I didn't give your name to the police."

Those alarming blue eyes opened wide. "Whoa, now. What is it that I can possibly have done to produce such a tirade from those genteel lips?"

"You know perfectly well what you've done," I said. "I have been a complete fool to think you might actually be interested in me. You were using me, weren't you? You pretended you came to the Featherstonehaughs' to see me, when you really wanted an excuse to get inside their house and help yourself to their valuables."

He frowned. "Their valuables?"

"Oh, come on, I'm not that stupid, Darcy. You tiptoe into the house, pretend to flirt with me, and then, miraculously, several valuable items go missing."

"And you think I took them?"

"You told me yourself that you are penniless and you live by your wits. I imagine your lifestyle with the nightclubs and the women is rather expensive to maintain. And who would notice an odd piece of Georgian silver missing? You're just damned lucky that I didn't tell the police, but now I'm their obvious suspect. It's bad enough that they think Binky and I murdered de Mauxville. Now they also think I do burglaries on the side. So if you really are anything of a gentleman, you'll return those items immediately and go and confess."

"So that's what you think of me—that I'm a thief?"

"Don't play the innocent with me. I've been stupidly naïve over too many things. Why else would you pretend to be interested in me after you found out I had no money? I certainly couldn't offer the delights of a Belinda Warburton-Stoke."

With that I fled before I started to cry. He didn't attempt to come after me.

Chapter 23

Rannoch House
Wednesday, May 4, 1932

I was overcome with gloom. Fig had arrived and made it clear that she didn't appreciate having my grandfather in the house. She'd found fault with everything, including the fact that the house was too warm and it was an unheard-of expense to run a boiler for one person. Grandfather beat a hasty retreat, telling me I was welcome to stay with him, and I was left alone with Fig and her maid. I don't think I had ever felt more wretched. What else can possibly go wrong? I wondered.

I didn't have long to wait. Fig's maid handed me a letter that had just been hand-delivered from the palace. Her Majesty would like to see me immediately. Strangely enough, Fig was quite put out by it. "How is it that Her Majesty wants to see you?" she demanded.

"I am a relative," I replied, rubbing in the fact that she wasn't.

"Perhaps I should go with you," she said. "Her Majesty is of the old school and would not like the thought of an unmarried woman going around without a chaperon."

"Kind of you, but no, thanks," I said. "I am not likely to be accosted going up Constitution Hill."

"What can she possibly want?" Fig went on. "If she wanted to speak to anybody about poor Binky's current situation, she'd speak to me."

"I have no idea," I said.

Actually I did have an idea. I suspected that she'd found out about Coronet Domestics and I was about to be dispatched to darkest Gloucestershire to hold knitting wool and walk Pekinese dogs. I put on my one smart black and white suit and this time I presented myself at the correct visitors' entrance on the left of the main forecourt, having successfully negotiated the bearskins on guard. I was escorted upstairs and around to the rear wing of the palace, to the queen's private study, overlooking the gardens. It was a simple, peaceful room, perfectly mirroring Her Majesty's personality. The only adornments were some lovely pieces of Wedgwood and a small marquetry table. One wouldn't speculate how or where they were acquired.

Her Majesty was sitting, straight-backed and severe, at her writing desk, with spectacles perched on her nose, and she looked up as I was announced.

"Ah, Georgiana, my dear. Do come and sit down. A bad business." She shook her head, then turned her face for the obligatory cheek kiss and curtsy. "I was most distressed when I heard the news."

"I'm sorry, ma'am." I perched on the striped Regency chair opposite her.

"It's not your fault," she said curtly. "You can't always be watching that fool of a brother. I take it he is innocent?"

I heaved an enormous sigh of relief. She hadn't heard about my domestic adventures, then. "Of course he's innocent, ma'am. You know Binky—can you imagine him drowning somebody in a bath?"

"Frankly, no. Shooting somebody by accident, perhaps." She shook her head again. "So what's being done for him, that's what I want to know."

"His solicitor has been notified. His wife has arrived and is currently tackling the police."

"Then if they are his entire defense team, I don't hold out much hope for a happy outcome," she said. "I'd like to help but the king says we must not intervene. We must be seen to have complete faith in our country's legal system and not pull rank just because it's a family member."

"I quite understand, ma'am."

She peered at me over her glasses. "I'm counting on you, Georgiana. Your brother is a decent sort of fellow, but not overly endowed with brains, I fear. You, on the other hand, have always had more than your share of wit and intelligence. Use them on your brother's behalf or I'm afraid he'll end up confessing to a crime he didn't commit."

This was all too true. "I am doing what I can, Your Majesty, but it's not easy."

"I'm sure it's not. This French person who drowned—do you have any idea who might have wanted to drown him in your bathtub?"

"He was a known gambler and blackmailer, ma'am. I suspect somebody took the opportunity to get out of a debt to him, but I don't know how I could find out who that was. I have no idea about gambling dens."

"Of course you haven't. But it must also have been somebody who knew your family—on equal terms, so to speak. You don't risk drowning somebody in a peer's bathtub if you are a laborer or a bank clerk."

I nodded. "One of our set, then."

"It must have been somebody who had at least passable knowledge of the workings of Rannoch House. Someone who knew your brother reasonably well, I'd say. Do you know which of his friends has visited the house on a regular basis?"

"I'm afraid I have no idea, ma'am. I've rarely been in London apart from my season, and have hardly stayed at Rannoch House since my father died. But from what I know of my brother, he doesn't come to London unless he has to. He much prefers pottering around his estate."

"As did his grandfather," the queen said. "The old queen had to practically issue a royal command to make him bring his wife to court to visit her mother. So you don't know which of your brother's friends is currently in London?"

"I'm afraid I don't even know who his friends are. If he meets them it would be at his club."

"Perhaps you could make discreet inquiries at his club, then. Brooks, isn't it?"

"Easier said than done, ma'am. Have you ever tried to persuade a gentlemen's club to tell you who is currently in residence?"

"I can't say I ever had to, not having the wandering kind of husband, but I'm sure my predecessor, Queen Alexandra, had to do so on a regular basis. But this may be one area in which the palace can help. I will ask the king to have his private secretary visit Brooks on our behalf. I believe he's a member. I hardly think they will refuse him the information, and if they do, he can always take a look at the membership book, can't he?"

"That's a splendid idea, ma'am."

"And in the meantime, keep watch. The murderer may want to know how the investigation is going. He may be enjoying your brother's current humiliation. They say murderers are vain fellows."

"I'll do my best, ma'am."

She nodded. "Well, let's see what Sir Julian can unearth for us, shall we? We should know something by the time you return from Sussex on Monday."

Sussex? I racked my brains to think of any royal relatives who lived in that county. Her Majesty frowned. "Don't tell me you have forgotten about the small assignment I gave you—the house party at Lady Mountjoy's."

"Oh, of course. The house party. The Prince of Wales. So much has happened in the past few days that it had slipped my mind."

"But you do still plan to attend? In spite of the current unhappy circumstances?"

"If Your Majesty wants me to, I'll be happy to oblige."

"Of course I want you to, and a few days in the country will do you good, and whisk you away from the scrutiny of the gutter press. Everything I hear about this woman is repugnant to me. I must know the truth, Georgiana, before the king and I attempt to nip any hint of romance in the bud."

"I have met her already," I said.

She removed the spectacles and leaned closer. "You have?"

"Yes, she came to my friend's clothing design salon."

"And?"

"She was horribly unpleasant. I couldn't stand her."

"Ah. Just as I thought. Well, by the end of this house party I hope she'll have laid out enough rope to hang herself. Oh, dear, not a good metaphor, given the current situation. Come to tea on Monday. I should be back from opening a mother and baby clinic in the East End by three. Shall we say four o'clock? Then we can exchange news."

"Very good, ma'am." I got to my feet.

"I'll ring for Heslop to escort you out. Until Monday, then. And don't forget—you are my eyes and ears. I am relying on you to be my spy."

⚬❀⚬

The moment I got home, Fig peppered me with questions.

"Her Majesty has a plan to rescue Binky, does she?"

"Yes, she's going to disguise the king as Robin Hood and have him swing into Scotland Yard from Big Ben."

"Don't be facetious, Georgiana. Honestly,

your manners have become appalling these days. I told Binky it was a waste of money to send you to that awful and expensive school."

"If you must know, Fig, it wasn't anything to do with Binky. It was something to do with the house party she wants me to attend on Friday."

I could see right away that this really upset her. "A house party? Her Majesty is inviting *you* to house parties these days?"

"Not inviting me. Sending me on her behalf," I said, enjoying every moment of this.

Fig's face was positively puce. "You are now representing Her Majesty at an official function? You, with a mother who was only a chorus girl?"

"Never a chorus girl, Fig. An actress. Maybe she thinks I've inherited my mother's talent for being friendly and gracious in public. Not everybody has that quality, you know."

"I just don't understand it," Fig muttered. "Your poor brother about to face the hangman's noose and Her Majesty sends you off to enjoy yourself in the country. I am obviously the only one who is going to stick by poor Binky." She put a lace handkerchief to her face and stalked out of the room in a huff. It was the only moment I had enjoyed in quite a long time.

But she was right. I really should be doing something constructive for Binky. If only someone could pay a visit to the gambling clubs de Mauxville had visited. Maybe something significant had happened there— he had cheated someone or he had collected blackmail money. Granddad had mentioned Crockford's, but I couldn't go to a place like that, could I? It needed someone with social ease and brilliance, part of that racy set. . . . Of course!

I set off for Belinda's place right away. She was awake and dressed, sitting at her kitchen table with a pad and pencil in front of her.

"Don't disturb me. I'm designing a new gown," she said. "I've actually got a commission. Some owner of a motorcar factory is going to be made a peer and his wife wants the kind of dress that the aristocracy wears. And she's going to pay me proper money for it too."

"I'm happy for you, but I wondered if you had any plans for tonight."

"Tonight, why?"

"I want you to go to Crockford's with me."

"Crockford's? Are you taking up gambling now? Out of your league, my dear. They cater to the gambling elite—very high stakes."

"I don't want to gamble, but the doorman at Claridge's said that de Mauxville frequented the place. I want to know who he met there and whether anything important happened—an argument, maybe."

"I'd like to help, but I'm afraid I have other plans tonight," she said.

I took a deep breath. "Then could you lend me a vampish outfit and I'll go on my own."

"Georgie, you have to be a member. They'd never let you in."

"I'll think of something. I'll claim to be meeting someone there. It's just important that I don't look like me or they'll recognize me. Please, Belinda? Someone has to do it, and my sister-in-law certainly can't."

She looked up at me, sighed, and stood up. "Oh, very well. I still think this is doomed to failure, but I suppose I could find something suitable to lend you."

She took me upstairs, tried various

dresses on me, and finally settled on long, black, and slinky with a red rouched cape.

"And if anyone asks you who designed it, you can hand them my card."

She then found a black cap with feathers to hide my untameable hair and showed me the cosmetics on her dressing table to make up my face. The result that evening was startling. Surely nobody would recognize the sultry young woman with the bright red lips and long black eyelashes?

I stayed at Belinda's place, leaving Fig to forage for her own supper, then at nine o'clock I paid out more hard-earned money on a cab and off I went, quaking in my boots—although I wasn't actually wearing boots but Belinda's high-heeled shoes, one size too big for me.

Crockford's was one of London's oldest and swankest gambling clubs, on St. James's Street, only a stone's throw from Brooks's. As my cab pulled up, chauffeurs were assisting other gamblers from their Rolls-Royces and Bentleys. They greeted each other merrily and sailed in past the uniformed doorman. I did not.

"Can I help you, miss?" He stepped out in front of me.

"I'm supposed to be meeting my cousin here, but I don't see him." I pretended to look around. "He said nine o'clock and it's already past nine. Do you think he could have gone inside without me?"

"Who is your cousin, miss?"

Obviously I couldn't use the name of any of my real cousins. "Roland Aston-Poley," I said, complimenting myself on my quick thinking. At least I knew he was in Italy on his honeymoon.

"I don't believe I've seen Mr. Aston-Poley tonight," the doorman said, "but if you'll step inside, I'll have one of the gentlemen look after you."

He led me in through the door into a gracious foyer. Through an archway I glimpsed a scene of sparkling elegance—the wink of chandeliers and diamonds, the clatter of chips, the rattle of the roulette wheel, excited voices, laughter, clapping. For a moment I wished I were the kind of person who had the means to frequent places like this. Then I reminded myself that my father had been that kind of person, and my father had shot himself.

A swarthy little man in a dinner jacket came up to us. There were muttered words between him and the doorman. The small man shot sideways glances I didn't much care for in my direction.

"Mr. Aston-Poley, you say?" He peered in through the doors. "I don't believe he's arrived yet, Miss . . . ?" He waited for me to supply my name. I didn't. "If you'd care to take a seat, I will go and check for you."

I sat on a gilt and satin chair. The doorman went back to his door. More members arrived. I watched them sign the book on a side table. The moment I was alone I jumped up and went over to the book. I started to turn back the pages. De Mauxville had been killed last Friday, so I would need dates before that. . . . I hadn't expected so many attendees each night. I was astounded at how many people had a suitable income to gamble here. But I spotted one name I recognized: Roderick Featherstonehaugh had been here on several occasions. And then another name I hadn't expected to see: the Hon. Darcy O'Mara had been here too.

Two men strolled past me, both smoking cigars. "I lost ten grand the other night," one said in an American accent, "but if the oil keeps on pumping, who's complaining?" and they both laughed.

My heart was beating so loudly I felt as if it must be reverberating around that foyer.

"I'm sorry, miss." I jumped at the voice close behind me. The dark little man had come back. "But your cousin doesn't appear to be here. I have just checked the *salle prive*. Are you sure you have the correct date?"

"Oh, dear, maybe I've made a mistake," I said. "Was he here last night?"

He turned back the pages, allowing me to peek over his shoulder. "Not last night, or the night before. It doesn't appear that he has been here at all this week. Not since last Saturday."

"Last Saturday?" The words blurted out.

He nodded. So it appeared that Primrose Asquey d'Asquey, now Roly Poley, had been honeymooning alone, at least for part of the time. No wonder her mother felt that she needed cheering up.

"I'm sorry we couldn't help you." The little man was now ushering me toward the front door. "If he does come in later, whom shall I say was waiting for him?"

I tried to come up with a name, then I had

a brain wave and produced a card. "Belinda Warburton-Stoke," I said.

His expression changed to one of hostility and suspicion. "Is this some kind of schoolgirl prank?" he demanded.

"What do you mean?"

"That you are most certainly not Miss Warburton-Stoke. That young lady is well known to us here. Good night to you."

I was deposited outside with my cheeks burning. Why hadn't Belinda mentioned that she frequented Crockford's? How could she afford to frequent Crockford's? And what else had she neglected to tell me?

Chapter 24

Rannoch House
Thursday, May 5, 1932

Fortunately Belinda was out for the evening when I returned the garments to her. I went home to find that Fig had gone to bed and I curled up in my own bed, feeling thoroughly miserable. It seemed there was nobody I could trust anymore and in the darkness my suspicions ran riot. It was Belinda who had sat beside me on that boat. I seemed to remember that she had bent to straighten her stocking at some point. Could she have tied that rope around my ankle? But why?

In the morning I found that Fig had turned the boiler down to a level at which lukewarm water came out of the hot taps. Not that I fancied having a bath any longer anyway. I looked forward to a few days of luxury—extravagant meals, warm house, amusing guests, and all I had to do for once was keep an eye on a certain American woman. I took the invitation from my mantelpiece and was reminded that there was to be a fancy dress ball. I had neither time nor money to hire an expensive outfit at the moment so I hacked at the skirt of the maid's uniform I had been wearing until it came up above my knee, found a white frilly apron, and decided to go as a French maid. Ooh la la.

I tried on the outfit and was rather pleased with my task when the doorbell rang. I answered it without thinking and found Tristram standing there. He opened his mouth in surprise. "Oh, I say, it's you, Georgie. I thought you'd got a new maid."

"I'd never hire anyone who wore her skirts this length," I said, laughing. "It's for a fancy dress ball. I'm a French maid. What do you think?"

"Rather fetching," he said. "But you need fishnet stockings and high heels to complete the picture."

"Good idea. I'll go out and buy a pair today."

"It's for the Mountjoys' do, I suppose."

"You know about the Mountjoys' house party?"

"Rather. I've been invited too."

"I didn't realize you knew the Mountjoys."

"It's obvious, really, with their place only a stone's throw from Eynsleigh. I used to play with the Mountjoy sons."

"The Mountjoys have sons?" This weekend might turn out to be quite promising after all.

"Both away, so I gather. Robert is in India and Richard is at Dartmouth." (These came out as "Wobert" and "Wichard," naturally.) "Navy family, you know. I came to ask you if you'd like a wide down to their place tomorrow. I've managed to borrow a car."

"How very kind of you. Thank you very much. I was wondering how I'd get there."

He beamed, as if I'd just given him a present. "That's splendid, then. About ten all right for you? I'm afraid it's only a little runabout. Couldn't rustle up a Rolls." (Which of course sounded like "wustle up a Wolls.")

"Perfect. Thank you again."

"Maybe we could stroll over to Eynsleigh together and relive old times."

"As long as you don't want me to run through any fountains with you."

He laughed. "Oh, goodness me, no. How embarrassing." His face grew serious. "I thought I should call on you because I realized you must be fwightfully upset about your brother. What an awful thing to have happened."

"Yes, it is pretty shocking," I said. "Binky's innocent, of course, but it's not going to be easy to prove. The police seem to be sure that he's guilty."

"The police are idiots," he said. "They always get it wrong. Look, I don't have to be back in the office for an hour or so. I could do what I promised and show you around London a bit, to cheer you up."

"It's very sweet of you, Tristram, but frankly I don't think I'd take anything in today. I've just too much on my mind. Some happier time, maybe."

"Quite understand. Beastly rotten luck, I say. But how about a cup of coffee? I'm sure there must be a café somewhere nearby and I'd certainly like a cup before I have to go back to work."

"There are plenty along Knightsbridge, including a Lyons."

"Oh, I don't think we have to descend to a Lyons. Let's go and see, shall we?—After you change your clothes."

"Oh, yes." I smiled, glancing down at my

outfit. "Do come in and wait in the morning room. It's the only room that's suitable for guests at the moment." I led him up the stairs to the first floor. "Take a seat. I won't be long. Oh, and my sister-in-law is in residence, so don't be surprised if a strange woman wants to know who you are."

I changed quickly and came down to find Tristram sitting with such a strained expression on his face that I knew he had encountered Fig.

"Your sister-in-law is a bit of a stickler, isn't she?" he muttered as we left the house. "She said she had no idea you'd been entertaining gentleman callers unchaperoned and that was no way to behave when they'd been so generous in letting you stay in the house. She positively glared at me as if I were Don Juan. I mean to say, do I look like Don Juan?"

"Oh, dear," I said. "More trouble. I can't wait to get away tomorrow and go to a place of peace, quiet, and jollity."

"Me too," he said. "I can't tell you how utterly dreary it is working in that office. Filing, copying lists, more filing. I'm sure if Sir Hubert had realized what it was like he'd never have sentenced me to be articled there.

He'd never have stuck it for two minutes. He'd have gone mad with boredom."

"How is he?" I asked. "Is there any news?"

He bit his lip, like a little boy. "No change. Still in a coma. I'd really like to go over to be with him, but there's nothing I could do, even if I could afford the fare. One feels so helpless."

"I'm really sorry."

"He's the only person I have in the world. Still, these things happen, I suppose. Let's talk about more cheerful subjects. We'll have a rattling good time at that fancy dress ball. Will you dance with me?"

"Of course, if you can bear my standard of dancing."

"Mine too. We'll both say 'ow' in unison."

"What are you going as?" I asked.

"Lady Mountjoy said she has some costumes we can borrow. I thought I'd take her up on her kind offer. I don't really have the time or money to visit the costume shops in the West End. She mentioned a highwayman and I must say that rather caught my fancy. Swashbuckling, don't you know."

We laughed as we reached the busy thoroughfare of Knightsbridge. We soon found a quiet little café and ordered coffee. A large woman was seated at the next table. Her face was too obviously made up, and a fox fur grinned at us from around her neck. She smiled and nodded to us as we sat down.

"Lovely day, isn't it? Just the right sort of day for young people like you to go walking in the park. I'm just off to Harrods myself, although they are not what they were, are they? Catering to the masses nowadays, I always say." She broke off as the waitress put a cup in front of her, and then gave us our coffees. "Ta, love," she said, "and don't forget the cream slice, will you? I must have my cream slice to keep up my strength."

"I'll get it for you," the waitress said.

Tristram glanced at me and grinned.

"Sugar?" Tristram dropped a lump into his coffee, then offered me the bowl.

"No, thanks. Don't take it."

I felt a tap on my back. "Excuse me, miss, but could I borrow your sugar? There doesn't seem to be any on my table. Really, standards are getting so lax these days, aren't they?"

I took the bowl from Tristram and handed it to her, noticing that her pudgy hands were covered in rings. She dropped several lumps into a coffee cup then handed the bowl back to me, looking up expectantly as the cream slice arrived. I had scarcely turned back to my own coffee when I heard choking noises. I looked around. The fat lady was turning almost purple, her hands waving in the air in panic.

"She's choking." Tristram leaped up and began slapping her on the back. The waitress heard the commotion and rushed out to help. But it was no good. The woman's choking turned to a gurgle and she collapsed onto her plate.

"Get help, quickly!" Tristram shouted. I stood there in a state of shock as the waitress ran out screaming.

"Can't we do something?" I demanded. "Try and remove what's choking her."

"Whatever she swallowed is too far down or it would have come up by now. I'm scared I'd only wedge it more firmly if I tried anything." Tristram looked ashen white. "How awfully horrible. Shall I take you home?"

"We should stay until help gets here," I said, "even though I don't see what we could do."

"I'm afraid she asked for it," he said. "Did

you see the way she was cramming that cake into her mouth?"

Help arrived in the shape of a policeman and a doctor who had happened to be passing. The doctor set to work instantly, then took her pulse.

"I'm afraid there's nothing we can do," he said. "She's dead."

We gave our statements to the policeman and tiptoed home. Tristram had to go back to work and I tried to pack for the house party. Fig was off somewhere, probably annoying Scotland Yard again. I wandered around the empty house, trying to shake off a feeling of dread that just wouldn't go away. If this had been my first brush with death, it would have been different. But within one week to have found a body in my bath, been dragged off a boat, then almost pushed under a train made this death almost too much of a coincidence. A disturbing thought crept into my head that the same killer had been aiming for me once again.

The sugar bowl—the woman had asked to borrow the sugar and I had handed her our bowl. Was it possible that someone had poisoned the sugar? The only person who could have done that was Tristram. I shook my head. That was impossible. He hadn't touched the sugar bowl until he took a lump himself and then offered it to me. He couldn't have known in advance where we were going because I had been the one that suggested Knightsbridge and chose the coffeehouse. And as far as I knew, Tristram hadn't been on the boat last Sunday.

Then I remembered something that made me feel cold all over. That first meeting with Darcy in Lyons. He had made a joke about being poisoned by their tea and how they carried out the dead customers. And Darcy had been on the boat last Sunday. I was very glad that I was getting away from all this to the safety of the country. Roll on tomorrow.

Chapter 25

Farlows
Near Mayfield, Sussex
Friday, May 6, 1932

I wasn't sure what to believe anymore. Yesterday's incident could be no more than a greedy woman choking to death, and yet it had happened after I handed her my sugar bowl. I was now almost ready to believe that there was a clever conspiracy against my brother and me. Perhaps Darcy and Belinda, maybe even Whiffy Featherstonehaugh were all in it together. It was just possible that Tristram was part of it too, although I didn't think he had been on the boat on Sunday. The only thing I couldn't come up with was a motive. Why would anybody want to kill me?

So it was with some apprehension when I climbed into the little two-seater beside Tristram and watched him strap my suitcase to the boot. He caught me looking and gave me a jaunty smile. How ridiculous to suspect him, I thought. But it was just as ridiculous to suspect Belinda or Whiffy. I didn't want to suspect Darcy either, but with him I couldn't be sure. At any rate Tristram would have two hands on the wheel, all the way to the Mountjoys'.

Fig had decided that traveling alone with a young man, especially one she had never heard of until this moment, was quite unsuitable. I practically had to wrestle the telephone from her grasp as she attempted to call a cab to take me to Victoria Station.

"Fig, I am over twenty-one and you and Binky have made it very clear that I am no longer your responsibility," I snapped. "If you wish to reinstate my allowance and pay for my household staff, then you can start trying to order me around. If not, then my activities and choice of companions are none of your business."

"I have never been spoken to like that before in my life," she spluttered.

"Then it's about time."

"I must say that your lack of breeding on your mother's side comes out now," she sniffed. "I've no doubt it will be one unsuitable young man after another, just like her."

I gave her a serene smile. "Ah, but think of the fun she's had doing it."

She couldn't come up with an answer to that one.

So now we were puttering merrily along. City gave way to leafy suburbs as we joined the Portsmouth Road. Then suburbs turned into true countryside with spreading chestnuts and oak trees in fields, horses looking over gates. I felt the weight of the last days gradually lifting. Tristram chatted merrily. We stopped at a bakery to buy some sausage rolls and Chelsea buns and then we puttered up one flank of the Hog's Back and pulled off at the top to admire the view. As we sat on the verge beside the road eating our impromptu picnic, I gave a contented sigh.

"It's good to be out in the country again, isn't it?"

"Absolutely. Do you dislike the city as much as I do?"

"I don't dislike it, in fact it could be rather fun if one had money, but I'm a country girl at heart. I need to ride and walk along the loch and feel the wind blowing in my face."

He stared at me for a long while before saying, "You know, Georgie, I wasn't joking the other day. You could always marry me. I know I don't have much now, but one day I'll be very comfortably off. Perhaps we could live at Eynsleigh and get those fountains going again."

"You really are sweet, Tris." I patted his hand. "But I already told you that I plan to marry for love. You feel more like a brother to me. And I won't ever marry for convenience."

"All right. I understand. Still, a fellow can always hope to make you change your mind, can't he?"

I got to my feet. "It's pretty here, isn't it? I wonder if there is a view through the trees."

I started walking down a little path. It was amazing how quickly the car and the road vanished and I was in the middle of the wood. Birds called from the trees, a squirrel raced in front of my feet. I'd been an outdoor girl all my life. Suddenly I sensed that the wood had gone quiet. It felt tense, as if everything were listening and watching. I looked around me uneasily. I was only a few yards from the car. I couldn't be in any danger, could I? Then I remembered a crowded tube platform. I turned and hurried back to the road.

"Ah, here she is," said a hearty voice. "We wondered where you'd got to."

Another car had parked beside us, this one driven by Whiffy Featherstonehaugh and containing Marisa Pauncefoot-Young and Belinda, who were now spreading out their own picnic mat on the grass.

"Where are you heading for?" I asked and was greeted with merry laughter.

"Same as you, silly. We're the rest of the house party."

"Come and sit down." Whiffy patted the mat beside him. "Marisa's mum has rustled up some spiffing food from Fortnum's."

I sat and joined them in a far better picnic than our own, but I couldn't really enjoy the cold pheasant or the Melton Mowbray pies or Stilton, because I couldn't shake off the thought that the very people I was trying to avoid were now going to be with me in the country.

We set off again. I stared at their Armstrong Siddeley as it drove ahead of us. Could it possibly be my Celtic sixth sense that made me feel uneasy the moment they arrived?

This was all so ridiculous. These were people I had known for most of my life. I told myself that I was overreacting. All those accidents this past week had been accidents, nothing more sinister. I had read more into them because of the body in the bath and because I was alone and out of my element. I was now going to have a few days of ease and fun and try to forget what had happened to poor Binky and me.

The more powerful Armstrong Siddeley left us behind and we puttered along leafy byways. At last Tristram slowed the car and pointed. "There, through the trees. That's Eynsleigh. Do you remember it?"

I looked down a long graceful driveway lined with plane trees. Beyond was a rambling Tudor mansion in red and white brick. Happy memories stirred. I had ridden up that driveway on a fat little pony called Squibs. And Sir Hubert had made me a tree house.

"I can understand why you love it so much," I said. "I remember it as a very happy place."

We drove on and were soon approaching yet another lovely house. This one was Farlows, home of the Mountjoys. It was Georgian, with elegant lines, its balustrade crowned with classical marble statues. There was a colonnade of more statues along the driveway.

"Quite an impressive showing, don't you think?" Tristram said. "There is obviously money in the arms game. There's always a war somewhere. Even the statues look violent, don't they? Even more alarming than that fierce angel at your place."

We passed an ornamental lake with fountains playing and came to a halt beside a flight of marble steps, leading to the front door. Liveried servants came out immediately, murmuring, "Welcome, m'lady," as they whisked away my luggage. At the top of the steps I was received by the butler. "Good afternoon, my lady. May I be permitted to say how sorry I was to read of His Grace's current plight. Lady Mountjoy is awaiting you in the long gallery if you'd care to take tea."

I was back in a world where I knew the rules. I followed the butler through to the long gallery, where Whiffy and his party were already attacking the crumpets with Imogen Mountjoy. Several older people were seated together. I recognized Whiffy's parents among them. Lady Mountjoy stood up and came to greet me.

"My dear, so good of you to come at such an unsettling time. We all feel for your poor, dear brother. Such a travesty. Let us hope they get to the bottom of it rapidly. Come and meet Imogen and our American guests."

Imogen pretended to be thrilled. "Georgie. How lovely," she said. We kissed the air somewhere near each other's cheeks. I glanced around, expecting to see Mrs. Simpson, but the Americans turned out to be a Mr. and Mrs. Wilton J. Weinberger.

"I understand your brother is the Dook we've been reading about," he said as he shook my hand.

"And these are our neighbors, Colonel and Mrs. Bantry-Bynge." Lady Mountjoy whisked me away before I could be interrogated on this subject. I had wondered why the woman had seemed vaguely familiar. I felt my face flushing and awaited doom. Colonel Bantry-Bynge shook my hand. "How de doo," he said heartily.

Mrs. Bantry-Bynge also took my hand. "Delighted to make your acquaintance, your ladyship." And gave a little curtsy. Her eyes were lowered and I had no way of knowing whether she recognized me as her former maid or not. If she did, she was obviously not going to say anything, given that I knew what I knew. I stood with the group, exchanging a few pleasantries on "your delightful British countryside and how disappointed Willy is that he couldn't try the hunting," then I was mercifully dragged away by Imogen to see pictures of her recent trip to Florence.

"Is this the sum total of male dance partners?" I whispered to her. "Whiffy and Tristram?"

She made a face. "I know. It's grim, isn't it. But Mummy says it's not really a young person's weekend and it all is for the prince and his pals, but she is trying to come up with a couple more men who are not old fogies in time for the ball tomorrow. Whiffy's not a bad dancing partner but Tristram is guaranteed to step on one's toes. He's hopeless, isn't he? I used to hate it when he was brought over to play with us. He was always breaking one's toys or falling out of trees and getting us into trouble."

"Imogen, why don't you show your friends to their rooms," Lady Mountjoy suggested. "I'm sure you young people have masses to talk about."

"Good idea. Come on, then." She led us up the stairs, marching in unladylike fashion. "Anything to get away from those awful people," she said, glancing back down the curved staircase. "Thank God it's not hunting season or that Wilton person would have ruined our horses. Utterly dreary so far, don't you think? I mean, one had hopes about the Prince of Wales, but one gathers that he has other interests."

"Who will be arriving with her own husband," Belinda said, laughing.

"Really?" Marisa looked fascinated.

"Absolutely. The poor thing is dragged around like a dog on a leash."

Marisa made a face. "Just don't let me drink too much and make a fool of myself in front of HRH. You know what I'm like."

We reached the first landing—a grand affair with marble busts in niches and a noble corridor going off in both directions. "You're down here, Georgie," Imogen said. "You get the royal treatment in the best bedrooms, along with HRH. The rest of us are up another floor, slumming it."

"I hope certain other guests will also be

on this floor," Belinda whispered, "or there will be a lot of creeping up and down stairs during the night."

"I'm not sure it's reached the creeping-up-and-down stage yet," Imogen said. "But I can tell you that a certain married couple has been given rooms on this floor, only on the other side of the great staircase, so it will still be a long hike, and cold feet on the marble floor." Imogen giggled. "If you hear a shriek, Georgie, that's what it will be—cold feet."

My room was at the far end of the corridor. It was quite delightful, with bay windows overlooking the lake and the park. My clothes had already been unpacked and put away.

"Did you bring your maid or do you want me to send one down to dress you?" Imogen asked.

"My maid's still in Scotland, but I've learned to dress myself," I said.

"Have you? Clever you."

"My maid's arriving by train," Belinda said. "You can borrow her if you like."

I could sense the strain between Belinda and myself and didn't know if it all came from me. I noticed she hadn't been her normal friendly self.

"We'll leave you to change then, while I take these two to their humble abodes up above," Imogen said. "Cocktails at seven. Have a nice rest first." At the doorway she turned back. "Oh, and there's a little staircase right beside your room, which actually leads into the long gallery, where we'll be having cocktails."

Left alone, I lay on my bed, but couldn't relax. I got up and paced around the room. From my window I spotted Whiffy Featherstonehaugh striding out away from the house. At one point he looked up at the house and then hurried on. I watched him, my thoughts churning. Someone I had known for most of my life—a Guards officer, a little stiff and stuffy, perhaps, but surely not a murderer. But he was also a frequent visitor at Crockford's, at times when de Mauxville had been there. And . . . I remembered one thing more . . . the impression on the pad beside the telephone in de Mauxville's room: *R—10:30*. Whiffy's name was Roderick. Somehow I had to confront him this weekend. I had to find out the truth. I was fed up with living with danger.

I put such thoughts aside and applied myself to the task of getting dressed for dinner. For once I had to look respectable. I had brought a cream silk dress with burgundy sleeves that complemented my coloring rather well and had enough shape to it to prevent me from looking like a beanpole. I ventured a little rouge to my cheeks, a dash of lipstick to my lips, and put my twenty-first birthday pearls around my neck. I was rather proud of doing the whole thing without help. Thus adorned, I went to meet and mingle. My end of the corridor was unlit and I descended the little spiral staircase with caution. One step. Two. Suddenly I lost my footing, pitched forward, and hurtled downward. There was no banister and my hands slid off smooth walls. I suppose it all happened quickly but it was almost as if I were flying downward in slow motion. I saw a suit of armor looming up ahead of me only an instant before I collided with it. I noticed that its ax was raised and I raised my own arms to defend myself. There was a crash, a clatter, and I found myself sitting with bits of armor raining down around me.

Instantly people came running up from below.

"Georgie, are you all right?"

Worried faces stared at me as I was helped to my feet. I brushed myself down and appeared not to have suffered any major damage, apart from some scrapes to my arms and a laddered stocking.

"I should have warned you about that staircase," Lady Mountjoy was saying. "The lighting is poor. I've spoken to William about it."

"Honestly, Georgie," Belinda said, attempting to laugh it off, "I swear you'd find something to trip over in the middle of a large polished floor. Oh, your poor arm. Lucky you weren't wearing long gloves or you would have ruined them. Let's go back to your room and get it cleaned up. And you've laddered your stockings. Do you want another pair?"

Everyone was being very kind. I let them minister to me and noticed how carefully they led me downstairs again.

"Here she is, safe and sound." Lady Mountjoy sounded relieved. "Come and be presented to His Royal Highness." She led me over to where my cousin David was standing with Lord Mountjoy and a couple of stiff young men who were obviously HRH's equerries.

"What-ho, Georgie," David said before Lady Mountjoy could do any presenting. "Been fighting suits of armor, so I hear."

"Just an unlucky tumble, sir," Lady Mountjoy said, before I could answer. "But all is well. A glass of champagne, or would you rather have a cocktail, Georgiana?"

"She needs a brandy after that scare," Lord Mountjoy said and one was brought to me. I didn't like to admit that I don't enjoy brandy and was grateful to have something to sip. Because it was going to take a lot to calm my nerves at the moment. As I was being ministered to upstairs, I picked something from my skirt. It was a piece of strong black thread. I couldn't think how it got there until it dawned on me that somebody could have strung it across the top of those steps—someone who knew that I would probably be the only person who used them tonight. My attacker was indeed in the house with me.

Chapter 26

Farlows
Friday, May 6, 1932

I had no time to think, however, as I was led away to meet the women. I spotted Mrs. Simpson instantly. She was dressed in a trouser outfit rather like the one I had modeled so disastrously, and was holding court on the most comfortable sofa, currently giving what sounded like an impression of the Duke of York's stutter. We were duly introduced.

"I think I've seen you somewhere before, haven't I?" she drawled, eyeing me critically.

"It's possible," I said, trying to sound disinterested and remembering all the rude things she had said.

"Let's see, now. You're the one whose mother was an 'actress' who snagged a duke, right?" She made the word sound as if it were a euphemism for something less reputable.

"She was indeed," I said. "If you get a chance to meet her, then maybe she could give you some pointers on how to act like a princess." I smiled sweetly. There was gentle tittering but she looked daggers at me. As I excused myself and walked on I heard her say loudly, "That poor girl, so tall and gawkish still. If she marries at all, she'll probably have to settle for some brute of a farmer."

"Who will be considerably better in bed than anything she has at the moment," said a voice in my ear and there was my mother, looking stunning in peacock blue, complete with a ruff of peacock feathers. "And what's all this nonsense about Binky? If he killed anybody I'd have expected it to be Fig."

"It's not funny, Mother. He could be hanged."

"They don't hang dukes, darling. He'd be let off by reason of insanity. Everyone knows the upper classes are batty."

"But he didn't do it."

"Of course he didn't. He's just not the violent type. He used to throw up every time the hounds got at the fox."

"What are you doing here anyway?" I asked, for once delighted to see her.

"Max has business connections with Lord Mountjoy. They're in the armaments game together, and he also hunts with HRH, so here we are," she said. "Come and meet Max. His English is atrocious, I'm afraid."

"And you don't speak German, do you? So how do you manage?"

She laughed, that delightful, infectious laugh that had filled theaters. "My darling, one doesn't always need to talk."

She slipped her arm through mine and led me over to a stocky but imposing blond-haired man, who was deep in conversation with the prince and Lord Mountjoy.

"Ya, de vild boar," we heard him say. "Bang bang."

"See what I mean?" my mother whispered. "A definite deficiency there. But the sex is heavenly."

The mention of sex reminded me of a pressing question. "I wonder who is supposed to escort me in to dinner tonight? I do hope it won't be Lord Mountjoy. I hate having to make polite conversation to older people."

"I gather he's escorting that awful American woman," my mother whispered. "Just as if she were officially with you know who. Poor old Mr. S, whom you'll notice skulking in the background over there, will be forced to make his own way in at the end of the procession. Damned bad form, I call it."

"Then it looks as if I'll be stuck with either Whiffy Featherstonehaugh or Tristram. Hardly scintillating conversation."

"Poor little Tristram. How's he holding up?"

"All right, I suppose. He asked me to marry him."

She laughed. "That's awful. Almost like incest. You had the same nanny, for God's sake. Still, I suppose he might be a good catch if poor old Hubie does die."

"Mother, he's very sweet, but can you imagine being married to him?"

"Frankly, no. But I thought Lady Mountjoy had said that they'd invited a partner for you."

At that moment the double doors opened, and the butler stepped into the room and announced, "His Serene Highness, Prince Siegfried of Romania."

Siegfried, his pale blond hair slicked down, his military evening jacket adorned with more orders and medals than any general's, strode into the room, marched up to Lady Mountjoy, clicked his heels, and bowed. "So kind," he said. From her he went over to the Prince of Wales and clicked his heels again. They exchanged words in German and then Siegfried was brought over to me.

"I believe you already know Lady Georgiana, Your Highness?"

"Naturally. We meet again at last." He bent to kiss my hand with those large, cold fish-lips. "You have been well, I trust?"

I was seething. The crafty old thing, I thought. She didn't want me to spy on David at all. She planned this so that I would be thrust together with Siegfried again. She knew I'd wriggled out of the encounter in Scotland and she simply wasn't going to let me escape. Well, you could lead a horse to water, but you can't make her marry anyone she loathes.

I had, however, been well brought up. I was polite and attentive as Siegfried talked about himself. "I had brilliant skiing this winter. Where do you ski these days? I myself am a magnificent skier. I know no fear."

The dinner gong sounded and we formed

up to parade into the dining room. I, of course, was paired with Siegfried, right behind the prince and Lady Mountjoy. We took our places and my eyes strayed around the table. Who had been devious enough to tie that black thread across those stairs? It was a miracle I was still alive. If I had landed slightly differently, that ax would have come crashing down on me or I'd have broken my neck. I stared at Whiffy then Tristram. Neither one was what I'd call a live wire when it came to brains. But Belinda—she had been one of the cleverest girls in school. I shook my head in disbelief. Why on earth would Belinda want me dead?

There was one place still vacant at table. The moment I noticed it the door opened again.

"The Honorable Darcy O'Mara," the butler announced and Darcy came in, looking dashing in his dinner suit.

"Mr. O'Mara," Lady Mountjoy said as he presented himself to her with apologies. "You managed it after all. I am so glad. Do sit down. They are only just serving the soup."

Darcy cast me the briefest of glances as he sat opposite me, then started talking to

Marisa on his left. I felt that my cheeks were flaming. What was he doing here? Who had invited him and why?

Over the polite murmur of conversation I heard Mrs. Simpson's strident voice. "So let me get this straight. Does one now have to call you 'Frau' or 'your ladyship,' or are you simply 'Mrs.'?"

She was, of course, addressing my mother, who had unwisely been seated within firing range.

"Simply 'Mrs.,'" my mother said sweetly, "and how about you? Are you still married to anybody?"

There was a moment's frosty silence before the table went back to talk of the weather and the next day's game of golf.

"Tomorrow we shall go out riding, do you think?" Siegfried asked me. "Myself I ride magnificently. I am a magnificent horseman. I know no fear."

This couldn't be happening to me. I was trapped in a room with my mother, Mrs. Simpson, Fish-Lips, Darcy, and/or someone who was trying to kill me. How much worse could things get?

Somehow I survived dinner. The redeeming feature was the magnificent food. For one who had been living on baked beans, there was one heady course after the next— turtle soup followed by sole Veronique followed by squab followed by roast beef followed by charlotte russe followed by anchovies on toast. I was amazed at the amount I was able to eat, given my nervous state. And wine to accompany each course.

I noted that Mrs. Simpson picked at her food and cast glances in the direction of the prince, who was doing a lot of cow-eyed gazing in her direction.

"I'm afraid I have to eat like a sparrow these days or I put on weight," she commented to those around her. "You're so lucky. Germans like their women fat." This last remark addressed to my mother, of course.

"In which case I should eat up if I were you," my mother said, glancing at the prince whose royal ancestor included the Elector of Hanover and Prince Albert of Saxe-Coburg-Gotha. She was clearly enjoying herself. I was relieved when Lady Mountjoy indicated that the ladies should withdraw and we followed her into the drawing room where coffee awaited us. My mother and Mrs. Simpson, now already sworn enemies, were still exchanging the most deliciously honeyed barbs. I would have enjoyed observing this spectacle, but Belinda was sitting beside me, offering to put cream and sugar into my coffee. I declined both.

"But I thought you always claimed that black coffee at night kept you awake," she said.

I looked across at my mother. Could I count on her as an ally? As a mother she hadn't exactly fulfilled the role, but surely she'd want to protect her only child. The men arrived soon after.

"David, come and sit here." Mrs. Simpson patted the sofa beside her. There was an almost discernible gasp from the rest of the party. Princes are "sir" in public, even to their closest friends. His Highness just smiled and hurried to perch on the arm at her side. Mr. Simpson was nowhere in sight. Gone to play billiards, so I was told. Darcy settled himself between Marisa and Imogen and didn't once look in my direction.

"I gather you had a nasty tumble," Whiffy said. "The lighting is so poor in the corridors, isn't it? Old Tris tripped over a suit of armor on our floor. That's par for the course for him. Clumsy as an ox. Have you seen him, by the way?"

At that moment he appeared, in animated conversation with Prince Siegfried. They were both heading in my direction. I couldn't stand it a minute longer. I excused myself as soon as I was able, and went to my room. I went up the little staircase, looking carefully for clues. It was too dark to see much, but I knelt down and examined the third step, which was where I had taken the tumble. There was no sign of a nail from which a string could be tied, but there were telltale holes in the walls. My adversary thought he or she had removed the evidence, but one can't remove holes.

I went into my room and locked the door, but I couldn't sleep. Every house has a set of skeleton keys that my killer could acquire, but at least I'd be ready for him. I looked around for a suitable weapon, then took a warming pan off the wall and laid it beside me. At the first hint of anyone near my door, I'd be waiting, armed and ready to bash him over the head and scream the place down.

The hours ticked on. An owl hooted and somewhere in the park there was a scream, probably a fox taking a rabbit. Then I heard the floorboards outside my door creak. It was the slightest of sounds but I was up in an instant, warming pan in my hands, standing beside the door. I held my breath, waiting, but nothing happened. At last I could stand it no longer. I unlocked the door as quietly as possible, and looked out. A figure in a dark robe was creeping down the hall as if he or she didn't want to wake anyone. My first thought was the Prince of Wales, returning from a visit to Mrs. Simpson, or vice versa. But I could see that the person was taller than either the prince or the American woman. The form passed the prince's suite and kept on going. At last it paused outside a door, tapped very gently, then entered.

I crept down the hall, counting doors, trying to make sense of what I'd just seen. I passed the Prince of Wales's suite. The room had to be Prince Siegfried's. And from the outline of the figure against the light on the landing, it could be none other than Tristram. I hadn't even realized that Tristram knew the prince. So why was he visiting him in the middle of the night? Naïve as I was, I could only come to one conclusion. And this was someone who only yesterday had proposed marriage to me. Like everything else at the moment, it didn't add up.

Chapter 27

Farlows
Saturday, May 7, 1932

I finally managed to sleep after placing a chair back under my doorknob and awoke to hear that doorknob being rattled fiercely and then a loud tapping on my door. It was broad daylight. I opened the door to find the maid with my morning tea. It was a lovely day, she said, and the gentlemen were off to play golf. The American ladies were joining them. If I also wanted to, I'd have to hurry.

I had no intention of straying from my mother, Lady Mountjoy, and Marisa. There had to be safety in numbers. I dressed and came down to breakfast to find Belinda busy attacking the kidneys. "Lovely spread," she said. "One forgets how much one misses this sort of thing."

I smiled at her and went to the sideboard to help myself.

"You've been awfully quiet," she said. "Are you worrying about your brother?"

"No, I'm worrying about me." I looked her straight in the eye. "Someone's trying to kill me."

"Oh, Georgie, surely you're imagining things. You're the type of person who has accidents, you know that."

"But several accidents in one week? Even I am not that clumsy."

"Horrible, I agree, but accidents nonetheless."

"Only not last night," I said. "Someone strung black thread across the top of those stairs. I found a piece on my skirt."

"And nails in the wall?"

"No, but there were holes where nails could have been. My attacker must have removed them. He or she is obviously very sharp."

"He or she? Who do you think it could be, then?"

"I have no idea," I said, still staring at her. "Someone who is somehow linked to the death of de Mauxville. Tell me, was Tristram Hautbois on that boat on Sunday?"

"Tristram? No, he wasn't."

"Well, that shoots that theory, then."

Belinda got to her feet. "I really do think you're letting your imagination run riot," she said. "We're all your friends. We've known you for years."

"And haven't been quite straight with me."

"What do you mean?"

"That you didn't tell me you frequented Crockford's. You were well known to the staff there."

She looked at me and laughed. "You didn't ask. All right, I confess I do adore gambling. I'm actually rather good at it. It's what keeps my head above water, financially. And I rarely have to come up with the money for my own stake. Older men love to befriend a helpless and charming young woman." She dabbed at her mouth with a napkin. "Did you find out anything there?"

"Only that several people I know gamble more than they should."

"One needs some excitement in life, doesn't one?" Belinda said. She got up and left me alone at the breakfast table, still not knowing if she was a suspect or not.

My mother came in before I had finished and I latched on to her. Max was off golfing so she wasn't averse to some time with her daughter. She whisked me up to her room for some "girl time," as she called it, and made me try endless jars of cosmetics and various perfumes. I feigned interest while trying to think how to tell her that my life was in danger. Knowing her, she'd just tell me not to be silly and go on as if nothing had happened.

"What are you doing with yourself?" she asked. "Not still working at Harrods in that awful pink smock?"

"No, I got the sack, thanks to you."

"I got you the sack? Little *moi*?"

"They told me I was rude to a customer and I couldn't very well tell them that you were my mother."

She gave a great peal of laughter. "It's too, too funny, darling."

"Not if you need money to buy food, it's not. I'm not getting anything from Binky, you know."

"Poor Binky. He may not be in a position to give anyone anything again. Such an awful thing to have happened. How did that terrible de Mauxville man come to be in your house in the first place?"

"You know him, do you?"

"Of course. Everyone on the Riviera

knows him. Odious man. Whoever drowned him did the world a service."

"Except that Binky is likely to be hanged for a crime he didn't commit unless I can find out who did it."

"Leave that kind of thing to the police, darling. I'm sure they'll sort it all out nicely. Don't worry about it. I want you to enjoy yourself—come out of your shell, start flirting a little more. It's time you snagged yourself a husband."

"Mother, I'll find myself a husband when the time is right."

"What about the Student Prince at dinner last night? You'd never find a man with more orders or medals."

"Or flabbier lips," I said. "He looks like a cod, Mother."

She laughed. "Yes, he does, rather. And deadly dull, I should imagine. Still, future queen isn't to be sniffed at."

"You tried duchess and you didn't stick with it for long."

"True enough." She looked at me critically. "You do need better clothes, now that you're out in society, that's obvious. I'll see if I can worm a little something out of Max. What a pity you're not my size. I'm always throwing away absolutely scrumptuous things that I can't wear because they are last year's. Of course, if poor Hubie actually dies, I'd imagine you'd be able to buy yourself a decent wardrobe, and a house to go with it."

I stared at her. "You said I was mentioned in his will, but—"

"Hubie is rich as Croesus, darling, and who else does he have to leave it to? Poor little Tristram will probably get his share, but I got the impression that Hubie wanted to make sure you were provided for."

"Really?"

"He was so fond of you. I probably should have stayed with him for your sake, but you know I couldn't take all those months with no sex while he was rafting up the Amazon or scaling some mountain." She pulled me to my feet. "Let's go for a walk, shall we? I haven't had a chance to explore the grounds yet."

"All right." A walk would be a good chance to tell her about my "accidents."

We went down the stairs, arm in arm. The house was remarkably quiet. It seemed that most of our party had gone to play golf. A blustery wind was blowing outside and my mother decided she had to return to the house to find a scarf for her hair or she'd look a fright. I waited outside the house, wondering about a lot of things. If I was going to inherit money from Sir Hubert's will, then Tristram did have a motive to want to marry me. But to kill me? That didn't make sense. He was due to receive his own share of the inheritance. Besides, he hadn't been on the boat, and I hadn't spotted him at that tube platform either. What's more, he seemed like the kind of person who would faint at the sight of blood. He had certainly looked as if he was about to faint when that woman choked to death beside us.

There was a sound above me. I started to look up. At the same time my mother's voice screamed, "Look out!" I jumped and one of the marble statues from the balustrade crashed to the ground beside me. Mother rushed down the steps to me, her face deathly white.

"Are you all right? What an awful thing to have happened! Of course, it's so windy today. That thing had probably been unstable for years. Thank God you're all right. Thank God I wasn't still standing beside you."

Servants ran out. Everyone was trying to

comfort me. But I shook myself loose of them and ran into the house. I was tired of being a victim. I wasn't going to take it any longer. I rushed upstairs, one flight then the next. And bumped into Whiffy Feather-stonehaugh, running down.

"You!" I shouted, blocking his way. "I should have known when you didn't jump in to try and save me on the boat. I can understand killing de Mauxville, but what have you got against Binky and me, eh? Come on, out with it!"

Whiffy swallowed hard, his Adam's apple jumping up and down, eyes darting nervously. "I'm afraid I haven't a clue what you're talking about."

"You've just been up on the roof, haven't you? Come on, don't deny it."

"The roof? Good Lord, no. What would I have been doing on the roof? The other fellows snapped up the good fancy dress costumes. Lady Mountjoy said there was another trunk of costumes up in the attic, but I couldn't find them."

"Good excuse," I said. "Quick thinking. You're obviously brighter than you make out. You must be, to have lured de Mauxville to our house and killed him. But why pick us?— that's what I want to know."

He was looking at me as if I were a new and dangerous species of animal.

"Look here, Georgie. I don't know what you're on about. I—I didn't kill de Mauxville. I had nothing to do with his death."

"You mean he wasn't blackmailing you?"

His jaw dropped. "How the devil did you know about that?"

I didn't like to say "lucky guess." It had suddenly come to me in a flash of inspiration as I noticed how tall and dark-haired and distinguished-looking he was. "They described you as visiting him at Claridge's, and I saw your name in the book at Crockford's, and de Mauxville had scribbled something about meeting 'R' on a pad."

"Oh, cripes. Then the police also know."

I was probably standing on a staircase with a killer. I wasn't stupid enough to admit that the police knew nothing. "I'm sure they do," I said. "Did you decide to kill him to end the blackmailing?"

"But I didn't kill him." He looked desperate now. "I can't say I'm not glad he's dead, but I swear I didn't do it."

"Was it gambling debts? Did you owe him money?"

"Not exactly." He looked away. "He found out about my visits to a certain club."

"Crockford's?"

"Oh, good Lord, no. Crockford's is acceptable. Half the Guards gamble."

"Then what?"

He was looking around him like a trapped animal. "I'd rather not say."

"A strip club, you mean?"

"Not exactly." He was looking at me as if I were rather dense. "Look, Georgie, it's really none of your business."

"It damned well is my business. My brother has been arrested for a murder he didn't commit. I'm in danger and so far you are the only one with a motive to want de Mauxville dead. I'm going straight downstairs to telephone the police. They'll get to the bottom of this."

"No, don't do that. For God's sake. I swear I didn't kill him, Georgie, but I can't let my family find out."

Suddenly light dawned. The conversation I had overheard at Whiffy's house . . . and last night Tristram tiptoeing down the hall to Prince Siegfried's room. "You're talking about clubs where boys go to meet boys, aren't you?" I said. "You and Tristram, you're both that way inclined."

He flushed bright scarlet. "So you see what it would be like if anyone found out. I'd be out of the Guards on my ear, and my family—well, my family would never forgive me. Military since Wellington, you know."

Another idea was forming in my head. "So how did you manage to pay off de Mauxville? Not on a Guards officer's pay."

"That was the problem. Where to get the money."

"So you took things from your family's London house?"

"Good God, Georgie—are you a blinking mind reader or something? Yes, I took the odd item, here and there. Pawned them, you know, outside of London. Always planned to get them back."

"And you don't know who killed de Mauxville?"

"No, but I'm bally glad they did. God bless them."

"And did you see anybody upstairs, when you were heading for the attic?"

"No. Can't say I did. But I'll come and look with you, if you like."

I hesitated. A strong Guards officer might not be a bad idea if I was to tackle a murderer, but I could also find myself trapped on the roof alone with him.

"We'll get the servants to search," I said and walked down the stairs with him.

The search revealed nobody hiding on the roof, but my attacker would have had plenty of time to sneak down while I was questioning Whiffy. Everyone but me seemed to think it was a horrible accident. I no longer felt safe anywhere and there was something I had to know. I slipped out of the house when no one was looking and walked the length of the driveway. Then, after half a mile or so, I followed the long drive to Sir Hubert's sprawling Tudor mansion.

The door was opened by a maid and the butler was summoned.

"I'm sorry but the master is not in residence," he said as he came to meet me. "I am Rogers, Sir Hubert's butler."

"I remember you, Rogers. I am Lady Georgiana and at one time I knew this house very well."

His face lit up. "Little Lady Georgiana. Well, I never. What a young lady you've grown into. Of course we've followed your progress in the newspapers. Cook cut out the pictures when you were presented at court. How kind of you to come and visit at such a sad time."

"I'm so sorry to hear about Sir Hubert," I said. "But I'm actually here on a very delicate matter and I hope you'll be able to help me."

"Please, come into the drawing room. Can I bring you a cup of coffee or a sherry, perhaps?"

"Nothing, thank you. It's about Sir Hubert's will. Something my mother said gave me to understand that I am mentioned in it. Now, I'm not after his money, I can assure you I'd much rather he lived, but strange things have been happening to my family, and it just occurred to me they may have something to do with this will. So I wondered if it was possible he kept a copy of his will on the premises?"

"I believe there is a copy in the safe," he said.

"Under normal circumstances I wouldn't dream of asking to see it, but I have reason to believe my life is in danger. Do you happen to know the combination?"

"I'm afraid I don't, my lady. That was the sort of thing that only the master knew."

"Oh, well, never mind." I sighed. "It was worth a try. Can you tell me who are Sir Hubert's solicitors?"

"Henty and Fyfe, in Tunbridge Wells," he said.

"Thank you, but they won't be available until Monday, will they?" I felt remarkably near to tears. "I hope that's not too late."

He cleared his throat. "As it happens, my lady, I know the contents of the will," he said, "because I was asked to witness it."

I looked up at him.

"There were small bequests to the staff, and a generous bequest to the Royal Geographical Society. The rest of the estate was divided into three parts: Master Tristram was to receive one-third, yourself one-third, and the final third was to go to Master Tristram's cousin, one of Sir Hubert's French relatives, called Gaston de Mauxville."

Chapter 28

Eynsleigh and Farlows
Near Mayfield, Sussex
Saturday, May 7, 1932

I stared at him, trying to digest this. "I'm to be left a third of the estate? There must be some mistake," I stammered. "Sir Hubert hardly knew me. He hadn't seen me for years. . . ."

"Ah, but he remained very fond you, my lady." The butler smiled at me benevolently. "He wanted to adopt you once, you know."

"When I was an adorable child of five and liked to climb trees."

"He never lost interest in you, not even after your mother moved on to—" he finished that phrase discreetly with a cough. "And when your father died, he was most concerned. 'I don't like to think of that girl growing up without a penny to her name,' he said to me. He hinted it was clear your mother was never going to provide for you."

"How very kind of him," I muttered, almost moved to tears, "but surely Mr. Hautbois should have been left the lion's share of the estate. He is Sir Hubert's ward, after all."

"The master felt that too much money might not be in Mr. Tristram's best interests," the butler said dryly. "Nor Monsieur de Mauxville's, even though he was his sister's only child. Addicted to gambling apparently. Moved in shady circles."

I fought to retain my composure while the butler took me downstairs to meet Cook and then had to eat a slice of her famous Victoria sponge I had always adored as a child. All that time my thoughts were in utter turmoil. The will gave Tristram a motive for wanting both de Mauxville and myself out of the way, but I had no proof that he had done anything. On the contrary, Tristram's slight build against the stocky de Mauxville made it hard to believe that he had carried out that murder. Unless he had had an accomplice. I remembered the pally conversation at Whiffy's house when I had been cleaning floors and they hadn't known I could speak French. So it could have been a conspiracy, beneficial to both of them. Which meant I had two sources of danger, not one, waiting for me back at Farlows.

The obvious thing was to go to the police, even to summon Chief Inspector Burnall of Scotland Yard, but I realized that everything I would tell him was pure supposition. How clever my assailant had been. Every one of those attacks could be passed off as an accident. And as for killing de Mauxville, there was nothing that linked Tristram to that crime.

As I turned out onto the road another idea struck me. Maybe Tristram wasn't the killer at all. I hadn't found out who would inherit Sir Hubert's estate if both Tristram and I were dead. Whiffy had mentioned something about Tristram falling over a suit of armor the night before. What if there was another person lurking in the background, waiting for an opportunity to get rid of Tristram and me?

I had reached the impressive stone gateway leading to Farlows and hesitated. Was it really wise to go back there? Then I decided I wasn't going to run away. I had to know the truth. I glanced up at the colonnade of statues as I walked past. There was something about them. . . . I frowned, but it wouldn't come. As I reached the lake I met Marisa, Belinda, and Imogen out for a walk.

"Oh, there you are," Marisa called. "Everyone wondered where you'd got to. Poor Tristram was positively pining, wasn't he, Belinda? He pestered everyone, asking for you."

"I just went for a walk to see a house where I once stayed. Where is Tristram now?"

"I don't know," Marisa said. "But he seems awfully keen on you, Georgie. I think he's really sweet—like a little lost boy, isn't he, Belinda?"

Belinda shrugged. "If that sort appeals to you, Marisa."

"And where's everyone else?" I asked casually.

"Most of the golfers aren't back yet. Apparently Mrs. Simpson wanted to go shopping in Tunbridge Wells—as if anything will be open on a Saturday afternoon," Imogen said.

"It's just an excuse to be alone with the prince; you know that," Marisa added.

"The only person whose whereabouts are certain is your dear Prince Fishface," Belinda announced with a grin. "He fell off his horse trying to make it jump a gate. He jumped the gate, but the horse didn't. I gather he won't be joining us for dancing tonight."

In spite of everything, I had to laugh.

"So you'll be stuck getting your toes trodden on by Tristram after all"—Imogen slipped her arm through mine—"unless some of the neighbors come. It's always so much easier when my brothers are here."

We started walking toward the house, past the last of the long line of statues.

"I gather one of our statues nearly toppled down on you today," Imogen said. "What awful bad luck you're having, Georgie."

Suddenly I realized what had been worrying me. I realized that Tristram had given himself away. He had compared those statues to the vengeful angel at Rannoch House. But he could only have seen that statue if he had been upstairs on the second-floor landing, where the bathroom was.

Now at least I was sure of my adversary. I was lost in thought all the way back to the house, where Lady Mountjoy appeared to tell us that tea was being served and to eat heartily, as supper wouldn't be before ten.

We followed her into the gallery and found my mother already tucking in. For a small, slim person she certainly had an appetite. Mrs. Bantry-Bynge was trying to chat with her, with little success. For someone who had been born a commoner, my mother was rather good at cutting dead anyone she considered common.

"If anyone needs a costume ironed, just let me know," Lady Mountjoy said. "You have all brought costumes, I hope. Those young men are always so helpless. Never bring anything with them. I had to throw together costumes this morning and then young Roderick complained that he didn't want to be an ancient Briton. Too bad, I told him. I had managed to put together a highwayman and an executioner for Tristram and Mr. O'Mara, but that was it, apart from the animal skins and the spear. I sent him up to hunt through the attic. You never know what you'll find up there."

So at least that much of Whiffy's story rang true. And I now knew that Darcy was going to be an executioner. He should be easy to pick out in that costume. I lingered over tea as long as I dared but neither Darcy nor Tristram appeared. When it was time to change, I suggested that the other girls might like to get ready in my room, since it was so spacious and had good mirrors. They agreed and that way I was guarded until it was time to go down to the ball.

They chatted excitedly, but I was a bundle of nerves. If I wanted to prove beyond doubt that Tristram was the murderer, I'd have to offer myself as bait. Only I'd need someone to keep an eye on me, who could later act as a witness.

"Listen, girls," I said, "whatever you say, I believe that someone in this house is trying to kill me. If you see me leaving the ballroom with any man, please come after us and keep an eye on me."

"And if we find you locked in passionate embrace with him? Do we stay and watch?" Belinda asked. She was still taking this as a joke, I could tell. I decided my only hope was Darcy. He was strong enough to tackle Tristram. But after the way I had treated him, had I any right to expect his help? I'd just have to throw myself on his mercy as soon as I got a chance to be alone with him.

I was still nervous as we made our way down the grand staircase, Belinda, Marisa, and I. A band was playing a lively two-step and more guests were arriving through the front doors. A footman stood at the bottom of the stairs with a tray, handing out masks to arriving guests who weren't wearing them. Marisa took some and handed them to us.

"Not that one," Belinda said. "It comes down to the mouth. I won't be able to eat any supper. The slim highwayman type will be better."

"There is a highwayman over there," Marisa whispered. "It must be Tristram. I didn't realize he had such good legs."

"I'm looking out for an executioner," I said. "Let me know when you see him."

"I hope you don't have a desire to follow your ancestors to the chopping block," Marisa said.

"It's Darcy O'Mara, you dope," Belinda said, giving me a knowing look.

I smiled and put my finger to my lips. The ballroom was filling up rapidly. We found a table and sat at it. Belinda was whisked away to dance almost instantly. Dressed as a harem dancer, she waggled her bottom seductively as she stepped onto the floor. Whiffy Featherstonehaugh approached us, looking very uncomfortable as an ancient

Briton with animal skins draped around his shoulders. "Care to hop around the floor, old thing?" he said to me.

"Not now, thanks," I said. "Why don't you dance with Marisa?"

"Right-o. I'll try not to tread on toes," he said, taking her hand and leading her away. I sat and sipped at a glass of Pimm's. Everyone was having fun, dancing and laughing as if they hadn't a care in the world. I was conscious of the highwayman, standing at the far side of the ballroom, watching me. At least I was safe among so many people, surely. If only I could find Darcy.

At last I saw the executioner's black hood and ax moving among the crowd on the far side of the room. I got up and made my way toward him.

"Darcy?" I grabbed his sleeve. "I have to talk to you. I want to apologize and I really need your help. It's very important."

The band struck up the "Post Horn Gallop" and couples started charging around the room whooping loudly and shouting out "Tallyho!"

I took Darcy's arm. "Let's go outside. Please."

"All right," he muttered at last.

He allowed me to lead us out of the ball-room and onto the terrace at the back of the house.

"Well?" he asked.

"Darcy, I'm so sorry that I accused you," I said. "I thought—well, I thought that I couldn't trust you. I didn't know what to think. I mean, you did come into Whiffy's house that day and I couldn't believe it was just to see me. . . . And all those strange things going on. I didn't feel safe. And now I know who was behind them, only I need your help. We've got to catch him. We've got to get proof."

"Catch who?" Darcy whispered, even though we were alone.

I leaned closer. "Tristram. He was the one who killed de Mauxville and now he's trying to kill me."

"Really?" He was standing close beside me and before I knew what was happening, a black-gloved hand came over my mouth and I was being dragged backward into the shadows at the edge of the terrace.

I squirmed to glance up at that black-hooded face. The smile was not Darcy's. And too late I realized that he had said the word "really" with a *w*, not an *r*.

"That beggar O'Mara grabbed the high-wayman outfit," he said as I flailed out at him. "But this worked out rather well, as it happens. I bagged his scarf."

I struggled to bite at his fingers, as the scarf came around my throat. I tried to thrash out at him, kick him, scratch his hands, but he had the advantage of being behind me. And he was much stronger than I had expected. Slowly and surely he was dragging me backward, away from the lights and safety, one hand still clamped over my mouth.

"When you're found floating in the lake, O'Mara's scarf will give him away," he whispered into my ear. "And nobody will ever suspect me." He gave the scarf a savage twist. I fought to breathe as he yanked me backward.

Blood was singing in my ears and spots were dancing in front of my eyes. If I didn't do something soon, it would be too late. What would be the last thing he'd expect of me? He'd expect me to try to pull away to break free of him. Instead, I mustered all of my failing strength and rammed my head backward into his face. It must have hurt him a lot because it certainly hurt me. He let out a yell of pain. He might have been stronger than I had expected, but he still didn't weigh much. He went down hard, with me on top of him.

"Damn you," he gasped and tightened his grip on the scarf again.

As I tried to get to my feet he yanked me down, growling like an animal as he twisted the scarf. With the last of my strength I raised myself up then rammed myself down onto him. My aim must have been good. He let out a yowl and for a second the scarf went limp. This time I scrambled off him and tried to get to my feet. He grabbed at me. I opened my mouth to yell for help but no sound would come out of my throat.

"And you pretended to play the innocent virgin," said a voice above us. "This is the wildest sex I've witnessed in years. You must teach me some of those moves next time we're together." And the masked highwayman stood there, holding out a hand to me. I staggered to my feet and stood gasping and coughing as he supported me.

"Tristram," I whispered. "Tried to kill me. Don't let him get away."

Tristram was also struggling to his feet. He started to run. Darcy brought him down in a flying rugby tackle. "You never were any good at rugger, were you, Hautbois?" he said, kneeling on Tristram's back and bringing his arm up behind him. "I always thought you were rotten. Lying, cheating, stealing, getting other fellows into trouble at school—that was you, wasn't it, Hautbois?"

Tristram cried out as Darcy rammed his face into the gravel with a good deal of satisfaction. "But killing? Why was he trying to kill you?"

"To get my part of an inheritance. He killed de Mauxville for the same reason," I managed to say, although my throat was still burning.

"I thought something strange was going on. Ever since you fell off that boat," Darcy said.

"Let me up. You're hurting me," Tristram whined. "I never meant to harm her. She's exaggerating. It was only fun."

"I saw the whole thing and it wasn't fun," Darcy said. He looked up as there were footsteps on the gravel behind us.

"What's going on here?" Lord Mountjoy demanded.

"Call the police," Darcy shouted to him. "I caught this fellow trying to kill Georgie."

"Tristram?" Whiffy exclaimed. "What the devil . . ."

"Get him off me, Whiffy. He's got it all wrong," Tristram yelled. "It was just a game. I didn't mean anything."

"Some game," I said. "You'd have let my brother hang for you."

"No, it wasn't me. I didn't kill de Mauxville. I didn't kill anyone."

"Yes, you did, and I can prove it," I said.

Tristram started to blubber as he was dragged to his feet.

Darcy put an arm around me as they led Tristram away. "Are you all right?"

"Much better now. Thank you for coming to my rescue."

"It looked as if you were doing rather well without me," he said. "I quite enjoyed watching."

"You mean you were standing there watching and didn't try to help?" I demanded indignantly.

"I had to make sure I could testify he was really trying to kill you," he said. "Quite a good little fighter, I have to say." He put his hands on my shoulders. "Don't look at me like that. I'd have intervened earlier if I'd seen you sneak out of the room. Belinda was doing a harem dance and I got distracted for a second. No, wait, Georgie. Come back here. . . ." He ran after me as I shook myself free and stalked away.

I strode out into the darkness until I stood at the balustrade overlooking the lake.

"Georgie!" Darcy said again.

"It's nothing to me what you and Belinda do," I said.

"Strangely enough I've done nothing more with Belinda than sit next to her at a roulette wheel. Not my type. Too easy. I like a challenge in life, personally." He slipped his arm around my shoulders.

"Darcy, if you'd come earlier you would have heard me apologizing. I thought you were dressed as the executioner, you see. I feel awful about the horrible things I said to you."

"I suppose it was a natural supposition."

I was very conscious of his arm, warm around my shoulder. "Why did you follow me into that house?"

"Mere curiosity and an opportunity to get you alone." He took a deep breath. "Look, Georgie. I've got a confession to make. After that wedding thing I got a tad drunk. I made a bet that I could lay you within a week."

"So when you took me back to your place, after the boat accident, you didn't really care about me at all. You were trying to win a stupid bet?"

He squeezed my shoulder more tightly. "No, that didn't cross my mind at all. When I pulled you out of that water, I realized that I really cared for you."

"But you still tried to get me into bed."

"Well, I'm only human and you were looking at me as if you fancied me. You do fancy me, don't you?"

"I might," I said, looking away. "If I felt sure that . . ."

"The bet's off," he said. He turned me toward him and kissed me full and hard on the mouth. His arms were crushing me. I felt as if I were melting into him and I didn't want it to stop. The hubbub that was still going on on the terrace faded into oblivion until there were just the two of us in the whole universe.

Later, when we walked back to the house together, our arms around each other, I asked him, "So who was the bet with?"

"Your friend Belinda," he said. "She said I'd be doing you a favor."

Chapter 29

Rannoch House
Sunday, May 8, 1932

It was almost morning by the time I finally fell into bed. I had spent the rest of the evening giving my statements to police. Chief Inspector Burnall arrived from Scotland Yard sometime during the night and I had to repeat everything. Finally Tristram was led away screaming and weeping disgracefully. Sir Hubert would have been mortified at his behavior. According to Darcy he'd been a rotten egg even at school, cheating on exams and get Darcy blamed for something he had stolen.

I drove home with Whiffy, Belinda, and Marisa the next afternoon and arrived at Rannoch House just in time to witness Binky's triumphant return. A crowd had gathered outside on hearing the latest news and when Binky appeared from a police car, everyone cheered. Binky went quite pink and looked pleased.

"I can't thank you enough, old thing," he said when we were safely inside and he had poured us both a Scotch. "You saved my life, literally. I'll be in your debt forever."

I didn't like to suggest that he find a way to resume my allowance as a small thank-you gift.

"So how did they find out it was this blighter Hautbois who killed de Mauxville? Did he confess?" he asked. "I've only had the most sketchy news so far."

"He was caught trying to strangle me," I said, "which was lucky, as they'd have had no way to link him to de Mauxville's death. Or to those other attempts on my life."

"Attempts on your life?"

"Yes, Tristram tried diligently to push me off a tube platform, poison me, trip me down the stairs, and be squashed by a statue. I'm glad to say I survived them all." The one thing he hadn't done, so it seemed, was to push me off the boat. That really had been a freak accident, but it gave him the idea that it might be simple to get rid of me. "I was known to be accident-prone so nobody would ever have suspected," I said, with an involuntary shudder.

"So they'd no proof he was the murderer?"

"Actually now they have. An autopsy revealed there was cyanide in de Mauxville's system, and in the poor woman he killed accidentally."

"Killed accidentally?"

"He meant to poison me with a cyanide-laced sugar cube, but some woman took the sugar bowl from me and died instead."

Binky looked astonished. "A poisoned sugar cube? How did he know you'd take the right cube? Had he poisoned the entire bowl?"

"No, he was lucky as well as opportunistic. He had the cyanide in his pocket, waiting for a chance to use it. When the woman at the next table started speaking to me, I turned around just long enough for him to taint one cube. Then he made a show of taking a lump himself first, leaving the poisoned cube sitting on top."

"Well, I'm dashed," Binky said. "Smart cove, then."

"Very smart," I said. "He played the likeable dolt so well that no one ever suspected him."

"And all for money," Binky said with disgust.

"Money is quite a useful thing to have," I said. "You only notice how useful when you don't have enough."

"That's certainly true," Binky said. "Which reminds me. I had a brilliant idea when I was locked up with hours to think: we'll open up Rannoch House to the public. We'll bring rich Americans for a Highland hunting experience. Fig can do cream teas."

I started to laugh. "Fig? Can you see Fig serving cream teas to charabancs full of plebs?"

"Well, not exactly serve them herself. Preside over them. Meet the duchess, you know. . . ."

But I was still laughing. Tears streamed down my face as I laughed myself silly.

Chapter 30

Buckingham Palace
Westminster
London
Later in May 1932

"Extraordinary," Her Majesty said. "From what one reads in the papers, one understands that this young man is a relative of Sir Hubert Anstruther."

"A distant relative, ma'am. Sir Hubert actually rescued him from France."

"French, then? And the man he killed was also a Frenchman, I believe. Well, that tidies it up nicely, doesn't it?" She looked at me over her Wedgwood teacup. "What one doesn't understand is why he picked Rannoch House to do the deed."

"He knew why de Mauxville was in London and realized that my brother and I would have a strong motive for murder."

"An intelligent young man, then." She

took a thin slice of brown bread from the plate that was offered her. "I always feel it's such a pity when good brains are wasted." She looked up at me and nodded approvingly. "You seem to have made admirable use of your brains, Georgiana. Well done. I see that your brother was given a hero's welcome when he arrived back in Scotland."

I nodded. For some reason there was a lump in my throat. I hadn't realized how fond I was of Binky.

"And I haven't had a chance to ask you about the house party yet, with all of this sensationalism going on," the queen said. "I take it my son and that woman were both in attendance?"

"They were, ma'am."

"And?"

"I would say that His Highness is infatuated. He couldn't take his eyes off her."

"And is she equally infatuated with him?"

I thought before I answered. "I believe she likes the idea of having power over him. He's certainly already under her thumb."

"Oh, dear. Just as I feared. Let us hope this is another of his passing fancies or that she'll tire of him. I must speak to the king.

This may be a good time to send David on a long tour of the colonies." She took another delicate bite of bread. I had just taken a second slice myself, in the hope that she wasn't counting.

"And what about you, Georgiana?" she asked. "What shall you be doing with yourself now that the excitement is over?"

"We've just had the good news that Sir Hubert has come out of his coma, and will be coming home," I said. "I thought I'd go down to Eynsleigh and keep him company. It will be an awful shock for him when he hears about Tristram."

"And it was all for nothing too," the queen said. "Sir Hubert is known for his strong constitution. I expect he'll now live for years."

"One hopes so, ma'am," I said, thinking that I'd have to go back to cleaning houses after all.

"Let me know when you return from Sir Hubert's," Her Majesty said. "I think I have another little assignment for you. . . ."